NEVER WAKE

NEVER WAKE

AMY PLUM

HARPER TEEN
An Imprint of HarperCollinsPublishers

HarperTeen is an imprint of HarperCollins Publishers.

"Enter Sandman" Words and Music by James Hetfield,
Lars Ulrich, and Kirk Hammett
Copyright © 1991 Creepy Death Music (GMR)
International copyright secured. All rights reserved.
Reprinted by permission of Hal Leonard LLC.

Library of Congress Control Number: 2018933337
ISBN 978-0-06-242990-2

Typography by Ray Shappell
18 19 20 21 22 PC/LSCH 10 9 8 7 6 5 4 3 2 1

First Edition

To Max, Jenna, Ant, and everyone else who illuminates our lives
and the world with their extraordinary minds

But dreams come through stone walls, light up dark rooms, or darken light ones, and their persons make their exits and their entrances as they please, and laugh at locksmiths.

—J. Sheridan Le Fanu, *Carmilla*

NEVER WAKE

CHAPTER 1

JAIME

THE LAST EIGHT HOURS HAVE BEEN A LIVING nightmare.

Early this morning, I witnessed seven teenagers simultaneously fall into a coma. Shortly after, one of them, a nineteen-year-old girl, died of a heart attack. Then, just moments ago, an eighteen-year-old boy almost died the same way . . . would have died if I hadn't used a defibrillator on him. It was an insane move, one I'm not sure I would have made if I'd had time to think it through, especially considering I'd only ever practiced on a plastic dummy.

Now here I am, standing in the darkened laboratory of the Pasithea sleep research facility, heart pounding like a speed-metal drum solo as I watch the six survivors on their hospital beds. They're fanned out like spokes on a wheel around the blinking, beeping column they are linked to by a jungle of wires and tubes.

There is a gap in the wheel now—one empty bed that held Beta subject three, BethAnn, before her body was carted away.

Dr. Zhu and Dr. Vesper have reconnected the IV tube that Fergus, the boy I just saved, ripped out as he flailed on his bed. Vesper is mopping up the puddle of feeding solution that spilled onto the floor. The way he crouches as he swabs the liquid makes him look even more vulturelike than usual. "We should give him a beta-blocker," he says.

Zhu nods and, going to her phone, calls someone to deliver the drug. They're acting so normal, while I'm trying to slow my pulse to a speed that won't give me a stroke. But I know that underneath their studiedly calm demeanor they're as scared as I am. I can read it in the sweat gleaming on Vesper's brow and the tentative way Zhu hovers over her keyboard instead of her regular speed-typing. She glances up, catching my eye, and I quickly look back at my monitor.

"You saved that boy's life," she had told me. But we both know that it could easily have gone wrong. Her shadowed expression suggests that she is torn between praising me and kicking me out: I might be too much of a loose cannon to keep in such a precarious situation.

If she makes me leave, it will be the end of all my dreams. If she writes me up for what I did, I'll never get into medical school. Forget about winning a scholarship. I can pretty much kiss that career good-bye.

Then what would I have left? Would it be back to the streets of Detroit? Or would I be able to find an office job, like my mom did? My mom, who is way too smart to be answering the phone and getting someone's coffee.

I have to win back Zhu's and Vesper's confidence. My future depends on it.

Their boss, Mr. Osterman, made it clear that he wanted me to stay. I'm the only witness—besides the doctors themselves—to the derailing of this cutting-edge insomnia treatment that not only threw the subjects into comas, but ended up killing one. I'm the only one who can stand up to say that it wasn't the researchers' fault. It was that freak earthquake, and they've done everything they can to keep the subjects stable while they try to find a solution. I'm a necessary evil. They can't get rid of me now.

Or can they? Maybe their boss was overreacting and they'll be fine without my testimony. Or maybe they won't even listen to him. I will have to be careful either way.

My eyes flit across the seven windows on my screen, and I focus on the one labeled "subject two": Fergus. I think back to the moment he opened his eyes. He looked directly at me and asked a question that confirmed my wildest theory about what was really going on—a theory I hadn't dared believe. "Did Beth-Ann make it?"

Those four words proved beyond a doubt that the seven teenagers are somehow connected, even though they appear to be comatose. How else could Fergus know something had happened to BethAnn—a girl he most likely had never met? In her last breath, she had spoken about being shot by soldiers in Africa.

When I finally dared mention it to Vesper, he said it was the delirious rambling of a dying girl's subconscious. That it didn't mean a thing.

But subject five, Remi, had lived through a genocide in Africa. His family had been killed by soldiers.

Fergus knew BethAnn was in danger. BethAnn knew about Remi's past. The subjects must somehow have access to one another's thoughts. Perhaps even be in a place where they are able to communicate. It sounds crazy. Impossible. But there's no other explanation.

When I told Fergus that BethAnn had died, he said, "It's the dreams. They're killing us."

According to the feedback monitors, their brain waves are so low that dreaming shouldn't be possible. But I began to think . . . and now I'm sure . . . that the monitors are wrong.

I wonder if they were damaged by the earthquake. Or maybe the subjects are experiencing a state of awareness that doesn't show up on regular brain-wave monitoring. A state that the makers of brain-wave monitors would never think of trying to measure. A shared consciousness in a subconscious state. Shared dreams.

But before Fergus fell into cardiac arrest, I told him what had happened and that the doctors were working on how to wake them up. More important, I warned him to be careful. That I had discovered one of the other teenagers trapped in there with him was dangerous. A psychopath.

I didn't have a chance to tell him who. Or that subject four was linked to the recent deaths of three other teenagers, and that his psychiatrist suspected he was responsible. If my suspicions are true, and they're all in there together, will Sinclair be capable of hurting the others? What kind of motivation would he need to kill them too?

I don't know much about psychopaths besides their trademark use of manipulation and lack of empathy. I don't know what it would take to set one off on a murder spree. But I can't imagine that being stuck inside shared nightmares would bring out the best in someone potentially dangerous and mentally unstable. I fear it could be enough to trigger even the most carefully hidden psychosis.

CHAPTER 2

CATA

I OPEN MY EYES. I'M LYING ON MY SIDE ON THE
ground staring at a row of rusted metal garbage bins. I try to move
but am pinned in place by a heavy weight on my back. Craning
my neck, I see brick walls stretching up five stories to touch a
cement-gray sky. I'm in a long narrow street that dead-ends a few
yards away.

Everything is hazy and red, like I'm peering through blood-
tinted sunglasses. I blink but my vision doesn't clear. And then I
smell smoke.

The trash cans are on fire. Their lids all fly open, one after the
other, clanging loudly while flames pour out, vomiting clouds of
smoke. I strain from side to side, then raise my hands to feel ropes
wrapped around my torso. I suddenly remember my plan to bring
Fergus into the nightmare.

In the Void, he had said something about his heart and then he lost consciousness. Afraid of what would happen if we left him behind, I had the others tie him to me with a rope just before the wind whipped us through the door into this place. The plan had worked—he made it through. But now he's putting us both in danger.

"Ant! Sinclair! Remi!" I yell, and hear voices coming from nearby.

Ant's small, worried face appears in my line of sight, flames billowing behind her head like a blazing halo. She looks like a saint wearing a chullo hat, flaps pulled securely beneath her ears.

"Cut Fergus free!" I yell, choking on the smoke. "Quick!"

Remi appears, crossbow slung across his back, and, pulling out his knife, begins sawing at the rope binding Fergus and me together. Ant draws her own knife from its sheath and kneels down to help.

Sinclair crouches next to my head. "Something's wrong with my eyes," he says, glancing down the alley. He cups his hand over his nose and mouth to filter the smoke.

"Mine too," I respond. "Is everything red?"

"Yeah. It's like I'm seeing through a gun sight."

"Same for me," says Remi. He finishes slicing through one of the ropes, and scrambles to free us. I feel the weight of Fergus fall from my back, and turn to see him slump sideways onto the ground, thick black hair fanning across his face.

Out of the corner of my eye, I see a haunting but familiar figure crouching in a doorway across from us. He flickers as I focus on him, his face changing from one of a boy my age to an amorphous blur with features that look like they were sketched in chalk then wiped away. The boy cradles his left arm with his right, blood flowing freely from a wound near his shoulder.

"Oh my God, it's him!" I hiss. Everyone turns to look.

A blast of static scrapes my eardrums, and the boy changes into a manlike creature with a freakish rooster head. He's wearing striped pajama bottoms, and his arms are bound in a straitjacket.

A man's voice reverberates through the alley, coming from midair above us. "Come out, Brett. We know you're in there. We know you can hear us."

It's followed by the voice of a woman. "Just open your eyes, honey. It's going to be okay. Talk to us. Try to tell us what you see."

"May I speak frankly?" another voice says.

"Why not?" The man's voice is burdened with sadness. "It doesn't even seem like he hears us anymore."

"As we have discussed with FFI, the brain cells that degenerate don't ever come back. We can't recover what is already gone. Gone. Gone." The voice echoes robotically, and then stops.

"Brett! His name is Brett!" exclaims Ant.

She has thrown herself down by Fergus, and is cradling his head in her lap. She directs her gaze at me. "The static monster . . . I kept thinking he was saying *red* in the dreams, but he was saying *Brett* the whole time. He's been trying to tell us his name!"

"Holy shit," exclaims Sinclair. "If those voices are talking to him, this must be his dream! What was it that you said, Cata?

About there being something wrong with him?"

"It was when Ant explained how we see each other in the Dreamfall," I respond.

Ant watches me, holding her gloved hand over her nose to filter the smoke.

"Didn't you say that we appear as we perceive ourselves, since we aren't using our . . ."

She comes to my rescue. "If everything in the Dreamfall is in our minds, then we don't have typical use of our sensory organs: noses, ears, eyes. Everything we hear and smell and feel is fabricated by our thoughts. And the way we appear to one another is just a projection of how we perceive ourselves."

Ant looks self-conscious. I give her a smile. She seems to realize she'll have to communicate in a more . . . normal way now that she no longer has George to translate for her.

The rooster head flickers like an old TV, before changing into a skeleton draped in rotting flesh. The corpse writhes and convulses, like it's having a seizure.

"Fuck. Me," groans Sinclair. "If that's how he perceives himself, then he's tripping. Or completely insane. Let's get the hell out of here."

"Watch out!" Remi yells. I turn to see something hurtling toward us from the street end of the alley. There is a pounding of hooves on pavement as a wall of horses races toward us.

"Help me with Fergus!" I shout over the din, and we all scramble, dragging and pushing Fergus's limp body until it's hidden between two of the flaming garbage bins. There's enough space for Ant and Remi to huddle beside him, but Sinclair and I stick out in the path of the oncoming animals.

"Quick!" yells Sinclair, and drags me across the alley. As we throw ourselves against the wall between another pair of burning bins, I lean too far sideways and scream as the sizzling metal sears my shoulder. Sinclair pulls me toward him, cocooning me with his body as the herd gallops past.

Echoing Brett's last transformation, the horses are skeletons with decomposing flesh draped across their bones. As they toss their heads and bare their teeth, their blood-encrusted maws emit unearthly screams that shake the walls around us. Loose bricks and dust come tumbling from above as the horses run full speed into the wall at the end of the alley and disappear.

"What. The," Sinclair begins, but even he is unable to find an expletive that rises to the level of horror we just witnessed. He lets go and holds me back to inspect me. "Are you okay?" His features are tight with fear.

I can't even speak. He rises cautiously, peers around to see if another monstrosity is about to come at us, then pulls me to my feet and presses me to his chest. I'm glad for the comfort, and bury my head in his shoulder, trying to catch my breath.

After a second, I lean back and look at him. "Where do you think we are?"

"Inside an insane person's dream," he replies. And then suddenly, his hands move up from my back to cradle my face as he leans in and kisses me.

I jerk backward. "What the hell was that?" I ask, wiping the taste of salt and smoke from my lips.

"I thought that's what you wanted. You were giving off a kiss-me vibe," he says with a sardonic twist of his mouth.

I take another step back, careful not to sear myself again on the bin, but desperate for personal space. "That was not my kiss-me vibe. We almost got trampled by rotting horse cadavers! What is your deal?"

He holds up his hands in innocence. "Misread you. Sorry. But you do taste good. Guess I'll just take a rain check."

"You'll be waiting a hell of a long time," I say, but he acts like he doesn't hear me.

I glance across the alley to where Remi and Ant crouch next to Fergus's body. Ant stares at me and Sinclair like she can't believe her eyes. I don't blame her. That kiss was so random. . . . So wrong . . . that I felt repulsed. I turn to Sinclair, but he's back behind his usual jokey mask and is completely unreadable.

Yanking up the hem of my T-shirt to shield my nose and mouth from the thickening smoke, I rush over to them. "You guys okay?" I ask. Ant and Remi nod.

"We can't stay here," says Remi, peering out from behind the bin toward the street. "It's too dangerous. We're penned in. Nowhere to escape."

"There's the door behind Brett," Sinclair suggests.

Across from us, Corpse Brett has transformed into an alien, with tentacles instead of arms waving around above his head. One of the tentacles is severed, and blood gushes from the stump.

"That's what he looked like when George hit him with the

pick in the graveyard," Ant says. As we watch, he stares back with multiple hooded eyes, and steps closer to the door, slapping the doorknob ineffectually with an appendage.

"We're in his dream," Sinclair says. "Maybe he wants us to follow him."

Remi looks unconvinced. "Why would he want to help us?"

"He saved Fergus's life back in the cathedral," I respond.

"Like you said, we can't stay here," adds Sinclair. "And whatever's behind the door can't be much worse than stampeding horse zombies. I say we go for it."

"How do we carry Fergus?" I gesture to the body sprawled on the ground.

"What do you mean?" Sinclair asks. He seems to have completely forgotten about the unconscious boy lying at his feet, and is already moving toward Brett.

"We can't bring him with us," says Remi.

Sinclair isn't even listening. He stops and turns, looking at me impatiently.

"Well, we can't just leave him here!" Ant exclaims.

Remi looks between us, face twisted in disgust, fists planted firmly on his hips. "What you don't seem to understand is that survival means strategy. George was the only one here who got it. And now she's gone. Or at least she's stuffed back into that oversized brain of yours," he says, glaring at Ant.

"Enlighten us," I say. "Just what is this strategy of yours?"

Now that he's got my attention, Remi straightens. "We should have left Fergus back in the Void. He almost got us killed right now—crushed by those . . . animals." He shivers at the memory. "If we take him with us, it will just slow us down."

Remi sees my horrified expression and picks up speed. "I'm not saying we leave him to get stuck in the nightmares again. We can come back for him once we find a safe place to wait for the Wall."

"What's wrong with you?" I look at Sinclair. "What's wrong with both of you? We are not leaving him behind."

"I wasn't . . ." Sinclair begins, holding his hands up in innocence, but Remi cuts him off.

"No, what's wrong with *you*?" Remi points his finger in my face. "You'd rather we all die than four of us get out alive? What would Fergus want?"

"I don't give a shit what Fergus wants," I growl. "We're taking him with us."

Remi sees I'm not backing down. He narrows his eyes at me and turns to Sinclair, shaking his head in defeat. Sinclair shrugs his shoulders and walks back to us.

"How are we going to carry him?" I ask Ant. "Can you make us a stretcher like you do in the Void?"

Ant closes her eyes. After a moment she opens them and shakes her head. "I have to feel relaxed. There is no way I can be calm enough here."

"Is there anything in our bags?" I ask, swinging the backpack off my shoulders and unzipping it. Inside are a flashlight, a light blanket, and a camping canteen. I hold it up, looking quizzically at Ant.

Sinclair bursts out laughing.

Ant shrugs. "I didn't know what we would need."

"That's okay." Eyeing Sinclair, I say, "We'll all help plan next time."

Ant points to where a rusty fire escape ladder protrudes from a pile of fallen bricks and rubble. "Maybe we could use that," she says. She picks her way over and shakes it loose. "It's not heavy."

"Perfect," I say, and help her carry it to where Fergus lies.

Sinclair seems resigned to helping us. "It's long enough to fit his body if his legs hang off the back," he remarks, and bending down, lifts Fergus by the armpits. "You get his feet."

We hoist Fergus up while Ant slides the ladder beneath him. "Let's give it a try," I say, and Sinclair pulls up the ladder by the front rung. I grab the side rails on the back, and we lift. It's heavy but doable.

Fergus's knees dangle over the back rung, his feet knocking against my legs. I wedge myself between his calves and nod at Sinclair. "Not a bad stretcher."

We set Fergus back down. The smoke is so thick now, my eyes are watering. "I'm all for going through the door, but shouldn't we check it out first?" I say, choking on my words. The fumes have begun to smell like burning plastic.

"I'll do it," says Remi, who has been watching our makeshift stretcher exercise dubiously. Even if he's not enthusiastic about bringing Fergus along, he wants to show he's still part of the team. "That boy monster . . . it's not going to hurt me, is it?"

"We're the ones who hurt him," Ant says, stepping forward to join Remi. "Brett," she calls, "do you want us to follow you? Through that door?"

Brett's shape levitates and drifts out of the doorway, leaving them room to pass. Ant looks back at us for reassurance as Remi steps forward and grabs the door handle. As soon as he touches it, our surroundings change. The red filter is gone and the alley has become a tunnel. Sinclair and I stand on a set of tracks.

Multifaced Brett lets out a high-pitched screech that sounds like metal scraping metal, a noise echoed by the screaming of train brakes. Twin beams of light shine from my right, growing stronger every millisecond.

"Grab the ladder!" I yell.

Sinclair gapes at me. He sees me grab my end of the ladder and, suddenly remembering we're supposed to be carrying Fergus, bends down to grasp the front rung.

"Remi! Go!" I scream.

"But we don't know what's behind . . ." he begins, and then looks around and sees the tracks. The oncoming train. He turns the handle, throws the door open, and flings himself inside. Ant tumbles in after him.

The front car of a subway train comes hurtling around a corner just yards away from us, lights blinding. Sinclair freezes, eyes glued to the oncoming train.

"Sinclair!" I scream, jolting him from his paralysis.

He bolts ahead, almost jerking the ladder from my grasp. Fergus's body tilts dangerously to one side. I tighten my hold and jerk up to tip him back onto the ladder as we pitch forward.

Brett and the train make the same metallic shriek, an earsplitting grind as the train locks its brakes. The boy-monster pushes me through the door just as the train crashes by.

CHAPTER 3

ANT

WE ARE IN A ROOM AS LONG AS TWO OLYMPIC swimming pools placed end to end (so approximately one hundred meters or three hundred twenty-eight feet) but only as wide as one pool (twenty-five meters or eighty-two feet). Two rows of cast-iron beds run the length of the room—one row down either side.

A single bed is generally ninety-nine centimeters wide (thirty-nine inches), and since they are spaced one bed apart from one another with gaps left on either end of the room, there should be forty-nine beds. But people generally prefer organizing groups in even numbers, so I predict there are fifty beds on each side, meaning one hundred in all.

The air smells like mildew and rancid pee.

The metal bed frames have peeling white paint and their thin mattresses are spotted with easily decipherable stains: blood, urine, feces.

On the two end walls are wooden doors. Closed.

A row of floor-to-ceiling windows runs along one wall. They are the length of two beds with half a bed space between them, so thirty-nine-point-six, round up to even number—forty windows. Some of the panes are broken. Others are so dirty they are almost impossible to see through. Although it's not dark outside, very little light is able to filter in.

A row of . . . I count . . . twenty-five lights with dirty glass shades hang down the center of the ceiling. Most are broken, except for one glowing steadily on the far end. The rest flicker on and off at different tempos.

These details—the stench, the decay, the sense that a disaster happened years ago, right here in this spot—trigger a visceral reaction in me. My chest is tight. My throat is clenched. I feel my pulse. My heart is beating faster than normal.

There is a buzzing sound, like static, coming from behind me. The monster . . . Brett . . . hovers next to the windows. He stands not really on the floor, but a few inches beneath the wooden floorboards. He reminds me of a ghost who doesn't realize that he aimed low. My heartbeat remains accelerated.

I begin to tap the floor, but stop after two because I don't remember what I've got with me. One tap for my hat. Two more for my gloves. I touch my pocket. Two more for my notebook and pen. That's five things. And with a stabbing feeling in my chest,

I remember. George. She's my sixth thing. My most important thing. And she's gone.

I sent her away. I had to. Fergus almost died for her. *Might still die*, I think, and turn to see Cata and Sinclair heaped on the floor on either end of the ladder. Fergus has rolled off it. He lies on his back, arms stretched out on either side and head facing away from me. Getting up, I walk quickly to him, turn his face toward the ceiling, and hold my hand in front of his mouth. Warm air puffs on my palm. The tight strap across my chest loosens a fraction.

Cata sits up and raises a hand to her forehead. She glances at me, red-eyed and shaking. I run through the facial recognition flash cards I memorized to help me identify emotions. Cata is in shock.

I should say something like, *Are you okay?* But the words don't come.

"That was too close," she says with a tremor in her voice.

Remi lies motionless on the ground a few feet away from us. I walk over to him and squat by his head, holding my hand over his lips. He's breathing too.

His eyelids flutter open and, seeing me so close, he jerks away. *Startled*, I think, classifying his emotion. He squeezes his eyes closed again. "Do you have to lurk?" he murmurs.

"I was making sure you were alive."

"I'm alive. Now can I have some personal space?"

I back off as Remi rubs his hand against his temple and holds it up to see it smeared with blood. His eyes grow wide. *Scared*, I identify. I should reassure him. "It's just a small cut."

"What is this place?" he asks, dabbing at the blood with his T-shirt. Reassured that his wound is not serious, he looks around.

"What is *anything* in a nightmare?" Cata replies, rising to her feet. "It could be one of Brett's memories. It could be a scene from a book he read or a film he saw. Or it could be a sample of his unleashed imagination."

All around us the room glitches, wavering and becoming solid again. "More like unleashed brain," remarks Sinclair in a voice quiet enough that he must not require a response from us.

I look back to where Brett hovers. He's staring at the far end of the room. There's an antique upright piano in the corner, and as I watch, a figure slowly materializes, crouched over the keyboard. It is dressed in a long-sleeved nightgown and has a shock of stringy gray hair. I can't see the face, but it reminds me of my great-aunt Ruby after she went crazy and my uncle found her living in the dog's house in her backyard. It was a Great Dane's doghouse, but still . . . doghouse.

The sound of piano notes unfurl *like a bandage*, I think, congratulating myself on the simile. I've been working on similes and metaphors as an exercise at nonlinear thinking. The song is played slowly but inevitably, *like a dirge*. The song is in a minor key and most of the keys are out of tune. It reminds me of the old-fashioned horror movies they show on TV late at night.

"Nice," moans Sinclair, dusting himself off. "All we need now is a chorus of creepy kids' voices and we'll be stuck in

Children of the Corn." I have not seen that film but suppose there are children singing in the soundtrack.

From the tilt of Sinclair's chin and ramrod-straight back, I think he's trying to act brave, but he avoids looking at the piano player. I glance back and notice that the elderly person's fingers aren't actually touching the keys, but the music is playing all the same.

Goose bumps rise on my arms, and my throat closes. *Fear.* I tap five times on the floor and, inhaling deeply, remind myself that this is just a dream. One that's going to end in . . . how long?

I access that place in my mind that always has a stopwatch running and make an adjustment for the heightened heart rate. "Twenty-eight minutes to go," I say, more to myself than to the others, but I can see the remark register in the others' silence.

"What can be going on in Brett's brain?" Cata asks after a moment.

"Sinclair suggested that his 'brain got fried' in the experiment," I say, avoiding using air quotes. People don't tend to like that when you're referring to their statements, even if they have used colloquial language. "But, seeing that none of the rest of us were affected, I think that's unlikely."

Sinclair nods, accepting my argument. He glances at Brett's writhing, flickering form. "I'll bet he was already messed up when he signed up for the test. And those voices out there in the alleyway . . . I'll bet those were his parents."

"This isn't just a regular old nightmare. What kind of insomnia would make someone's dreams this . . . bizarre?" Remi asks.

"Maybe he hasn't slept for a really long time and it made him delusional," Cata offers.

"No," I say, shaking my head. "I've studied insomnia, and . . ."

Sinclair is looking at me funny.

"What?"

"Nothing," he replies, lifting an eyebrow at Cata.

She frowns and shakes her head. "Go ahead, Ant," she urges.

"It's completely normal to try to understand a disorder after you have been diagnosed with it," I insist.

"You're totally right!" Sinclair says. I can't tell from his expression whether he means it or if he's being sarcastic. A lot of his expressions are not on my flash cards.

I shake my head. "It doesn't matter."

"Come on, Ant," pleads Cata.

I sigh and try to phrase it in a way that won't make them stare. "One of the voices mentioned FFI and brain degeneration. FFI stands for fatal familial insomnia. It's like mad cow disease, eating up parts of the brain. The person can't sleep and finally dies. There's a whole phase before that happens where they're hallucinating and delirious."

We all look at Brett. He is Rooster Head again. Sinclair says, "Well, that would definitely qualify someone for a cutting-edge insomnia study."

"And if we appear in the Dreamfall the way we perceive ourselves, it explains how he looks. There has to be something really wrong with his brain if he sees himself like that," Cata says. After giving Fergus a once-over, she walks over to one of the beds, wrinkling her nose at the stains and choosing a clean patch to perch on.

"If he doesn't have much of a rational brain left . . . if he's in the delusional stage of the illness . . . maybe that's why he can't get into the Void," I suggest. "He's stuck in the dream phase."

Everyone looks at me like I just created electricity. *(Simile.)* "It's just a hypothesis," I say. The room starts glitching again. A large mirror appears above each bed on the nonwindow side of the room. Contained in each mirror is an identical full-length image of a teenage boy.

He is blond and emaciated, and his eyes are empty and unfocused. He wears striped pajamas identical to the ones Rooster Head wears, but no straitjacket. He takes something invisible out of the pajama top pocket and mimes combing his hair.

I don't understand why something so simple affects me so strongly, but the combination of his hollow gaze and the ineffective use of an imaginary comb on his bed hair makes me shudder involuntarily.

I glance over at where Rooster Head floats, and for once his twitching seems minimal, just an occasional glitch as he stares intently at the mirrors.

"The kid in the mirror is Brett in real life," guesses Sinclair. "At least, it looks like what you can see of his face when he's human."

"Yep, that's him," agrees Remi.

"He definitely *looks* crazy," confirms Cata as the boy in the mirror stops combing his hair and starts pretending he's buttoning his pajamas. They're already buttoned up to the collar, but he's miming the action with great concentration.

"I don't know what's scarier. The old hag playing show tunes or Mime Boy dressing himself for a day in the mental asylum," Sinclair comments.

"Unicorn," comments Remi.

"What?" asks Sinclair.

"It's a unicorn now. Playing the piano," Remi says, pointing.

The stringy gray hair has been replaced by what looks like the head of one of the corpse horses from the alley, but there is a horn protruding from it. A band of dried blood circles the neck like a scarlet ribbon (*simile*) where the head has been stitched onto the body in the nightgown with thick black thread. As if sensing our stares, the thing turns its head slowly to us, the head pivoting one hundred eighty degrees . . . way farther than it should be able to go. Its mouth opens and closes as it sings, "Waaaaaay down upon the Swanee River. Far, far awaaaaaaay." It has a rich, nasal Broadway-singer voice.

"Fuck. Me," yelps Sinclair. He is no longer trying to act brave. He looks completely "freaked out."

"Show-tune unicorn is definitely scarier," Cata murmurs as it turns slowly back to the piano and continues singing.

The boy in the mirror has started using an invisible toothbrush. From above us comes the same voice we heard in the alley. It's so loud, it feels like my eardrums are going to burst. I press my hat flaps hard against my ears to muffle the sound.

"Do you think Brett can hear us, honey?" the woman's voice

says. But now her voice is warped. . . . It sounds like it's been slowed down.

"Dr. Zhu says he can hear our voices, but she's not sure if Brett understands what we're saying," the man responds.

"What do we do if this doesn't work?" the woman asks. "The clinic says their staff isn't trained to care for this severe of a condition."

"Zhu mentioned the Priory," the man says.

"We can't send him there. That place is an asylum!" the woman's voice responds, getting lower and slower until it kind of grinds to a stop. Mirror Brett continues brushing his teeth, his eyes wide and vacant.

"We're in an asylum," I say. Although I used some deductive reasoning to come to my conclusion, I am still extrapolating, so there remains some epistemic uncertainty. But George would say it isn't the time to bring that up, and now that she's gone, I've begun to think about how she would do things. So I keep quiet.

Cata nods. "I think you're right. This must be straight from his imagination. This is probably what he fears most—being put into a place like this." She raises her hand to her mouth and stares between the boy in the mirror and the floating static monster. "That is so incredibly horrific. I can't even imagine what he's going through."

"This whole dream is coming from someone whose brain is being eaten up by a disease," Remi says.

Sinclair moans. "Oh man. We are well and truly screwed."

A clicking sound starts up in the direction of the door next to the piano player, who has switched to a high-pitched rendition of "Moon River." A dark liquid starts pouring into the room from the crack beneath the door as the clicking sound grows louder.

"What is . . ." Remi says, and then as we all realize what it is, he scrambles to his feet and runs toward the windows. Climbing up to perch on the windowsill a couple of feet off the ground, he cowers as the stream widens. The clicking noise morphs into a metallic scuttling as millions of cockroaches pour under the door and spread outward to fill the width of the room with their teeming mass.

"Quick! Get Fergus onto a bed!" I yell. Cata and Sinclair unfreeze and rush to pick him up. They manage to yank his rag-doll body onto one of the mattresses before stepping up onto it themselves, and watch with expressions of horror as the wave of insects floods toward them.

I scramble onto the mattress of the closest bed and clutch the metal headboard, more for emotional support than for physical. The cockroaches are swarming up and over everything in their path. The unicorn continues to play as the cockroaches scale its body. As they reach its face and pour into its mouth, it starts gagging, coughing, and spitting. It stands abruptly and begins flailing like it's having an epileptic fit.

The insects reach Brett. Even though his body doesn't seem to be solid, they start climbing him too, and he flails in the same way the piano player did before it toppled over to lie thrashing on the ground.

"They climb!" I scream, as the insects reach my bed and begin scaling the metal posts. They pour across the mattress and swarm over my feet, moving up my bare legs, scratching my skin as they surge up my shorts, under my shirt, up my neck. I cup my hands together and seal them over my nose and mouth, squeezing my eyes shut.

The bugs squirm up under my earflaps and into my ears, and I let go of my nose and mouth to scoop them out. My face is covered in an instant and now I too am flailing, swatting at my head . . . slumping down to the mattress as I hear the others' terrified screams through the deafening scuttling noise.

My chest is pushing this muffled shriek through my windpipe as I fight to breathe through blocked nostrils and pursed lips, when a crashing boom comes from all around.

The cockroaches pause, as if they are all linked by a collective mind. I use the precious seconds to knock them off my face and shovel them away from my eyes.

I look around and see Cata and Sinclair cowering on the bed on either side of Fergus. It looks like they're on a life raft floating in a heaving sea of shiny brown.

On my other side, Remi has scaled the window, positioning himself just above where the cockroaches have risen halfway up the wall. He rubs his palm across the pane next to his face, peering out through the grimy glass. "The Wall!" he yells. "It's just outside the windows!"

The cockroaches suddenly spring into action, retreating down everything they've scaled, and rush toward the far door. They drop off me like I'm a magnet that has suddenly lost its pull. I turn to see Brett in his corpse state, cockroach-free, and buzzing with static as if nothing happened. The rotting unicorn-in-a-nightgown is on the floor, unmoving.

The bugs clear away like they know something bad's about to happen, crowding under the far door so fast that they create a writhing mound, trying to squeeze its bulk through far too small of a space.

That's when everything starts to melt.

It begins with the mirrors, which drip like they're from one of those surreal Salvador Dalí paintings. Mirror Brett is pretending to drive now, hands on an invisible steering wheel, eyes empty, mouth gaping slightly open as his image stretches and begins to leak onto the floor.

Then, with an earsplitting grinding noise, the wooden floors at both of the doors begin to cave in. Beneath is a black pit that swallows the mountain of cockroaches, along with the door they were trying to squeeze through. On the other end of the room, the piano crashes with a splintering noise through the floorboards, and the unicorn disappears into the gaping hole so quickly that it looks like it was sucked down by a giant vacuum. Inch by inch, the floorboards disappear, the black hole spreading inward toward us.

Remi has jumped down and is trying to wrench the window open. He steps onto the lower sill and feels up above his head for some sort of catch or lock. "I don't know how to open it!" he yells, running to the next window and searching futilely for its nonexistent lock before banging on the place where the upper and lower sill meet, trying to unstick them. I run over to help him and, grabbing the brass handles at the bottom of the sill, we struggle to lift, but the window won't budge.

Another deafening knock shakes the room so violently that the hanging lamps swing back and forth. The black hole forming on either side of the room has swallowed up half of the beds and is closing in on us.

A roar comes from behind me. It's Sinclair, who has flung himself off the lifeboat bed. Scooping up the old rusty ladder he and Cata used to carry Fergus, he yells, "I'm not dying in a psycho's nightmare!" And lunging toward a window, he rams the unwieldy ladder through the glass.

The window, wooden frame and all, explodes under the pressure. It bursts into the air in a million diamond fragments, spraying out around Sinclair as he pitches himself through the hole in the jagged glass. Mid-jump, he disappears. Remi was right: the Wall is just outside the windows.

"He left us!" Cata exclaims. She looks down at Fergus and then back at the window. The grinding noise of the disintegrating floors almost drown out her words. "Come help me carry Fergus!" she yells, eyes flitting from Remi to me.

"Leave him!" Remi shouts back, positioning himself in front of the broken window. "He could be gone for good. But we're still alive!"

Cata looks hard at Remi and then bends down to grasp Fergus under the arms and starts shifting him sideways. I run over and grab his feet. Between us, we half shove, half yank him off the bed.

"Come on!" yells Cata, and starts dragging Fergus toward the window. I take his ankles and we careen across the room as the floor disintegrates on either side of us, leaving us nothing but a tiny bridge of floorboards for the last couple of yards. "Help me lift him!" Cata yells.

I eye the wicked shards of glass lining the lower edge of the window, and shake my head. "That'll rip him to shreds! Remi, grab a mattress and drape it across the glass!"

"No time," Remi says. He had been wavering, waiting to see if we would give up and come with him. But a look of panic has seized his face. "Seriously," he urges, reaching out as if to grab our hands. "Come on!"

Cata ignores him and turns to me. "It doesn't matter if Fergus gets hurt. He'll be healed in the Void."

"Not if it kills him here first!" I argue.

Cata uses her tennis shoe to kick the biggest shards of glass outward. "That has to be good enough!" she says. But shoving him through the window is more difficult than dragging him across the floor. We struggle with his weight as we try to roll him over the jagged window sill. His body catches on it, and one arm lands heavily on a shard of glass, releasing a spurt of bright red blood.

"It's not going to work!" I yell. I want to tap on something so badly I feel nauseous, but I won't let go of Fergus.

The third knock comes with a sound like an atomic bomb.

Corpse Brett launches himself toward the broken window, and, seeing the rotting flesh lurch toward him, Remi throws himself through, disappearing into the blackness as he clears the window ledge.

Brett hits the window and rebounds, like an invisible force field suddenly materialized before the yawning gap. He hovers next to it, flailing and ripping out his nonexistent hair with heart-wrenching shrieks.

A wind rises from nowhere, sucking up the millions of tiny glass shards and hurling them through the air. They spray against my face and sting like a swarm of bees as they lodge into my skin. Cata's face and arms bloom red as she shrieks and holds her hands up to shield her eyes.

There's a look on her face, and I know we're both thinking the same thing. *Should we leave Fergus here and save ourselves?* I press my lips together and shake my head no. "Shift him sideways!" I order. Cata takes him under the shoulders and I grab his calves. "Swing him like a hammock!"

A flash in Cata's eye tells me she understands. "On three," she yells. Hefting him up a few inches off the floor, we swing him in toward the room, out toward the window, in and out once more—"Two!" Cata yells—and then, "Three!" With all our strength, we swing him forward, letting the follow-through of the gravitational force lift him through the window. Fergus disappears into the blackness. Cata grabs my hand, and, with a running start, we dive through after him.

CHAPTER 4

JAIME

A MEDIC ARRIVES AT THE LABORATORY DOOR, carrying a vial and syringe. Zhu takes them and shoots the liquid into Fergus's feeding tube. The beeping of his machines decelerates to a rhythm that is markedly slower than the others.

"This drug is propranolol," Zhou says, glancing at my notebook.

I pick up my pen and write it down, then take bullet-point notes on her explanation.

- *Propranolol = beta-blocker*
- *Often given after heart attack*
- *Makes heart beat more slowly, lowering blood pressure*
- *Dose given to Fergus only lasts an hour*
- *Gives heart a break, reducing chances of another heart attack*

Once I've got this down, Zhu asks me to join them in front of their monitors. "I would appreciate it if you could take notes on this conversation, Jaime," she urges.

I nod.

"You saved that boy's life," she says, "and, even though it was a rash decision, it was the right one. We will not put you in that dilemma again. We won't leave you alone in the lab."

Vesper's forehead is beaded with sweat. I realize that, with the amount of stress they've been through, he and Zhu must be fighting to keep it together. I'm guessing they're now running on pure desperation.

"Subject two's heart rate is back to normal, but the rest of his feedback is not in tune with the others," Zhu states.

"Besides subject seven, of course," Vesper adds.

"Yes," affirms Zhu. "But as you might have read in the test file, subject seven is an exception. He has brain damage that is possibly irreversible. This test was an effort to stabilize him—to halt the progression of his disease long enough to search for a cure. His feedback can not be compared to the rest."

"I read his diagnosis: fatal familial insomnia."

Zhu nods. "So, ignoring his feedback, up until now the other subjects show very similar heart rates, muscle tension, breathing, and brain waves. We don't know if this means that subject two is going the way of subject three . . ." She pauses. What she means is if Fergus is going to have a heart attack and die like BethAnn did. But she's not about to say that out loud. She closes her eyes and breathes in through her nose, then continues. "It's not clear if this is the eventual risk for all of them. We hope subject two will stabilize, but for the moment, his safety hangs in the balance."

She looks at Vesper. He presses a few keys on his keyboard, and a printer begins whirring on a table to his right. Retrieving a sheaf of papers, he hands copies to Zhu and me and keeps one for himself.

"These charts give a side-by-side overview of the subjects' feedback during the last couple of hours. Although there are inconsistencies and irregular cycles, it is obvious that the overall feedback is waning. The subjects are declining. Being in a non-waking state is wearing down their hearts . . . their metabolisms. It's as if they have been sleep-deprived over the space of several days instead of several hours. If this deterioration continues, they will be in grave danger. Something must be done to stabilize them until we can figure out how to wake them up."

He looks meaningfully at Zhu, and then back to me. "Although I was not a fan of the idea in the beginning, I see no other option but to go along with Dr. Zhu's plan to repeat the initial electroshock waves at a higher level and hope that that will have a stabilizing effect. The goal is for it to facilitate REM sleep and the healing effects it has on a sleep-deprived brain."

"What if they're already dreaming?" I blurt it out before I have time to think. The researchers stare at me, dumbfounded.

"They aren't dreaming, Jaime," says Zhu cautiously. "Look at the brain waves."

"What if the monitors are faulty?" I ask. I've already stuck my foot in it. I might as well follow through.

"Why would they be?" Vesper asks. "There is nothing to indicate they are."

"Both BethAnn and Fergus spoke to me."

Zhu looks puzzled.

"Like I said, BethAnn's words were the ravings of a dying brain," Vesper says, giving Zhu a look that says he's got this handled.

"But what if not?" I press on, even though their mood is quickly souring. "Could we reset the monitors, just to be sure?"

"Even if there was good reason," Zhu says sharply, "that can only be done by shutting down the electricity in the room. And that's not going to happen again."

Vesper claps his hands once, as if adjourning our meeting. He glances up at the clock on the wall. "It's already two fifty p.m., and we haven't taken time for lunch. Why don't I order something?"

"I brought my own," I reply.

"Well, then why don't you go eat outside?" Zhu suggests quickly, obviously relieved at the chance of getting rid of me for a little while. "Take a break. This has been hard on us, so I can imagine it has been difficult for you as well. Get some fresh air. Take a half hour. Forty-five minutes if you want. By then, Vesper and I will have been able to check with more colleagues before we come to a decision on a plan of action." *A decision that you will have no part in deciding*, she is really saying.

Fair enough. Who am I to even make a suggestion? I shouldn't have spoken up, I don't know why I did. Okay. Yes, I do. It's this sense of responsibility I feel for the kids in the test. I think of what my mom has counseled me about so many times in the past. "You don't have to make everyone else's problems your own, Jaime. You need to learn to care for people without getting emotionally involved each time, or you'll be carrying the weight of the world on your shoulders. And believe me, that can get heavy."

I nod, realizing that I could use a break. Some sunlight and fresh air would be good for me, after hours in this hermetically sealed basement lab.

I walk back to my desk, pick up my satchel, and, with one last look at the sleepers, leave for the outside world.

CHAPTER 5

CATA

BACK TO THE VOID. BACK TO WHITE NOTHING-
ness stretching for so far that I doubt there's actually an end to
it. At least it's light and not dark like it was the first time we got
here. Ant wished there to be light, and as if she were a tween version of God, there it was.

A circle of couches is off to the side, still here from when Ant
thought them out of the nothingness. Sinclair lies sprawled
across one of them, arm thrown across his eyes as if he's blocking
the light. Remi sits perched on the edge of another, holding his
head in his hands.

Fergus lies in a heap between Ant and me. As I predicted, he
is unhurt, the blood gone, no cuts or scratches from where we
dragged him over the broken glass. Ant doesn't even bother to
stand up. She crawls to him, rolls him over, face to ceiling, and

once she's reassured that he is breathing, flops onto her back and closes her eyes.

Sinclair moans, "We are *not* going into that crazy dude's dreams again. Someone tell me that's not going to happen."

I push myself up, stalk over to his couch, and punch him in the shoulder. Hard.

"Ow!" Sinclair exclaims, glaring up at me. "What was that for?"

"That was for leaving us to fend for ourselves!"

"Punch him too, then. He got here right after me." He gestures at Remi.

"Brett chased him through the window. *He* had an excuse. *You* didn't."

"Ugh," moans Sinclair, draping the arm back over his eyes. "Roaches. Show-tune unicorns in granny nightgowns. I've gotta say, I, for one, am glad Brett's locked inside the nightmares and can't drag the contents of his freaky subconscious in here."

"Oh my God!" I say. "That's so coldhearted!"

"Coldhearted, maybe, but honest. I'm knackered, as the British would say. I just want to lie here like a slug until the next door comes to whip me away." He pats the couch cushion next to him. "Want to join me?" The dark pools of his eyes and those chiseled cheekbones that make him look like a mischievous god might be enticing to some. But not me. Not any more.

"You know, Sinclair, I have the feeling that you're used to girls ignoring your bad behavior and doing whatever you ask.

But even if I didn't hate your guts right now, if Fergus weren't lying unconscious on the ground, and Remi weren't holding on to his head like it was about to explode, I'd still say no."

He just smiles. "Rain check?" he says, winking.

Oh my God, the gall. I suppress the urge to punch him in the face this time and walk away. "Remi. Are you okay?"

"We almost didn't make it. Again." He raises his head from his hands and looks at me. He has the same terrified look he did when we were stuck under the floorboards of his house several dreams ago, when I still barely knew him. Not that I've really gotten to know him any better. Up until now, he seemed like a good kid, though cranky and direct. But the fact that he wanted to leave Fergus behind? It makes me trust him a lot less.

Sure—our survival is important, but at what cost? It feels like one of those ethics exercises where you have to choose between steering a train with a hundred people off a ravine or onto a side track to safety, but running over four children on the way. No . . . we didn't know if Fergus would ever wake up. But it felt like the right thing to do, to bring him with us. No matter what.

I hear a groan and turn to see Ant hovering excitedly over Fergus. "He's waking up!" she exclaims. She touches his shoulder like she's afraid he'll give her an electric shock, and he lifts a hand to press his palm against his forehead.

"Are you okay?" I squat down to look him in the face.

He squints and moves his head from side to side to peer around me. "The Void," he rasps.

"Yep," I confirm.

"How long was I out?"

"Fifty-nine minutes," Ant says.

Fergus sits up abruptly. "What?" He presses both hands to his temples. "Ouch. Splitting headache," he moans. He peers at Ant. "What do you mean fifty-nine minutes? I thought the Void only lasted twenty. Did the dreams stop? Have we been here the whole time?"

"No," Sinclair calls. He rolls onto his stomach and, propping himself on his elbows, peers over the arm of the couch. "We most definitely have not been here the whole time. We were in that freak monster Brett's nightmare, and we brought you with us."

Fergus stares at him, confused. "Brett?"

Ant clarifies. "We thought he was saying *red*. His name is Brett."

Fergus cops on. "The static monster. The missing seventh subject. We were in his dream?"

"Yes," confirms Sinclair. "And you're lucky to have missed it. The kid is unquestionably psychotic."

Fergus thinks it over. "How did I get there?"

"They tied you to my back," I respond. "We went in together. And then once in the dream, Sinclair and I carried you around. And when the Wall showed up, Ant and I tossed you through."

"You . . . tossed me through," Fergus repeats, looking between Ant and me.

"After I cleared the way for you," Sinclair says.

40

"You jumped through and left the rest of us to fend for ourselves," I rebut.

"Not true," Sinclair says, sitting up. "When Remi said that the Wall was outside the windows, I didn't realize he meant *just* outside. I was going to break through and then come back and help carry this lug." He gestures to Fergus.

He meets my eyes and sees my doubt. He sits up and his face is framed in what seems astonishingly like pure, unadulterated sincerity. His words are earnest. "Listen, Cata. I'm being one hundred percent honest. I was as scared as you. But I forced that fear aside. I was willing to sacrifice myself because I knew it was up to me to save you. But, like I said, I miscalculated and went all the way in."

We have a brief stare-down. I speak my lingering doubt. "From the way we found you, lounging on the couch, shielding your eyes from the light, it didn't look like you were terribly worried about whether we'd get through."

He gives me the deep-eye gaze for another few seconds, and I feel something switch inside me. He's telling the truth. And surprise, surprise, underneath that sarcastic hard shell, I see that he really cares. At least about me.

Then he looks around at the others, and the shell is back. "Think rationally," he says. "What could I have done from here to help you? Nothing! Except prepare for the next dream by resting. Because I don't know about you guys, but I am fucking exhausted."

41

The warm fuzzy trusting feeling dissipates with his return to tough-skinned asshole. "I can't believe that mouth ever actually touched mine," I say.

Sinclair smiles a lopsided smile.

"You kissed him?" Fergus exclaims.

"He kissed me."

"It was a panic kiss," Sinclair says. "We had nearly been trampled by zombie horses. I was just expressing my relief at still being alive."

"By launching yourself onto my face," I charge.

He huffs and gives me a sour look. "Don't worry," he says. "It won't happen again."

"Good," mumbles Remi, looking more himself now that Fergus has regained consciousness. "Because that was almost as disturbing as the corpse horses galloping by."

Fergus stares at Remi, incredulous. "Did you just . . . make a joke?"

Remi gives a barely decipherable grin.

"I wouldn't be making friends too quickly, Fergus," Sinclair said, raising an eyebrow. "This kid wanted to leave you behind. Twice!"

Fergus's smile disappears.

Remi drops his head back into his hands. "As you reminded me repeatedly before the others got back." He looks up at Fergus. "I'm sorry, man. I was just thinking about the survival of the rest of us since we had no way of knowing if you were going to ever wake up."

Fergus nods, like he agrees, and then a weird look steals over his face and he frowns at Remi.

"This isn't the time to argue," I say. "We have twenty minutes to—"

"—take a nap!" Sinclair butts in, flopping onto his back.

"I'm exhausted too," admits Remi.

I suddenly realize how tired I am. I haven't felt it this strongly before. Maybe because of the adrenaline. We just escaped . . . barely . . . and hauling Fergus around seems to have drained all my energy.

"I was going to suggest we get ready for the next nightmare," I say. "We were totally unprepared in there. We didn't even use the weapons Ant made for us."

"Remi used the crossbow to try to break the window," Sinclair counters. "Which should win him the award for most original use of a medieval weapon."

"Cata's right; we should prepare," says Ant, and something in her voice shuts everyone up. "But we don't have twenty minutes. I wanted to tell you in the last Void, but too much was happening." She fidgets. "And I didn't want to scare you."

Our silence is deafening.

She exhales. "The Voids are getting shorter and the nightmares are getting longer."

"What do you mean?" asks Remi. His voice is cold with fear.

"At first I thought that there were just slight variations in time with each Void and nightmare, since some seemed longer and others shorter. But then I saw a pattern. The Voids have been getting shorter by a minute each time, and the nightmares longer by a minute. This Void should only last fourteen minutes." She gazes upward, calculating. "Five more minutes to go. And Brett's nightmare lasted fifty-five minutes."

Everyone is silent for a moment, and then Fergus speaks up. "Are you saying that before long we'll be in the nightmares non-stop?"

Ant doesn't reply.

Fergus turns to the rest of us. "We have to find a way out of here. The person in the lab told me that the researchers were working to wake us from our comas. But if what Ant says is true, we only have a few hours left before we're continuously fighting for survival. Who knows if they'll succeed in waking us before that happens? And even if they do, we can't just wait helplessly for them to rescue us without coming up with a contingency plan."

I try to drum up some energy, but realize I have none in reserve. I'm utterly exhausted. "Okay. We only have five minutes."

"Four," corrects Ant.

"And Fergus has just regained consciousness," I continue. "I second Sinclair's suggestion to rest for a couple of minutes."

"Smartest plan I've heard all day!" Sinclair crows. He stretches his limbs lazily, and then curls up in a fetal position, facing the couch. "Night, night."

Somewhat stiffly, Remi follows his example, lying on his back and plopping a couch cushion over his eyes.

Fergus stares at him for a second, and then waves me over. Ant has moved a few feet away and is scribbling furiously in her notebook.

I sit down next to him, and he scoots toward me until our shoulders and knees touch. "The person in the lab . . ." he whispers, his voice so soft I can barely make out what he's saying. ". . . they gave me a warning."

"What was it?" I whisper back.

"They told me to be careful. That one of us is a dangerous psychopath."

"What?" I ask, too confused to be shocked. And then I follow the path of Fergus's stare to the boy who urged us to leave him behind. The boy hiding his head under a pillow. Remi.

I shake my head. "I seriously doubt that."

"Then who?" Fergus asks, glancing between Sinclair and Ant.

"How do you know it's not me?" I ask, playing devil's advocate.

"I don't know much about psychopaths, but isn't empathy one of the biggest tells?" he asks. He lowers his voice again. "Even though you hide it under your well-developed protective shell . . ." He sees me flinch and reaches over to fold my hand in his. ". . . which is a pretty smart self-preservation technique, in my opinion."

There is sincerity in his eyes. A small flame sparks to life inside my chest.

He continues. "I can tell you have empathy . . . by the truckload . . . but these three?" His eyes travel from Remi to Fergus to Ant. "I can't really read any of them."

And following his gaze, studying each of these people we're trapped here with, I have to agree. We all have our problems. Problems that could be hiding something darker beneath. And I know without a doubt that we'd all do anything to get out of here.

CHAPTER 6

JAIME

STEPPING OUTSIDE THE CLINIC FEELS LIKE returning to my home planet after years of space travel. Everything looks somehow alien. The sun is brighter, the grass greener, even the bubbling fountain in the clinic's drop-off traffic circle looks like it was conceived by a different life-form.

Since waking up this morning, I've witnessed a medical catastrophe, experienced a natural disaster, watched someone die, and saved someone's life. I wonder if I look ten years older, because it feels like a decade's flown past.

There is a park adjoining the clinic, and I find a bench with a view of the building. For some reason, I don't want to let it out of my sight. On the street that runs past the clinic, I see the aftereffects of the earthquake: A couple of telephone poles lie in people's yards. A utility truck is parked beside a traffic light that dangles dangerously from snapped cables. The light stutters green-amber, green-amber-red as men in blue jumpsuits emblazoned with the city seal work to detach it. A new traffic light sits on a nearby curb, ready to install.

I set my lunch bag next to me and turn on my cell phone, which I recovered from the front desk on my way out. I had been ordered to leave it there this morning "for security purposes" when I arrived. Aka, *We don't trust you not to post online about the things you see here.* I type my security code and get a flood of push notifications alerting me to new texts, emails, missed calls, and instant messages.

I answer the first of a string of worried texts from my mom with a quick reply: *I'm surprised you saw the earthquake on the news—it was pretty minor. I'm safe. Don't worry. Not allowed phones in the lab, but I'll call you tonight.*

That doesn't quite qualify as a lie. Just a sin of omission. With Mom's boss being one of the clinic's biggest donors, she's sure to find out about the earthquake's effects if she checks in with her favorite charity. Which obviously hasn't happened. But if I say anything more, I'm going to spend the rest of my lunch break talking Mom down, so a slight prevarication will have to do for now.

Next. A voice mail from my adviser. That's weird. He always communicates by email. I didn't know he even had my number.

I press play and listen as the posh British accent everyone mimics when he's out of earshot speaks through my iPhone.

"Yes, Jaime, Dr. Trevayne speaking," he says, sounding like

Gandalf on a caffeine high. "I just received word from the clinic director, Mike Osterman. He explained that there was an emergency with the trial you are monitoring today for your field experience paper. He complimented you on your apparent calm and said that you had agreed to allow them to use any documentation you produce if they might need it."

My adviser clears his throat. "I have no idea what's going on there, but I just wanted you to know that . . . as always . . . I support you. If your field experience is compromised by whatever has happened, don't worry. I assume you've already been there six hours, so you don't have to stay until the end of the trial if you feel uncomfortable. My connections with the lab would not be strained by your decision. And writing up a failed test is just as instructive as (if not more so than) a successful one. So do what's best for you. No pressure.

"If you want to check in with me, please feel free to phone me at this number. Take care, Jaime."

I put down my phone and pick up my sandwich. I take a bite, chew, and try to swallow, but my throat is clenched so tight that I choke and have to chug my bottle of water to get it down.

My adviser has given me permission to leave this disaster of a situation behind. He said I don't have to complete the trial. But now that the pressure of a good grade is no longer hanging over my head, I realize that's not why I'm staying. It's because I've begun to truly care.

The doctors have no clue as to what's really going on—that the sleepers . . . at least some of them . . . are sharing a consciousness within their coma. And I have an awful feeling that, by the end of this, BethAnn will not be the only one dead.

So . . . do I stay silent and take notes like I'm supposed to? Or do I investigate further? Try to find proof for my hypothesis? Zhu and Vesper have been unreceptive to my theory so far. I'll have to be sure of myself before I say anything else. I just hope I can come up with something to convince them . . . in time.

CHAPTER 7

ANT

I OPEN ONE EYE. EVERYTHING'S GREEN. I OPEN the other. Still green. Blindingly green. It isn't until I move my head that I realize I'm lying on my back looking straight up. Where could we be where the *sky* is *green*?

It smells like the mulch my dad uses in the garden. Mulch and rain.

And then I hear a wild animal screech that has me up on my feet in an instant.

Hat, gloves . . . I reach in my pocket . . . *notebook, pen.* I tap five times on the side of my leg, which isn't satisfying, but it's better than nothing.

The animal sounded like one of those shrieking monkeys on National Geographic. I look around and see that I am in the

51

middle of a forest. No, wait . . . there are vines hanging from the trees. It's a jungle. And I'm in a clearing that looks the same size as the quad at school, which measures four hundred square feet. (The principal let me come the weekend before school started so I could measure everything. Which, as my mom pointed out, he didn't have to, so I did everything she suggested to appear grateful.)

Cata stands up beside me, adjusting her backpack, and I turn to see Fergus and Sinclair brushing dirt off their clothes.

Remi makes a guttural sound like a groan. "No!" he moans. He swings around, taking in where we are with eyes so wide that I easily recognize the expression from my flash cards. Not just fear. Terror.

"Do you know where we are?" Cata's voice is strained. You can tell she hopes he says no. Because if we're in one of his dreams, it's definitely not a good thing.

Remi wipes sweat off his forehead—it is pouring off of him—and says, "We are back in my country."

"This doesn't look like the desert we were in last time," Fergus says.

"It is the jungle a half day away. It is the base of the antigovernment rebel forces."

"Would those be the same rebel forces who were shooting at us last time?" Sinclair asks.

"The ones who killed BethAnn?" Fergus adds.

Remi nods. He's clenching his teeth so tightly, his jaws stick out.

I glance around at the four-hundred-foot square clearing. My stomach twists: I'm nervous. I step toward Fergus, who lays a hand on my shoulder. I don't flinch. "We're in the open. Shouldn't we hide?" I ask.

And then there is a crack so loud it sounds like a tree just broke in half right next to us. Sinclair screams and falls to the ground. Men wearing camouflage and holding guns emerge from the trees. We're surrounded. My eyes flick around the clearing. There are twelve of them. Although they look menacing, they also look surprised. I suspect the last thing they expected to stumble across in this jungle was a group of teenagers dressed like they're out for a trip to the local shopping mall.

"They fucking shot me!" Sinclair yells, thrashing around and holding his upper arm in his hand. Bright red blood spurts from between his fingers.

I want to tap, but I know I shouldn't. Instead, I clench my hands together. One of the camouflaged men notices and yells something. Remi translates: "Hands in the air!"

We all put our hands in the air.

More yelling. "They say to drop our weapons, one by one."

"What weapons?" Cata asks, and then, remembering the knife I made her, slowly lowers her hands and unbuckles the belt. She drops it to the ground at her feet.

"Backpack too," Remi translates, and she shuffles that off and lets it drop.

One by one, we strip everything away and throw the items to the wet jungle floor.

A man standing behind Sinclair steps forward and butts him in the back with his rifle. "He wants you to take the sword off," Remi says.

"How am I supposed to do that when I'm bleeding out?" Sinclair growls.

"He'll shoot you again if you don't."

Sinclair lets go of his arm and, one-handed, unstraps the belt and lets it fall to his side. He curls up in a ball, clutching his wound and rocking back and forth, moaning.

The guard behind him yells something to the leader, and all twelve of them laugh.

Sinclair looks up at Remi and, forcing the words through his teeth, asks, "What'd he say?"

The man pointing the gun at Remi nods, giving him permission to respond.

"He says he doesn't like your pretty face. He asked if he could shoot you instead of taking you prisoner so he won't have to look at you any longer." Sinclair scowls, and all the soldiers laugh.

The leader addresses Sinclair's captor.

"He says they have to take us back to headquarters. The big leader won't like it if they kill us before they find out what we're doing here."

"Well, if they want me to live, they'd better stop my bleeding or else *big leader*'s not going to get any information from me," Sinclair retorts.

Remi translates and responds. "He says use your shirt."

Sinclair attempts to shuffle his shirt up one-handed, with little success.

"Ask if I can help him," Cata tells Remi. With the gunman's assent, she goes over to unbutton Sinclair's shirt, maneuvers it over his wound, and tears it into wide strips. She pauses before wrapping one around his arm. "I don't know if the bullet is still in there."

"Just wrap it," Sinclair begs.

"Sinclair, lie down and raise the arm up. It needs to be higher than your heart," I interject. I can't help myself—Cata's going to make things worse.

"Cata, tie one strip into a tourniquet around his arm just above the wound. Then tie another strip or two around the wound itself." Everyone stares at me, including the armed men, who obviously didn't understand. "Girl Scout first aid training," I say simply.

Sinclair lies down, and Cata gets to work. When she finishes, the men line us up and march, two of them for each of us, guns at the ready, with one leading the way. The twelfth stuffs all our things into a couple of our backpacks and brings up the rear.

We don't walk far. We happened to land five minutes from their camp. I count four hundred twenty-eight steps, but I tripped a few times, so I estimate one quarter mile. Approximately. It worries me that I'm not one hundred percent sure, so I tap five times and try to do what my mom always suggests: let it go.

The camp is so well camouflaged that we're practically on top of it before I make out the cabins. I scan the rows . . . five by seven, so forty wooden huts and a dozen other buildings dotted around the huge rectangular clearing. The whole thing is surrounded by a barbed-wire fence, trucks and jeeps parked around the perimeter.

Two armed guards stand at the gate. Judging from their expressions, they're as surprised by their comrades' catch as our captors were when they stumbled upon us.

They hustle us in through the gates and, with some shouted discussion, herd us toward a hut near the center of the enclosure. We are shoved inside, and the door slams behind us. There's enough of a gap between the door and its frame to see that one man has been left behind to guard us. He stands with his back to the door, gun in hand.

I turn. The cabin is one empty room . . . I hold out my hand to provide scale and multiply—seven by seven: forty-nine square feet. No windows. The roof is made of bamboo stalks lashed together with vines, and the sun streams through the cracks between them, striping the floor with bright white lines. It smells like my grandpa's boat fuel. I rub my nose and sneeze.

The others crowd around Sinclair, who sinks to the ground, his back against the wall.

"Should I have a look at it?" Fergus asks.

"What, are you a doctor or something?" Sinclair grumbles.

"Um. No. It's just that Cata said she didn't see anything. Maybe now that the bleeding has slowed, we can see if the bullet is in there or not."

"It doesn't matter," I say.

Everyone shuts up and stares at me. I'm getting used to that reaction.

"That's kind of hard-hearted," says Fergus slowly.

My stomach drops. I don't like it when he looks at me like that . . . suspiciously. "I'm not hard-hearted," I rush to explain. "It's just that we only have thirty-six minutes before the next Wall. If the bullet hit a major artery, Sinclair would already be dead. If it hit an organ, he wouldn't have long. But it's the arm, and the bleeding has been contained. In normal circumstances, if we kept the tourniquet on much longer, an amputation might be necessary. But by then we'll be in the Void."

Remi raises his eyebrows and nods once. "Respect," he mutters.

"What if we can't get to the Wall?" Sinclair asks.

"Have you noticed?" Cata says. "It's always nearby. At least . . . near enough that it's possible to make it through."

"I wonder if it always appears within a certain distance," Remi says.

I close my eyes and think. The cave. Remi's village. The graveyard. The circus. The asylum. "The Wall was the farthest from us outside Remi's village and in the graveyard. And those times I'd say it was less than a quarter mile away."

"Okay," says Remi. "If we only have a half hour, the immediate goal is to get outside this hut. If the Wall shows up inside the encampment, we just have to reach it without getting shot. If it appears outside the fence, we'll need to find a way out."

"I wonder if other people can see the Wall," Fergus says.

That makes everyone hesitate.

"The only dream where there have been other people was in Remi's village," I say. "The men in the jeep were chasing us. But who knows if they actually saw the Wall, or if they just saw us disappearing?"

"Even if they do see it, they won't know what it is," Cata suggests, "and they won't know they need to keep us from it. If one of them gets sucked through, I doubt he'll show up in the Void."

"Depends on how much of this is real," Fergus replies.

"The bullets are real enough, I can say that much," says Sinclair. "And so would BethAnn, if she could talk."

Cata squishes her nose. Sinclair's joke is in bad taste.

Just then, there's a noise outside the door. Our guard is talking to someone else in a clipped, submissive tone. The door swings open, and a tall, thin man walks through, ducking so as not to bash his head on the lintel.

Remi's eyes grow wider, and beads of sweat pop up on his forehead. He clearly recognizes this stranger.

The man's voice is menacingly low as he addresses Remi. Remi answers back, gesturing to the rest of us as he speaks. The man's eyes shift from person to person, as he weighs Remi's explanation. When they land on me, I feel a chill like I've never felt before. Usually, it's a chore to try to figure out what emotion is behind an expression. But here, it is clear there is nothing behind the eyes: they're as empty and cold as an ice cave.

The man says something to Remi, who sets his jaw, nods, and

turns to explain to us. "He says I have to come with . . ." The man cuts him off with a sharp word, and turns to stride out of the hut, the guard holding the door open for Remi and him. Once they're outside, he slams it shut.

"How much longer?" Fergus asks me.

I take my pulse and calculate. "Thirty-one minutes."

"Well, Remi's the one who's always thinking about strategy," Sinclair says hopefully. "Maybe he'll come up with some story that will get us out of here."

Fergus shakes his head. "Nope, he's abandoned us. That's the last we'll see of him."

"What?" Cata asks. "What are you talking about?"

"Don't any of the rest of you speak French?"

"Spanish," Cata responds.

"Me too," I say.

"Foreign languages aren't my thing." Sinclair frowns.

"Well, our captors in the jungle spoke to Remi in some language I didn't understand. But this man here was speaking French. And from what I could make out, he was asking Remi who the white people were."

"I'm not white," says Cata.

Fergus rolls his eyes. "Me neither. He meant foreigners."

"What did Remi say?" asks Sinclair, his eyes narrowing.

"He said we had captured him and forced him to bring us to the camp," Fergus says quietly. "He betrayed us."

"It's like you said in the Void," Cata says with amazement.

"What did you say in the Void?" Sinclair asks.

Fergus runs a hand over his head and frowns. "When I woke up in the lab, I was told there was a psychopath in our group. To be careful." He hesitates and looks toward the door. "Now we know who it is."

CHAPTER 8

CATA

"WHAT DO YOU MEAN BY *PSYCHOPATH*?" ANT ASKS with a curious expression. "That's exactly what the person said?"

"Word for word," Fergus says, holding up his hand like a Boy Scout pledging.

"Why, Ant?" I ask.

"It's just that not all psychopaths are dangerous. In fact, their lack of empathy and delusions of grandeur are valuable traits in some professions. If a surgeon is a psychopath, their lack of empathy prevents them from experiencing any distracting emotions when they cut into a patient, and they are so sure of their capability that their scalpel doesn't waver."

Ant looks at us. "What?" she asks defensively. "I studied it!"

"Why?" asks Sinclair. "Because you were diagnosed with it along with chronic insomnia?"

"No." She pulls her hat lower over her ears. "Because it interested me."

Sinclair raises an eyebrow.

"Cut it out, Sinclair," I say.

He shrugs, then says to Fergus, "It is interesting how Remi voted to leave you behind in the last nightmare. That's pretty cold. And he's so single-minded about this survival thing that it makes me wonder if his story is true."

"What do you mean?" I ask.

"Well, his whole family was slaughtered and he was the only one who escaped. Maybe he pulled something like this in order to save himself."

"Are you saying that Remi betrayed his own family?" I ask. "That he handed them over to the militia so that he could escape?" I feel a shot of rage course through my veins and am not sure whether it's directed at Sinclair for suggesting such a horrible thing, or at myself for halfway believing him.

"I wouldn't be surprised in the least," says Sinclair.

"No. He wouldn't do that," I rebut. "I was there with him under the floorboards of his house. He acted too traumatized to have done something like that."

"Aren't psychopaths supposed to be master liars?" Fergus replies, seemingly buying Sinclair's theory more easily than I do.

"His own survival has always meant more to him than anything else," Sinclair says.

"Well, you're the one who jumped out the window to save yourself in the last dream," Ant rebuts.

"Like I said, I was clearing the way for YOU all!" yells Sinclair, losing his temper. He cradles his wound for support.

"None of that matters," Fergus says, holding his hands out as if to put the matter to rest. "We're on our own now. Remi's the only one who had a chance of talking us out of it."

"Okay, let's plan, then," I suggest. I feel shaken, unwilling to believe that Remi would betray his own family, but unable to refute his coldheartedness.

I try to focus my thoughts. "Ant, are you sure you can't create something out of nothing here in the nightmares?"

Ant shakes her head. "I've tried before."

"Try again," urges Fergus.

"What should I try to make?"

"A machine gun would probably come in handy right about now," suggests Sinclair.

Ant looks at Fergus, then at me. We nod our agreement.

"I understand your hesitation before," I say. "I don't like guns either. But in this case, I think they're justified."

She tilts her head, considering, then sits down on the earthen floor, near where Sinclair is slumped. Fergus and I join them.

Crossing her legs and setting her gloved hands lightly on her knees, Ant closes her eyes and meditates. It's stifling hot inside the hut; her face is flushed red with heat. I see a rivulet of sweat roll out from under her knit hat. Without opening her eyes, she wipes it off with the back of her hand, and then after a second, rips off the gloves and hat and poses her hands back on her knees.

Once again, I'm shocked by the short strawberry blond hair

pulled back with barrettes. She looks so tiny and defenseless without the ubiquitous hat and gloves that I feel sorry for her. She needs so much armor to feel safe, and without George she must feel more defenseless than ever.

For a second, something seems to be taking form in the air in front of her. A glimmer of metal, although it could be a freak ray of sunlight coming through the bamboo roof. And then it's gone. Ant opens her eyes. Frustrated, she shakes her head.

The door to the hut flies open, and our guard stands in the doorway, signaling with his rifle that we're to stand. He gestures us out one by one. A pair of soldiers greet us outside the door. One grabs us roughly by the shoulders and forces our arms behind our backs, while the other binds our wrists together with a zip tie. Sinclair gestures toward his wounded arm, but the guy's lips spread into an evil smile, and, treating him rougher than necessary, he jerks Sinclair's arms back to bind them as Sinclair roars in pain.

With their guns in our backs, they march us over to a corner of the enclosure where Remi and the leader stand talking next to a watchtower elevated high off the ground on stilts. It is bordered by thin slabs of wood and topped with branches and leaves, camouflaging it to blend in with the surrounding jungle. Two men armed with machine guns stand perched up in it, surveying the surrounding area for danger. Beneath it, a uniformed man sits at a table, pen and papers set inexplicably in front of him.

Remi and the thin man look up as we arrive. Our guards

gesture for us to stop in front of them. The man addresses us in heavily accented English.

"This boy," he hesitates, then places a hand on Remi's shoulder. "This *man*," he corrects himself, "has exposed you for what you are: spies sent by foreign governments. Our enemies are wily, sending young people who look like students. But we always discover the truth."

He waves one of our guards forward. The man bows his head submissively, and the leader grabs the man's beret and places it carefully on Remi's head. "He will be rewarded for his assistance. And you"—the man runs his eyes across our group—"will be shot."

My stomach drops. I'm glad I haven't eaten anything lately, because, judging by the way my bowels unclench all at once, I would be in big trouble. "Wait! We're not spies!" My voice comes out in a croak.

The man ignores us and, turning, leads us to the table. "You will write out your confession so that we can notify the media of your acts of hostility, and the international community will accept why we took your lives." One of our guards grabs Ant and forces her into the chair to face the man with the papers.

She glances up at the leader, narrowing her eyes and jutting her jaw forward. Ant left her fear back in the hut with her hat and gloves, it seems, because she spits out her words with an uncharacteristic fury that would suit George to a T. "How am I supposed to write if my hands are tied behind my back?"

The thin man glares at her guard, who shrugs and, unsheathing

65

a huge knife, slices cleanly through the plastic band.

"That's better," she says, rubbing the circulation back into her wrists. "Next question. Why should I confess if you're just going to shoot me anyway?" Ant has the bland, bored look she gets when she's calculating something. I wonder if it's a strategy she's learned to deal with fear. Or maybe it's not a strategy at all—maybe the situation's lack of logic has triggered her need for things to make sense.

Whatever, it's pushing the leader's button. His lip twitches as he says, "Because I choose who shoots you. It can be him"—he tips his head at Ant's guard, holding his knife expertly like it's a natural appendage—"or Thomas there." He nods at a little boy struggling with a bucket of water. "Thomas has never held a gun. I'm assuming it will take him a few shots before he gets his aim right."

The man sitting behind the table picks up the pen and shoves it into Ant's hand. "Sign," he grunts.

"I thought I was supposed to write my confession," Ant says, looking confused.

"We will write it for you," the leader growls. "Just sign at the bottom to make it official."

Frowning, Ant signs the paper, then stands and makes room for Fergus.

The leader turns and walks away, yelling orders to a group of men who are huddled around watching us. One of them grabs Ant and forces her up against the fence, his gun in her face. She yelps as her back brushes the barbed wire, but she shows no emotion, training her eyes on Remi, who has sidled over to where Sinclair and I wait our turn to sign the papers.

"How could you?" I hiss at him. My guard looks cautious for a second. Then, once he cops on to what's happening, he laughs.

"You don't care about anyone but yourself!" I continue.

"Don't tell me you're as gullible as the leader," Remi says in a low voice, but it's obvious the guard doesn't understand English.

"You saved your own skin by handing us over," Sinclair says. And then he spits at Remi. The guards both start laughing now.

Remi reaches up to wipe off his cheek and lowers his voice. "You seriously think I'm handing you over?" Either there's pain in his eyes or he's a champion bluffer. Having witnessed his grief in his first dream, I'm tempted to believe him.

But the others obviously don't. With a cold look at Remi, Fergus stands and allows himself to be herded over to the gate and positioned next to Ant. He looks like he's going to throw up. I hope he doesn't faint again.

"Cata," Remi pleads. "What do you think I've been doing this whole time?" He sees my hesitation and continues. "Like I already said, I'm sorry for suggesting that we leave Fergus behind."

He watches as Sinclair sits down and takes the pen before turning back to me and looking me straight in the eyes. "Yes. I do care about my own survival," he whispers. "But my whole family died, and I'm the only one who's still alive. How much guilt do you think I feel? Every day. Waking up in my nice cozy room in

America. And knowing my family lies under the ground in that place. In *this* place. Slaughtered for a meaningless rebellion. And I can't do anything about it."

"Then why are you doing this?" I ask.

"Don't you get it? I'm buying us time. The Wall should be here in just a few minutes. I got you all out of that hut and into the open. If they hear the booming when it starts, there will be chaos. We might have a chance to escape."

I stare at him. There's something in his expression that isn't quite right. "I'm not sure I believe you."

Sinclair is led off toward the fence. My guard grabs me and, slicing off my wrist cuff, pushes me roughly into the chair. Remi comes to stand beside me as I sign my name and slam the pen back down. "If you're lying, I'll never forgive you," I say, looking up at him, but he's not listening. He's looking at Ant, who's staring back at him. She holds two fingers toward the ground and, as I look, pulls one in to leave only her index finger. Remi nods at her as my guard yanks me to my feet and shoves me toward the fence.

"If I'm lying, you're dead," Remi says from beside me. "Listen, Cata, I failed my family, but I won't fail you. I'm not going to be the sole survivor again." My eyes are on Ant as she pulls up the finger pointing one—no fingers left—and the air is shattered by a sonic boom.

There is a split second where the camp stands motionless, like a giant pause button has been pressed. Then all hell breaks loose. Men are running in all directions. Those who had guns sprint toward the entrance or jump in the vehicles, and those who were milling about scramble to get their weapons. No one pays any attention to us.

I make a break for it and duck behind a hut positioned near the fence. Remi joins me, and I wave the others over from where they stand, deserted by their guards. We hunker down in the space between the hut and the fence.

"There's the Wall!" I yell, spotting it about ten feet away from the watchtower . . . on the other side of the fence.

"What do we do?" Ant asks Remi.

"Wait. Why are you even here? You betrayed us! You should be out there with your buddy, the supreme leader," Sinclair spits.

Ant ignores him. She watches Remi, waiting for his response.

"What's going on?" Fergus asks, looking between Ant and Remi.

I can see it on Ant's face: she trusts him. My thoughts are going a million miles an hour. I speak up. "I'm not sure he *did* betray us. No time to explain, but I think we can trust him . . . at least with this."

"I only had a plan up to this point," Remi says to Ant. He looks toward the camp's main gate. It's clogged by men running in and out, weapons drawn.

"The only choices I see are climbing the barbed wire or digging our way under. Neither of which are actually viable options," I say.

"The watchtower," Remi says, pointing to the hut on stilts. Only one guard remains. He squats low, swinging his rifle around, looking for something to shoot. The Wall extends from the ground all the way up past the trees just ten feet away from him, but he doesn't seem to see it.

"What are you suggesting?" I ask Remi.

"We can get over the fence by climbing the watchtower and jumping down."

"This isn't like the cathedral," Fergus responds. "There's nothing we can use to swing through the Wall."

"And the Wall's not close enough to the watchtower to jump through," I say, "like in the asylum."

Remi turns to me, his expression grave. "I meant we'll have to jump down and then make a run for the Wall."

Sinclair laughs incredulously. "That thing's got to be twenty-five feet tall. We'll break a leg. Or our feet, if we manage to land on them."

"I know," Remi responds. "I'm scared of heights, remember? But it's the only solution I can see."

"How do we know this isn't a setup?" Fergus says quietly.

"What do you mean?" asks Remi, perplexed.

"How do we know you're not collaborating with the rebels? And that this isn't a way to get us all shot?"

Remi's face darkens. "Why would I do that?"

"I don't know," says Fergus. "Why would you?"

"I'll go if Remi goes first," Sinclair says.

Remi gets a trapped look. Then he shrugs and, resigned, admits, "I don't know what to do about the soldier guarding it."

We peer out from behind our hiding place at the guard in the

tower. He's holding the gun sniper-style, studying the jungle surrounding the camp. Gunshots ring out from a distance. All the
men seem to be shouting, and the noise adds to the general confusion.

"We're not going to send you up there on your own," Sinclair
says. "What if you already have a deal worked out with the guy,
and he just shoots us once we're out in the open?"

Remi's face twists in anger. "What is all this talk? Why don't
any of you believe me? Like I said, the only thing I've been thinking about is how to keep us . . . *all* . . . alive."

Sinclair looks at me and Fergus, one eyebrow raised. "I'll be
right behind you," he says to Remi. "Just go."

Remi closes his eyes and blows out a few puffs of air, pumping
himself up. He darts out from behind our hut, running toward
the watchtower. Sinclair follows closely behind, holding his
wounded arm carefully. Halfway to the tower, he bends over to
scoop something off the ground.

"What's he doing?" asks Fergus as we watch, paralyzed in fear.

The guard is so focused on the imagined foe outside the camp,
he doesn't see Remi arrive at the top of the ladder, or even turn
around as Sinclair, using his good arm, aims the pistol he picked
up off the ground at the back of the man's head. The commotion
in the camp is so loud that we don't hear the gunshot. We just
watch as the man sinks to the ground like a deflated balloon.

Remi spins and stares at Sinclair in shock. Sinclair boosts himself inside the watchtower, takes a look around, and then gestures
quickly for us to come. When no one budges, he turns to talk to

Remi. They are discussing something, pointing at us and then at the Wall.

My mouth is completely dry. I look at the others. They are as shocked as I am. I can't believe what just happened.

Sinclair waves his hand at us like *Come on!* Then, giving up on us, he turns and steps over the wooden barrier enclosing the watchtower and balances on the bamboo pole edging the floor.

He jumps.

He is midair, flailing his arms to stay upright. He lands and rolls over on his side, hugging his knees up to his chest with his good hand. He stays there for a second, and then slowly, achingly, pushes himself up. He looks our way, his face drawn with pain, and gives a thumbs-up. Then he hobbles toward the Wall, his hair and clothes whipping around in the wind, before disappearing into its blackness.

I glance around to see if the soldiers noticed, but no one is paying attention to our end of the camp. Remi crouches low and waves for the rest of us to come.

The second boom rocks the jungle, shaking water loose from the trees so that it seems to be raining. More screams of fear and anger come from the rebels. Several trucks and jeeps barrel off into the jungle.

"Go!" Fergus yells, and we all move at the same time, dashing across the yard toward the watchtower and scrambling one by one up the ladder.

From the top, we have a panoramic view of the area, with doll-sized men scrambling around.

"I don't know if I can do this," Ant says, looking green.

Fergus takes her hand. "I'll go with you."

She presses her lips together doubtfully, but nods. They swing their legs over the side, balancing on the bamboo rod for just a second before Fergus says, "Go!" Then they're in the air, plummeting toward the ground on the other side of the fence. They land, Fergus on all fours, before he rolls to the side, holding one hand in the other and stifling a scream. Ant lands on her feet, crumpling like a rag doll as soon as she hits and lies there. Fergus forces himself to scramble to his feet and begins to help Ant up.

My turn.

I hear the wind whip by me, and try my best to stay upright, but hit the ground on my side and hear my arm crunch beneath me. Blinded by pain and unable to breathe, I lie there for a second before hearing Remi land beside me with a thump and a groan.

I look up to see Fergus holding Ant to his side with his one good arm. He glances around to see if we made it. Our eyes meet. His are full of pain, but also concern. He's waiting. For me.

The wind whips my hair around my face, and the noise is so loud that I take the risk and yell. "Just go!" Fergus nods and pulls an ashen-faced Ant through the Wall.

I flip onto my stomach and push myself to my knees, using my good hand. Every inch of me feels broken, and tears are streaming down my face even though I can't feel myself crying. I look over at Remi. He's upright already, and takes a hop toward me, bending his right foot up behind him. His face is tight with pain.

"Let's go!" he urges, and I take a step toward the Wall. But something catches my eye a short distance to our right. I stop in my tracks.

The soldiers have surrounded someone, and are standing in a circle, guns pointed inward. Just visible between them is Brett. He stands there in his pajamas, but not as Rooster Brett or Corpse Man. He looks like the boy in the mirror, blank-eyed and lost.

He points at the Wall. He's showing the soldiers he wants to go that way. They look at where he's pointing, and I flinch, but they don't notice me standing off to the side. One of them yells something and, lifting his gun to eye level, points it at Brett's head.

"I can't let them kill him!" Remi shouts and takes off limping in Brett's direction.

"Remi! He can't come into the Void anyway!" I call.

"Don't you see? He's not a monster. Maybe he could make it!" Remi yells over his shoulder. And then turning, urges, "Go, Cata! You have to get through!"

"I'm not leaving you!" I yell back. I take a step toward him, then stop as pain shoots through every part of my body.

"Go, Cata," Remi says, jaw set and voice determined. "This is all my fault. If only one of us is going to make it out of here, it's not going to be me." He has begun hobbling back in Brett's direction when the third boom comes.

The wind whips me inward, toward the Wall, and I let myself stumble backward in its direction, refusing to turn away from Remi. With each step, a fiery white tongue of pain sears through me.

Remi has almost reached the circle of men around Brett, when all of a sudden Brett transforms into his squid state, and a single gunshot rings out. Remi screams, "No!" as Brett collapses to the ground.

The men spin and see Remi. They raise their guns. The wind is so loud that I don't hear the second gunshot. I just see Remi crumple to the ground as I lean back and let the blackness swallow me.

CHAPTER 9

JAIME

"CELL PHONE, PLEASE," SAYS THE RECEPTIONIST, robotically reaching out her hand as I sign back in to the visitors' book. My name is near the top of the paper-clipped left-hand page marked March 31:

Jaime Salvator Time In: 6:00 a.m. Time Out: 2:45 p.m.

I proceed to the next space, halfway down the right-hand page, and write my name again, signing in at three fifteen. Without thinking, I peruse the list of names sandwiched between my two entries. My eyes stop on a name that was entered late this morning: "Lindstrom." It was scrawled so quickly it was barely legible. There was no "out" time.

Lindstrom was BethAnn's last name. Her parents must have rushed to get here when they were notified of her death. They probably followed the funeral attendants out a back exit.

Hospitals never bring corpses out the front door.

The receptionist slips my cell phone into a drawer, and I make my way down the stairwell to the basement laboratory with renewed resolve. I need to figure out if my theory is right. It seems too crazy to be true. But there are two things tipping me off to the fact that all is not as it appears.

The first is the subjects' feedback. They keep experiencing periods of heightened . . . and then lowered . . . heart rates, blood pressure, eye movement, and muscle tension. It is the cyclical nature of these periods that makes me suspect something abnormal is going on.

When I noticed these periods lasted around fifty and twenty minutes, that triggered a memory. The manual said the trial was meant to induce twenty-minute cycles of REM sleep punctuated with fifty-minute periods of NREM. Because of the earthquake, that pattern was never established. But . . . and this is the weird part . . . even after the electrodes were disconnected, it looks like the cycles continued, but in reverse. The feedback read as if they were having twenty-minute periods of NREM and then dreaming for fifty.

The researchers didn't pay much attention to this, because the brain waves said they were comatose. They thought the ups and downs were the bodies' reactions to having the electrical current abruptly interrupted.

The second big question for me is . . . if they are dreaming, why do the brain waves read delta and theta—states that would make dreaming impossible? Either the system crash caused a bug in the brain-wave feedback machine, or—my previous theory—the subjects' brain activity is so atypical the machine can't read it.

Only one of those theories can be tested. Another machine could be brought in. Or the current one could be rebooted, a plan that Zhu shot down when she said it would mean cutting the electricity again . . . something she's not prepared to do.

I need more proof before I say anything else. I need to organize the available feedback better than the rough chart I threw together from estimated times and inconsistent notes.

I need to access the readouts. Video and audio of each subject is being recorded—I can see it happening on my screen. If I can pinpoint the moment of BethAnn's death and Fergus's period of consciousness, I could show it as evidence to Zhu and Vesper. Along with the consistent cycles, maybe it will be enough to convince them to check further into the brain-wave feedback. Or even to consider options that I'm not aware of as a premed student.

I have to do something, though. I push open the door and see Zhu standing next to Fergus, studying his screens on the Tower. She nods at me, acknowledging my return. "The beta-blockers seem to have done their job. Subject two is stable."

Vesper gets off the phone as I take my place in front of my screens at the monitoring station. "Murphy agrees that repeating the electric currents at a higher level is the best option," he calls to Zhu, who finishes making her rounds. She spends an extra minute beside subject seven, shakes her head, and then comes over to join us.

"That makes five colleagues in agreement," she says. "Are you convinced?"

Vesper pauses. "Well, we haven't gotten clearance from all of the legal guardians yet, so it's a nontopic until then."

Zhu sighs, then asks, "Would you mind writing this down, Jaime?" Which I take to mean, *Write this down so we can cover our asses.*

I get out my pen and open my notebook.

"BethAnn died of a heart attack. We won't know why until a full autopsy is carried out. Fergus almost died of the same thing. We are wondering if a contributing factor is the fact that their bodies seem to be wearing down, considering the wild fluctuations of their vitals that they have experienced in the last eight hours. Because of this, it appears that waiting for them to wake up on their own is not the best solution.

"Everyone, including our director, Mr. Osterman, agrees that the best plan for moving forward is proceeding with another round of electroshock, this one at a higher intensity than last time. Using laymen's terms, the hope is to bump their brains out of the rut they seem to have gotten stuck in. The technique has been demonstrated successfully with test animals. Never with humans, which is why we haven't acted so far. But time is of the essence."

She had mentioned the ups and downs in their vital signs. Now was my chance to push the matter further. "Just so I can understand what you're talking about . . . for my notes . . . is there any way I can see what you mean about the fluctuation of the vitals?"

She nods and comes over to my desk. Leaning over me, she opens a window on the fancy lab computer and types in a password. "This accesses our internal server."

She clicks through a few screens, and then stops on a list of links labeled one through seven. She clicks the top one. A page entitled "Beta subject one, Catalina Cordova" pops up. It has several subwindows, one of which is the image on my monitoring screen: a real-time video of Cata lying on the bed. The time ticks away in seconds beneath her image. The rest of the windows show diagrams of the feedback that is being monitored: heart rate, blood pressure, eye movement, muscle tension, brain waves.

Zhu pulls the scroll bar under the "heart rate" window, showing the zigzags of Cata's heartbeats moving in reverse.

"You can see the history of each subjects' feedback on their individual page. Once the trial is over, we pull all of them together into one chart to analyze overall individual feedback, giving us a better picture of how they reacted throughout the trial. We can also layer one subject's vitals over another's to analyze their reactions and draw comparative data. However, while the feedback is still being collected, you can only study one at a time."

That isn't going to be good enough. I notice a printer icon in the corner of each window. "Can I print?"

Zhu nods at a large-format printer in a corner of the room. "Knock yourself out," she says. "Right now we're on hold, trying to get in touch with all of the parents."

She reassures me that I'm logged in as a guest, so I can't accidentally delete or change data, then goes back to her chair. I sit there for a moment, jotting down my thoughts to form my strategy.

And then, one by one, I click into each subject's file and print out the history of their heart rate monitor. When I'm done, I collect the long strips of horizontally printed paper off the printer and bring them back to my desk. I begin by lining them up one on top of the other, and then realize the paper is so thin that if I layer one graph atop another, I can see through to the one underneath. I take my pen and trace the bottom graph onto the top one, and then label the new line "subject two."

Opening the desk drawer, I find an assortment of pens and pencils. Perfect. Using a different color of ink for each subject, I trace them one by one onto the graph until I have a picture of the entire group's heart rate feedback from the beginning of the experiment until now.

Across the bottom of the graph, the seconds, minutes, and hours are printed, starting with :00 at the beginning and ending at 7:20:05, which, though it was an hour ago (the timer on my screen currently reads 8:26:33), gives me more than seven hours of data. That should be enough to draw a conclusion.

Satisfied with my work, I start on the next category of feedback: eye movement. And glancing over my shoulder at the teenagers lying on the beds, I think, *Hold on. We're all doing everything we can.*

CHAPTER 10

ANT

PAIN. SO MUCH PAIN. I'VE NEVER BROKEN A BONE in my life. But when I jumped out of the watchtower and hit the ground, my body felt like it was made of porcelain, exploding upon impact.

How could I move? I was a pile of shattered shards. But Fergus scooped me up, and, even though his left arm was hanging limp by his side, he carried me toward the Wall.

My body hurt so bad it was like a fire blazed behind my eyes. The world around me was one big bright spot: Even the black emptiness of the Wall seemed to dance with orange banners of light.

I would have doubted that I was even conscious, but I glanced back to see Cata and Remi throw themselves off the tower too. Once I knew they were behind us, I let go of any attempt at control and let Fergus save me.

When I open my eyes, I am lying facedown across him. My first thought is that the pain is gone. My second thought is, *Oh my God, I'm lying on top of Fergus.*

My face flames with embarrassment, and I begin muttering something to the effect of, "Sorry. Getting off," when he raises his arms and wraps them around me.

"Are you okay?"

"I'm not sure. I think so," I respond. But the memory of the torturous brokenness is still reverberating in the pain centers of my brain. I was broken. Now I'm not. Nothing makes sense in this place.

I don't dare move. Fergus is hugging me. No one hugs me except my parents and my sister, Penny. And my neighbor, Edward, who has been in love with me since we were toddlers, but I only let him hug me on my birthday. I hug Dog, of course, but that's different. He's a dog.

It's not that I can't stand human touch. If someone shakes my hand or brushes up against me, I don't freak out. It's only affectionate touching that makes me cringe. But Fergus is affectionately hugging me and I'm not cringing.

He lets me go, and we sit up. Holding me back by my shoulders, he inspects me like he expects to see bones still broken. He exhales, looking visibly relieved.

"What?"

"Your legs," he says. "You had two compound fractures. Your shin bones were actually sticking out of the skin."

My head starts swimming and my stomach twists. I knock feebly five times on the floor.

He doesn't even seem to notice. Which is kind of nice, because I know how my knocking bothers people. "I'm sorry," he says. "I probably shouldn't have told you that."

"It's okay." I say and hesitate.

"What?" asks Fergus.

"Did it look as gross as those slasher films you watch to desensitize yourself?"

He looks like he's about to laugh and then catches himself, glancing down at his tattoo. He trades the laugh for a smile. "Twice as gross as *Halloween*, but only half as bad as *Saw*."

Our weapons and backpacks that had been seized by the rebels lie in a heap between us and Sinclair, who lies on his back looking straight up into the whiteness. He breathes heavy, one hand on his heart, like he's recovering from a heart attack. "You okay?" asks Fergus.

"I'm alive," Sinclair responds, not moving.

I blink, and there is Cata, lying a few feet away. As soon as her eyes flutter open, she is on her feet, peering around. "Look!" she yells, pointing.

Two forms lie on their backs side by side. Remi is covered in blood. His eyes are open but stare upward, unseeing. His lips move, but no sound comes out. He begins to fade at the same time as the boy next to him starts thrashing his head from side to side. It's Brett—the boy version from the mirror—and his eyes look just as wild and empty as they did back in his dream.

His mouth moves, but unlike Remi's, his throat actually produces sounds. "Mama," he says in a little boy's voice. "Papa." And then, like that, he's gone. While Remi still has a ghost of a form, Brett disappears all at once.

Cata kneels next to Remi and puts her hand on him. It passes right through. "Oh my God," she says, her face turning as white as the Void.

Fergus puts a hand on her shoulder. She looks like she's about to shake it off, then reaches up and grabs hold of it.

"I can't stand this anymore," she says. "I'm not going through the door again. I don't care if the Void swallows me whole."

"Won't work," Sinclair says. "It sucked me in even though I was running away."

"I can't take it," Cata repeats. "I'm too exhausted. I can't run. I can't fight. I can't watch anyone else die."

Fergus waits until the last wisps of Remi disappear. "What happened back there?"

"Brett was surrounded by gunmen. Remi said he couldn't let him die because it was his fault, and went to save him," Cata says, not bothering to tell the end of the story. It was obvious that Remi's attempt had failed.

"Told you," Sinclair adds. "He as much as admitted it to me when we were up on that watchtower. He manipulated the whole thing. Sounds like a typical psychopath move."

Cata seems not to hear him. She's back in the dream, trying to

85

remember the details. "Brett showed up not far from the Wall. He must have been trying to get through it again. He actually looked like a boy this time . . . not a monster."

"He must have had a moment of clarity," I say, pulling my notebook out of my pocket. I sit down on the ground and turn to the right page. At the top, *static monster* is crossed out. Twice. I replaced it with the name *Brett* after the last dream. Underneath, I had jotted a few guesses at what was wrong with him. They're all crossed out. Only *fatal familial insomnia* is left.

Underneath that is written: *Saw at informational meeting.* I have ticked that with a check mark and written beside it: *Must be the two parents without child. He was probably too sick to come.*

A box under that lists each nightmare we've had, and at what point Brett appeared. And finally, I list his incarnations—at least the ones we saw—with my thoughts about them. My notes don't have to make sense. Free association is often more enlightening than trying to form a thought before writing it down.

Skeleton: fear of death. Realization of oncoming death.

Octopus: reaching, grasping, trying to keep hold on reality, on the people he loves, on this world.

Picassoboy: boy who is splintered, trying to put himself back together, broken.

Roosterhead: awake, crow, animal, alarm clock for farmer, NO IDEA.

I write under *Roosterhead: appeared as human boy in Dream #8.* "What happened next?" I ask Cata before looking up and seeing her expression. I flinch. She and Fergus are watching me like I'm some sort of exotic animal species that hasn't yet been categorized.

"You're figuring this thing out for us, aren't you?" Fergus asks.

"I'm figuring it out for me." I hesitate, then admit, "I can't help it. I have to make sense of things or I get too many problems circling in my head and then I get overwhelmed. But yes . . . it might help us if I can get things straight."

Sinclair makes a huffing noise. I know he's making fun of me, even if he apologizes when the others point it out. I don't care. People have made fun of me since I was little. Unless it's someone I care about, I don't give a flip. And I definitely don't care about Sinclair.

"You look like you're about to fall over," Fergus says to Cata. Taking her by the hand, he leads her to one of the couches and sits at one end. She flops down, stretching out and using his leg as a pillow. Fergus perches there like he's not sure what to do. He reaches out to pet her head, then pulls his hand back, looks uncomfortable, and crosses his arms.

He can hug me with no compunction, but with Cata there's awkwardness. I guess that's normal. She's his age, and I look like a little girl. I mean, I *am* a little girl. I'm just not a child in my head. I feel unwanted for a second, then remember how moony-eyed he looked at George and feel better.

I sit on the ground next to them, cross my legs, and close my eyes. A blanket of calm wraps around me. I focus on relaxing, starting with my toes, working up toward the crown of my head. I breathe in through my nose and out through my mouth. And, like I do when I introduce specific desires when I meditate—a goal, something from my wish list—I imagine the object I want right now appearing in my hands. My palms grow warm and my fingers tingle.

When I open my eyes, I'm holding a box of tissues. It is pretty and has an intricate floral design on it like one of those coloring books for adults. I hand it to Cata and read her raised eyebrows and the little O she makes with her lips as surprise.

"I'm not crying, am I?" she asks.

I shake my head. "But you looked like you were about to."

She plucks out a tissue, blows her nose, and balances the box on her stomach. "I forced myself to stop crying years ago, and now, unless I get hurt like I did back there . . . no tears. They're gone. But I kind of wish I could." She closes her eyes as if trying to squeeze a few tears out, then opens them again, dry-eyed. "I know Remi might have been a psychopath, but I feel gutted—like I just lost a friend," she admits. "It's tragic. Every dream he had was practically the same. They've all been set in the genocide. Even in the first one, when we were all separate but could see one another, he was hiding from the soldiers."

"I wonder if he kept dreaming the same dream over and over because he was trying to figure something out. Or solve something," I say.

"Looks like he already solved it," Sinclair says. "He's the one who escaped. His family didn't."

Cata considers this. "I don't think he really meant for us to be killed. I think he was just trying to save himself. And do you blame him? After all of the death he's seen?"

No one answers. I don't know what to say. I could tell that Remi was secretly helping us, but that's because I read his face. Maybe people who find it natural to decipher others' emotions forget to stop and really look when they're distracted. Like when they're being marched around with guns to their backs.

Cata sniffs back a nonexistent tear. "What do you think happened to Brett?" she asks me.

"Like I said before, I think Brett had a degenerative brain disease that leads to the person hallucinating before they descend into delirium and finally death. I'll bet he had a moment of clarity when he showed up looking real. Maybe that means he was on the verge of death anyway. Sometimes that kind of thing happens to old people with dementia who are about to die. But the fact that he changed back into Roosterhead means he lost touch with reality again."

"Which might be a good thing if he was about to be shot to death," she concludes.

"I just need a minute," I say, and shift my attention back to my notebook. I draw a thick diagonal line across Brett's page. Then I turn to Remi's page. I glance at my notes.

15 years old.

PTSD.

From central Africa.

Brought by paternal aunt to America. Lives Minnesota.

Dream: #3. Genocide.

Interpretation: survivor's guilt, fear, post-traumatic stress,
  flashback.

Saw at informational meeting. Was with older woman:
  aunt.

I jot down *#8. Militant camp*, next to the "Dream" category. Then, with a tightening of my throat that means I'm sad, I draw a thick diagonal line from the upper left corner of the page to the lower right.

Turning to another section of the notebook, I jot down *Dream #8, Militant camp Africa, Remi's dream, lasted 56 minutes*, and then close the notebook and stick it, with the pen, in my pocket.

When I look up, Sinclair is sitting on the couch at Cata's feet. I realize that they've been talking, but I was so focused on my notes that I didn't catch what they said. I look at them one by one. "You guys look awful."

"Lay off the compliments. They're going to my head," says Sinclair, glancing over to see if Cata thinks he's funny.

"No, really, Fergus. You have dark circles around your eyes. You too, Cata. And there's something different about you," I say to Sinclair. He looks at me strangely, but whatever it is escapes me, and I yawn and rub my eyes, suddenly feeling very tired.

"Well, I, for one, am exhausted," Fergus responds. "Like, much more than in the other Voids."

Cata nods and reaches back to touch Fergus's arm with her fingertips. This means she feels comfortable with him. It might also mean that he makes her feel secure. I'm not sure. But when she feels him there, her face smooths out.

"I'm emotionally exhausted," she says. "But I also feel like I do after not sleeping for days and days."

"Ditto," says Sinclair, who has noticed Cata's fingers and is frowning.

I flip to the timetable I've made at the back of the notebook. "We've been in here for nine hours and twenty-one minutes, with seven-eighths of our time spent in the dreams and only one-eighth here in the Void—time where we can slow down and rest. Since our brains have been behaving like we were aware this whole time, it's like we've been running a marathon. In real sleep, the activity—the REM sleep—only happens in short intervals. But here, we're running on two hundred percent energy almost all the time, only taking short breaks. We're wearing ourselves out."

"That doesn't bode well if we're going to be spending more and more time in the dreams. That is . . . if we hope to survive them," Cata replies.

"Come on, guys, we have to train," Sinclair says. "I am the only one who has been actively fighting the things threatening us in our dreams. Besides when George attacked Brett, that is." He looks at me with an expression of superiority.

"She thought he was a monster," I say.

"Well, *she* was wrong." Sinclair winks at me. I don't know why. I look away.

"Well, if 'actively fighting' means violently striking out like you have, you're on your own as far as I'm concerned," Cata says to Sinclair. "I don't want to be like that."

Sinclair looks defensive. "What the hell are you talking about?" he asks. And then recognition dawns. "The tiger. Like I said, it was either us or it!"

"No," Cata says, shaking her head. "We had a plan. And it was working. I distracted the tiger, and you could easily have run right past it. But you killed it."

"Oh, for God's sake," Sinclair says, and then, seeing that she's not going to back down, continues, "What's the difference between that and big game hunting? Ask any hunter. Ask my dad! There's something about the thrill of the hunt. The thrill of the kill."

"Was it just as thrilling to kill that guard?" I ask. "Because you didn't look too bothered about doing that either."

Sinclair shoots me a look of pure hatred. "There's something you guys don't seem to realize. We. Are. In. A. Dream. This shit isn't real. That tiger deflated like a balloon at the end of the circus nightmare. And the guard was just a figment of Remi's imagination. It wasn't like some guy in the real world fell down dead when I shot him."

We're all quiet for a moment, running over that possibility in our minds.

Sinclair breaks the silence. "The difference between them and us is that we exist in the real world. And from what Fergus says, if we die in the dreams we die out there. The monsters don't. The

zombies and clowns or red-eyed monks are here in the Dreamfall. They die with the dream. They're not out there wandering
around in real life. Come on, you guys. You can't argue with
that!"

No one argues.

"There's a huge difference between killing imaginary tigers
and soldiers and betraying the group or leaving one of the others
behind," he continues. "And I don't hear you ragging on Remi."

I hold my tongue.

"So what we have to do is be ready. We need to be able to fight,"
Sinclair prods.

"You're right," Fergus agrees, his shoulders slumping.

Cata closes her eyes and then nods tiredly.

"It's just the four of us now," Sinclair says.

"How long?" Cata asks me.

"We had thirteen minutes." I check my pulse. "Only two left."

"Okay. We start training next time," Sinclair says, heading
for the pile of supplies and slinging the crossbow Remi had been
carrying over his shoulder. Everything is there, even the stuff sep-
arated out by the soldiers is back in the backpacks.

"Whatever we bring in comes out with us," I say to no one in
particular. It's something I already knew. I mean, my gloves and
hat burned to a crisp. But that was clothing. That seemed to be
an established rule since the beginning. I make a mental note to
add it to my notebook when I have time.

If I have time.

The first knock comes, and we rush to arm ourselves. But how can we ever actually be prepared? Who can prepare for a night-mare?

The whipping wind sucks up our silence as we brace ourselves for whatever horrors await us next.

CHAPTER 11

JAIME

MY CONCENTRATION IS BROKEN BY THE ACCEL-
erated beeping of heart rate monitors. I look around to see a red
light flashing on Vesper's screen. As Zhu leans over to have a look,
the monitors go crazy, accelerating so quickly they sound like a
rocket taking off. All three of us run down to the test area to
locate the noise. "It's subject seven!" yells Zhu from next to Brett.

"No, subject five," calls Vesper, standing next to Remi's head.
The doctors look at each other in shock.

"They're both in cardiac arrest?" Zhu asks.

"Quick . . . defibrillators!" says Vesper.

"Jaime, call for emergency backup!" yells Zhu, already ripping
the blanket from Brett and detaching the paddles from the defibrillator.

I race up the stairs and ask the operator to send backup. "Tell them we have two patients in cardiac arrest!" Zhu yells. I relay the message and hang up. The doctors have applied the first round of shock and are studying the screens on the Tower.

"What can I do?" I half expect them not to answer.

"Go to your desk," Zhu yells. "Write everything down. Times, everything."

I throw myself into my chair and flip to an open page. I register the time on my screen and start writing.

The doctors apply a second round of charges. One of the monitors has stopped accelerating, and the chilling steady tone of the flatline begins. I look up to my screen and see the boy in window seven thrashing his head back and forth as Zhu drops the paddles and tries to hold his head still. She picks up an instrument and forces it between his teeth, preventing him from swallowing his tongue.

"Subject five's mouth is moving," Vesper says as paramedics burst through the door. The doctors start the third round of charges. The team of four EMTs surround the doctors, leaning in to check the monitors before taking the doctors' place at the paddles.

"How many rounds have you applied?" one asks.

"Three," Zhu responds frantically.

There are now two flatlines whining from the Tower's speakers. The paramedics apply one more round and wait.

"This cannot be happening," Zhu says to Vesper. He remains silent, his eyes trained on Remi.

The flatlines continue until the paramedics put the paddles away and turn off the machines. They carry out a cursory check of vital signs. Then one of them turns to the doctors and shakes her head.

CHAPTER 12

CATA

I OPEN MY EYES. I DON'T KNOW WHY I CLOSE THEM every time we go through the door, but I do. And this time, when I open them and see we are in my bedroom, our little circle standing arm in arm next to my bed, my knees turn into noodles.

"Cata's falling," Sinclair says from my right, tugging as he tries to hold me upright. Fergus supports me until I remember how to breathe and can stand on my own.

"I'm guessing this is your dream?" Ant says. Without waiting for my answer, she crouches down to knock on the floor five times. Fergus meets my eyes, but we barely notice it anymore. It's just part of Ant. Something she needs.

Fergus keeps his arm around my shoulders as he looks around the room: high ceiling, hardwood floor, giant windows that open to the darkness, the white linen curtains moving with the breath of the night: sucked outward on the inhale and fluttering in on the exhale. "Is this your room?" he whispers.

"Yes," I respond. My voice sounds hollow. Like I'm hiding somewhere far away, in an invisible cobwebbed corner of my body.

"Can you stand?" he asks.

"I'm okay. It was just the last place I wanted to see when I opened my eyes." I say. But I don't move, preferring his arm to stay where it is.

Fergus nods, understanding. "What do we need to know?"

"Yeah," says Sinclair. "What are we looking at here? Fanged statues? Monks with glowing red eyes? Prepare us."

I take a deep breath and nod toward the bathroom. "The skinless man you saw me running from in the first dream. He's probably in there."

Sinclair swings the crossbow off his back and checks it over. Then, getting down on one knee, he aims it toward the bathroom. Nothing happens.

"Should I go check?" Fergus asks.

"I wouldn't get close to the door," I say. "He has this way of moving really fast without warning."

"Cover me," Fergus says to Sinclair, pulling the short sword from the scabbard on his belt. Ant and I draw our knives and position ourselves on either side of Sinclair. Fergus inches his way toward the bathroom. I hear the slap of a bloody foot on the tile floor. Fergus turns toward me. I nod and whisper, "That's him."

Fergus inches forward, holding the sword in both hands. He

is close enough to see inside the bathroom. He leans to one side, and then to the other, searching. "There are bloody footprints on the floor, but they stop at the threshold," he says in a hushed voice.

"It always comes from in there," I insist.

He reaches forward with one hand and pushes the door inward. It swings all the way back, banging against the wall. "There's nothing in there now," he says.

That's when I see the prints. They have skipped half the room, and reappear to the right of where we're standing. I turn and scream. The Flayed Man stands directly behind me, the white linen of the curtains billowing out from behind him like demonic wings.

His lidless eyeballs bulge out of their bloody sockets, and his cheekless jaw drops open to let out an earsplitting screech as he lashes forward. The long, jagged fingernails jutting from his bloody finger bones pierce the thin fabric of my T-shirt and carve deeply into my chest.

It all happens so fast that I don't have time to think. My body reacts faster than my mind. My hand holding the knife whips out and meets his wrist, slicing cleanly through the exposed muscle and—somehow—the bone. The hand falls to the ground and writhes on the floor like a dissected worm, spattering blood in an arc around the stump.

"Duck!" yells Sinclair. I don't need his warning—I am already careening toward the bed, knocked aside by the force of the

Flayed Man's blow. I hear the twang of a string and a whoosh overhead, and see the crossbow's arrow lodge deep into the center of the monster's forehead. The man roars and his hands fly upward, grasping at the bolt and trying to pull it free. Another bolt flies and hits him in the chest, embedding itself so deeply that it disappears into the bloody muscly gore.

As the Flayed Man stumbles, his back brushing against the window, Ant acts. Grabbing my floor lamp, she flips it around and uses it like a battering ram. She slams it against the Flayed Man's chest, putting all her weight behind the thrust. Already off balance, the monster topples backward, crashing through the thin panes of glass and falling out of the second-story window, folded into the darkness of the night.

"Are there more of him?" Sinclair asks, rising from his kneel.

I shake my head. "No."

"Will he be back?" Ant asks.

"Possibly," I respond. "I've never been able to hurt him before."

"Okay, then let's get out of here," Fergus says. "Are you going to be okay?"

"What do you mean?" I ask, pushing myself to my feet.

Resheathing his sword, he takes me by the shoulders and turns me around so that I'm facing my vanity table mirror. Four evenly spaced slashes are ripped into my shirt, and I'm drenched in blood. It isn't until I see it that I feel it and double over with the burning pain.

"You can use that shirt to mop up the blood if you tell me

where to find you another one," Ant suggests.

I hesitate, glancing at the boys, before thinking, *What the hell?* Slipping the shirt over my head, I stand there in my bra. My chest is a bloody mess. I dab at the blood with my balled-up T-shirt.

Ant sucks air between her teeth, experiencing my pain vicariously.

"Ouch," Sinclair comments.

"My T-shirts are in the second drawer," I say to Ant, gesturing toward my dresser.

"How much time do we have?" Fergus asks.

"Fifty-seven minutes for this nightmare. Twelve down," Ant replies, throwing me a shirt. It's my favorite—a vintage T-shirt of this movie *Flatliners* I found at Goodwill. It's so worn-out that the cotton feels like silk.

"Unless that thing has poisoned claws, I doubt you will bleed out or get infected in the next forty-five minutes," Fergus calculates. There is something in his eyes that goes beyond pity. It almost feels like care. I nod and slip the fresh T-shirt over my head, and though the wounds still burn, I immediately feel better. "So you've had this dream before?" he asks.

"I've been having this dream for the last few years. This is my old house."

Sinclair looks around and shudders. "I can see why you guys moved. It's creeptastic, to put it lightly."

I look down at the ground. "My family still lives there. I left them."

Everyone stares at me. "Well, if that crypt nightmare family is anything like your real one, that seems like a reasonable decision," Sinclair says.

Fergus touches my arm. "You don't have to tell us everything now. But we have a while to go, and your warning about the Flayed Man probably saved our lives. So anything you can tell us about this place could be helpful."

I'm not sure where to start. Should I tell them that the monster we just saw wasn't the real monster in this house? That living here was its own nightmare?

As my father's face flashes through my mind, a high buzzing sound flicks on inside my head. My eyes shift out of focus. I try to breathe, but it feels like I'm sucking molasses through my nostrils instead of air.

Ant taps my dresser five times and glances at the window.

"I hate to rush you," Sinclair says, "but I have a feeling that Ant and I are on the same wavelength here, being that there is a skinned monster out there that could be crawling back this way."

"Dude, give her a minute," Fergus says. He takes me carefully by the shoulders and looks me straight in the eyes. "Cata. Your eyes look weird. Are you doing that thing . . . dissociating?"

"My face feels fuzzy," I hear myself slur.

"Cata," Fergus says, and his grip tightens on my shoulders. "This is a nightmare. It's not real. You just said that you left this place, and I imagine it was for a good reason. But however shitty it was for you back then, this time we're here with you. You need to focus and tell us what to do. Come back. *Now.*" He snaps his fingers in front of my eyes, and that's all it takes. I shake my head, and the fog lifts.

"What else can happen here?" he asks, staring intently into my eyes.

"The house," I respond, filling my lungs with the fresh, cold air streaming in from the window.

"What else is in the house?"

"It's not what's in the house. It's the house itself."

"What do you mean the house itself?" Sinclair raises the crossbow defensively.

I swallow, and break Fergus's gaze. "My dad believed in spirits. Evil spirits," I say to Sinclair. "When we moved in, the place was trashed. The people who lived here before us left hypodermic needles, condoms, and other stuff that my dad said was proof that the house had been under the devil's influence. He had a priest come with a Bible to exorcise the place.

"I was just a kid. And all I could think was, 'They forgot to do the attic.' I was sure there were still evil spirits lurking up there that would float down during the night."

Sinclair laughs. "So you were scared of the ghosts in the attic?"

"Yeah. When I couldn't sleep. But in my dreams, it was the house itself that was possessed."

"What's that mean, exactly?" asks Ant, her eyes growing wide. "I mean, I understand the concept. But in practical terms." As she speaks, the wall behind her begins to bulge . . . slowly and smoothly, like a lava lamp . . . and a bloodred gel begins to ooze from the bubble forming behind the plaster.

I grab Ant's hand and pull her toward me. "It means that," I say, pointing to the frothy gel seeping from the pores of the room.

"What the hell is that?" Fergus yelps.

"I don't know," I say keeping my eyes on the blob, "but in one of my dreams I couldn't get away and it ate my skin."

"Holy shit!" swears Sinclair as the other walls begin to heave and crimson phlegm oozes out, steaming and hissing as the substance hits the floor. Black, burned holes begin to spread over the hardwood planks.

"Let's get out of here!" Fergus yells.

I throw myself toward the bedroom door, grab the knob, and pull. It's locked.

"Figures," growls Sinclair, grabbing for it. I step aside and let him try the handle, which he attempts to force while slamming his shoulder against the door. A ticking sound jogs my memory, and I yell, "Let go of the handle!"

But I'm too late. Sinclair's scream drowns out my words. A blade has popped out and sliced through the back of his hand. Another flashes up, barely missing his thumb. He yanks back, but he's pinioned there and thrashes ineffectually. Then, just as quickly as they appeared, the blades retract back into the doorknob.

Sinclair spins and, holding his hand by the wrist as blood pours from it, yells at me, "That came from *your* brain? You sick bitch!" But for a second, he's not Sinclair. For a split second he transforms into a shorter, freckled boy with dirty-blond hair. I blink and he's back to his tall, dark-haired self, his face twisted in pain and anger. "What the . . . ?" I murmur.

"It's open!" yells Ant as the door swings outward.

"How'd that happen?" Fergus asks me.

"The house," I say, not meeting his eyes. "It wants blood."

Sinclair lets out a string of expletives and throws himself out the door. The rest of us follow close behind. "Which way?" he shrieks. Blood from his hand splashes on the floor as he looks between the winding staircase and the door to my parents' room.

"Down!" I say, and we rush down the spiral staircase. "Don't touch the bannister!" I yell as Fergus grabs on to it. He lets go just in time, the spikes that flick upward just grazing his hand instead of impaling it. He curses and pulls his sliced hand to his chest.

Sinclair arrives at the base of the stairs and hurls himself toward the front door, which bursts into a wall of flames. He slams to a stop. Fergus almost runs over him. Ant perches two steps up from the floor, looking between me and the boys as if waiting for instructions.

Hearing something behind me, I look up. Standing at the top of the stairs is my father. His gray hair sticks up on end, and his ice-blue eyes stare down at me. In his hand is the razor strap. He folds it in half and gives it a snap, the corners of his lips curving cruelly. The buzzing comes back to my ears and my vision swims.

I stumble numbly down the last few stairs, sweeping Ant along with me, and stand before the bonfire that used to be my front door. The windows on either side ignite with a whoosh, and the four of us stumble back, blinded by the heat.

An unearthly shriek comes from behind the flaming door as a man-sized form takes shape in the blaze. A bloody hand, fingernails as long and sharp as switchblades, thrusts through the fire toward us, and through shivering waves of heat steps the Flayed Man.

CHAPTER 13

ANT

"THIS WAY!" SCREAMS CATA, GRABBING MY HAND and dragging me through a doorway leading away from the front hall. I stumble behind her, trying to map the house out in my mind but there's no time. I don't like being in a space I can't measure. But she doesn't give me the chance, and it's hard to quantify dimensions with the heat from the fires making the air all wavy.

The skinless monster lunges through the flames and lets out a shriek that makes me jerk my hand back from hers to cover my ears. Luckily, Cata doesn't give up and leave me. She grabs my arm with both hands and yanks me through the door.

The boys follow us as we careen into a living room fronted with windows that ignite one by one as we enter. Fergus spins around and, avoiding the ticking knob, kicks the door closed.

Grabbing a high-backed chair, he wedges it under the doorknob.

The walls bulge and ooze red mucus, which is even grosser when I realize it reminds me of an exploding bloody zit. A ripping noise comes from behind the flowered wallpaper. Seams protrude from beneath like inflating varicose veins, and then wires break free and start flailing around like a tromped-on nest of snakes. One grazes my arm, and the electric charge knocks me sideways off my feet. I land in a mound of the red slime. The smell of burning flesh hits my nose before the pain blazes up my left side. It hurts so badly that my mouth opens, but the scream sticks in my throat.

Fergus scoops me off the ground and carries me to the center of the room, plopping me down on an overstuffed floral couch. He whips my hat off my head and uses it to wipe my face and neck, and then, turning it inside out, scrapes the slime off my arm before tossing it away in disgust. He lifts my other arm, where the electrical wires cut a deep gash near my elbow, and uses the hem of his T-shirt to mop away the blood. "Does that hurt?" he asks.

"I can't feel it at all," I respond. "It's numb. I think I got electrocuted."

"Can you walk?" he asks, pulling me to my feet. I take a tentative step and nod.

"Then let's go!"

Cata and Sinclair stand in a doorway, waving us toward them, as the red slime burns holes in the floor between us. Dodging to avoid the flailing electrical wires, Fergus pulls me by the hand, sidestepping a lava flow of acid slime that I'm forced to leap across.

We follow the others into a kitchen where every surface is on fire—old iron stovetop, marble counters, enormous stainless steel refrigerators—everything spews flames so hot they're white. Coughing from the smoke, Cata heads toward a door leading to the backyard, but it explodes into ice-white flames before she can get to it.

"Everything leading outside is on fire," Sinclair yells over the whooshing, crackling sound of the flames. "Where else can we go?"

Cata swings around and looks at a door next to the stove that looks like it leads to a pantry. "Down!" she says, and lunges toward the door handle before stopping abruptly. She turns and sprints back into the room we just came from, reappearing a second later with a pair of fireplace tongs.

Taking it in both hands, she grabs the doorknob in its metal teeth. Long blades snap out of the doorknob like a throwing star, the metal glowing cruelly in the firelight. Cata turns the knob, and the door opens outward, revealing a stairway.

"What's down there?" Sinclair asks. He's grabbed a dish towel off a rack and is wrapping it around his bleeding hand.

"Basement. Laundry room. The shower rooms for the pool."

"Sounds lovely," Sinclair comments, wrinkling his nose. But, glancing back at the flaming-kitchen option, he says, "Let's go!"

As we pile down the stairs, Fergus grabs the side of the door and slams it behind us. We emerge into a cellar with cement walls and floor. A quick guess would be a hundred-foot square, but I don't allow myself to calculate further. Damp-looking towels are strewn around on the ground like rugs. It smells strongly of mildew. I sneeze and, realizing I don't have a tissue, wipe my nose on the back of my glove. Then, feeling dirty, I tap four times on the wall. No one looks.

"At least there aren't any windows," Sinclair says. He's right. There is no fire. The walls aren't seeping corrosive pus, and there are no live wires flailing around. It's so quiet down here that we seem to have passed into another dimension from the heaving, flaming, bleeding house above us.

He looks at me and flinches. "Damn, girl, that's gotta hurt," he says, studying the burned side of my face.

I touch it with my fingers. It feels wet and raw, and, where I rub it, bursts of pain shoot from my cheek to my jaw. But that doesn't bother me as much as the fact that my hat is gone. My head feels exposed. I knock on my leg four times. Glove. Glove. Notebook. Pen.

Sinclair watches me with scorn.

I want to turn away, to ignore it, but I force myself to stare right back at him. "How's the hand?" I ask, and have the weirdest feeling that George is speaking through me. He lifts the bloodied dish towel and narrows his eyes.

"How much time?" Fergus interrupts.

I search the clock space in my mind and feel my pulse to double-check. "Thirteen minutes."

"We need to get outside," Fergus says to Cata. "I doubt the Wall is going to show up inside your house."

Cata nods toward the far end of the room, where there is a dark opening without a door. "The shower rooms," she says. "At the far end are steps that go up and outside to the pool." The way her face constricts (*disgust? fear?*) when she says *pool* strikes a chord of horror in my heart.

"Swimming pool?" I ask.

"It used to be a swimming pool. It's been left to rot for the last twenty years," Cata says, squishing her nose and shuddering. Disgust and fear. "It's more like a swamp."

"Let's go," Sinclair says, but Cata shakes her head.

"We might need our weapons."

"You said we should go downstairs. You didn't say there was a catch," Sinclair says.

"There are things in the walls. But they've never gotten out."

"Things in the walls? Could you be more specific?" asks Sinclair.

Cata gives him a frown. "Just draw your weapons."

I pull out my knife, Fergus unsheaths his short sword, and Sinclair manages with his towel bandage to pull the crossbow from his back, swing it around, and aim it in front of him.

"How do you know how to use that?" I ask, hardly knowing how I had even created it after only having seen one in a museum.

"Like I said, I've gone hunting with my dad," he replies.

"You actually hadn't told us *you* went hunting with him," I say.

He shrugs and falls into line behind Cata, who leads us with her knife clutched before her in both hands. She steps over the threshold and flicks a switch to her left.

A naked bulb hangs from a wire in the middle of a cement corridor. Three doorless openings punctuate the wall to our right, and on the far end, a stone staircase leads upward.

Cata approaches the first opening and peeks in. Sinclair follows her, pointing the crossbow into the room and swinging it around like a TV cop doing a drug bust. "Nothing here," he says.

They continue down the hall and Fergus and I poke our heads into the room. There is a showerhead on one side, with a concrete bench across from it. In the far wall, a vent is embedded near the ceiling. It was probably meant to let out steam and moisture, but with years of disuse, it's become completely encrusted with dirt and moss.

Ahead of us, Cata and Sinclair peer into the second room. I hold my breath. Cata looks back at us. Shakes her head no. They move on to the third room. Sinclair lowers his crossbow and looks at Cata cynically.

"Good job, Cata. You had me crapping myself over the 'things in the walls.' Maybe they got fried by the inferno upstairs," he suggests. "Or turned into goo by the bloody slime."

Cata scowls back at him. "It doesn't happen every time." She turns to Fergus. "You told me to tell you guys everything I could think of to prepare."

He holds up a hand defensively. "Hey, I'm not the one in danger of crapping my pants. I say the more information, the better."

Their arguing is making me nervous. I try to focus on my knife, holding it in both hands like Cata. But as they squabble, a pressure builds up inside me until finally I can't resist. I knock on the wall four times.

Something reaches out and grabs my wrist.

"Help!" I yell as the cement fingers entrapping me grow outward from the wall into a hand, and then a wrist, and then an arm. The form of a very tall, very thin man starts to emerge as I struggle to free myself.

There is a twang, and one of Sinclair's bolts bounces off the cement arm and ricochets off the ceiling onto the floor of the shower room.

I look over at Sinclair. A shape is emerging from the wall beside him—a cement head leaning forward like it is trying to free itself from a membranous web. It tips its head upward, and its mouth stretches open in a silent scream. "Behind you!" I yell.

Now shapes are bulging out of the walls on all sides. "How do we fight them?" Fergus yells.

"We run!" Cata responds.

"Pull as far back as you can, Ant!" Fergus orders.

I lean back from where the cement man has me trapped. Fergus swings his sword above his head in both hands and brings it down with all his strength. The arm crumbles under the force of his blow, leaving a hand still clamped around my wrist. "Go!" Fergus yells, and I dart toward the stairs at the end of the hall.

Cata and Sinclair are fighting the grasping hands, Sinclair using his crossbow as a club to hammer them away as he struggles toward the stairway. Cata screams, and I grab her arm as I run past. I drag her away from where she has just freed herself from a hand by stabbing at it with her dagger. We make it to the stairs before I see that her arm is bleeding profusely. "I stabbed myself," she explains, looking like she's about to faint.

"Three minutes," I pant, out of breath.

She nods, and avoiding looking at her arm, takes a deep breath.

A shout comes from beneath us. We look back from where we perch just inside the stairway and see that one of the cement men is halfway out of the wall and has Sinclair trapped. One hand is clutched around Sinclair's chin, and the other is cupped around the back of his head, forcing his face up to stare the man in what would be his eyes if his face weren't a smooth plane of cement. The man is sinking back into the wall, pulling Sinclair with him.

Fergus swings his sword and breaks off the fingers of a cement man grabbing at him. Then, dropping the sword, he grabs Sinclair around the waist and tries to wrestle him away from the man. Sinclair is struggling and trying to scream through clenched jaws, but his arms have already disappeared inside the wall, and with a suction-sounding slurp, his head is dragged in too.

"No!" Fergus yells and, wrapping his arms more tightly around Sinclair's waist, gives another hard pull. Cata and I stumble down from our perch into the hallway, dodging grasping fingers with our knives drawn, ready to help Fergus, when all of a sudden the bulging forms recede into the concrete walls.

Sinclair remains there, half swallowed by the wall, before a wet belching noise comes from the cement around him, and he drops backward onto the floor, holding his throat and gasping for breath.

"What happened?" I whisper in the sudden silence. "Why did they all disappear?"

A dripping sound comes from the far end of the hallway. Cata's eyes flit from my face to the space behind me, and her eyes grow wide. I turn to see a red puddle spreading slowly into the hall from the darkness beyond. Above it, a form emerges.

The weak light of the hanging bulb illuminates the liquid whiteness of his bulging lidless eyeballs. Then the exposed teeth with no lips to hide them emerge from the shadow. Dark red bands of muscle drip with blood as the skinless man's arm slowly rises, pointing a bony finger, and then he runs full tilt toward us, shrieking his spine-chilling scream.

I stand frozen in terror until Cata grabs me and pulls me toward the stairs. Fergus and Sinclair are already scrambling up the staircase into the cold air of the night, and we barrel out behind them as the first boom sounds.

A full moon drifts overhead in a sky the color of a three-day bruise. A breeze stirs up the carpet of dead leaves covering the lawn. The wind blows against my bare ears, and I feel like screaming from the exposure.

"Over there!" Sinclair yells, pointing across the lawn to where the Wall has appeared. Just in front of it is a swimming pool that looks like something out of an old black-and-white movie. The large stones paving its edges are cracked and crumbling.

Cata moans. "Why does the Wall have to be *behind* the pool?"

I glance back at the stairway leading down to the house, but the skinless man has disappeared.

We dash through the whirlwind of leaves toward the Wall. Cata steers us toward one end of the pool so we can skirt around it. The cement hand weighs heavily on my wrist, the burn on my face is aching, and the sensation is returning to my electrocuted arm, searing pain stabbing at the bloody gash from the cords. *It doesn't matter*, I remind myself. *Once I'm through the Wall, I'll be whole again.*

I'm almost to the pool when I see something in my peripheral vision moving at a fast pace toward us from a far corner of the yard. For a second, I wonder if Brett is back. But I turn my head to see the skinless man running at us from far away, then glitching and appearing just a few yards to our right.

"Watch out!" I yell as he glitches again and reappears next to Cata. He takes a swipe at her, tearing the flesh of her shoulder with his fingernails and sending her toppling over the side of the pool. He lets out a wild shriek and turns to face the rest of us. Fergus has his sword out in a flash and takes a swipe at the monster, slicing cleanly into its arm. Thrown off balance, it teeters and, clawing the air, falls over the edge of the pool. It lands a few feet away from where Cata lies flat on her back, unmoving, in several inches of algae-coated water.

The skinless man lies still for a moment and then begins scrabbling onto his side and pushes himself up. A thwang rings out, and one of Sinclair's arrows hits the monster square in the forehead. He stands motionless for a moment and then crumples. The algae moves out from him in green waves, splashing slimy water over Cata's face. She doesn't react.

"Is she dead?" I ask, and then realize that the boys can't hear me over the wind. I spot a ladder on the deep end of the pool, and run for it, slinging myself down its metal rungs. Halfway to the bottom, I feel something brush against my fingers, and look up to see a large brown rat clinging to a broken piece of tile on the side of the pool. I freeze and look around. There are rats everywhere.

They are only large rodents . . . like guinea pigs, I tell myself, forcing my foot down another step. *People keep them as pets.* But rats are the thing I am most afraid of, after dentists and clowns. The pain radiating from my face, my arms, my side, helps me shut the fear into a small corner of my mind and keep moving. That, and the knowledge that Cata needs me. I can't turn back now.

I land at the bottom of the pool with a splash, the green water covering the tops of my shoes. It smells like infection down here, and I stifle a gag and try to breathe through my mouth. I slosh over to Cata and bend down to hold my hand in front of her mouth.

"She's alive!" I yell up to Fergus and Sinclair. "She must have just knocked herself out."

The second boom rings out, and hundreds of rats squeal as one and plummet from their sideways perches on the wall down to the floor of the pool.

I scream as they begin swarming toward me and kick them away from Cata's head.

Fergus appears by my side and, unslinging his backpack, pulls out the coil of rope. "Prop her up," he says, ignoring the fact that

118

I'm having a meltdown. Rats scurry over my feet, and another scream tears from my chest.

Fergus looks up at me. "Ant, I need you to channel George for me. I know she's somewhere inside you. And she's brave enough to do this. *You're* brave enough to do this. Now help me prop Cata up."

I reach down into the writhing mass of rats and pull Cata up by the shoulders. Fergus loops the rope under her arms and around her torso and ties it in a tight knot. "Up the ladder, Ant!" he yells.

I'm off, climbing like a monkey up the metal bars, barely touching them I'm going so fast.

Fergus shuffles Cata over to the side of the pool directly under where Sinclair squats, reaching for the rope. Fergus throws it, and it slips through Sinclair's fingers. Fergus curses and throws it again. Sinclair catches it. I grab the rope from behind him, and the two of us start pulling Cata up the side of the pool.

We've gotten her halfway up when Fergus arrives and takes over for me. They drag her over the rim of the pool, not even being careful, bumping her head hard on the side as they reach over and pull her up. She'll be fine once we get through the Wall . . . if we get through the Wall.

The third boom rings out, shaking another flurry of leaves from the trees and causing a squealing mass exodus of the pool by the rats, who come pouring over the sides.

Fergus and Sinclair have Cata by the arms and legs, and we only have a few feet to go. The wind whips around us so hard it feels like a tornado, and I get sucked up and turned backward just before I pass through.

That gives me the perfect view of the pool as we leave Cata's nightmare. The perfect view of the skinless man, who has risen to his feet and stands there shrieking and flailing as he watches us disappear.

CHAPTER 14

JAIME

THE PARAMEDICS ARE GONE. THE DEATH CERTIFI-
cates have been filled in and signed. The nursing assistants move
at a pace that befits death, slowly settling Remi and Brett into
body bags. They are the opposite of the efficient, bustling paramedics. It's like if they go slowly enough, avoiding any abrupt
movements, it will buffer what just happened. That it will ease
the realization that those two people who were just there, no longer are.

But the researchers are all too aware of what has happened
and what it means. They look like they've aged twenty years in
the last twenty minutes. After asking, "Did you get all of that,
Jaime?" they forget I'm here. Vesper leaves to notify Osterman
and alert the bereavement team, and Zhu alternates between typ-
ing data into her computer and making phone calls.

I look up at my screen. It is now a patchwork of squares: Windows three, five, and seven are dark. Windows one, two, four, and six are lit up, displaying the remaining subjects: Catalina, Fergus, Sinclair, and Antonia. They're in the period of accelerated feedback. I wonder what they're dreaming about.

Catalina with her violent father and dead mother. Fergus with his severe neurological disorder. Antonia with her high intelligence and behavioral tics. And Sinclair . . . Sinclair with his possibly murderous past.

Based on what BethAnn said about soldiers with guns and Fergus's statement that the dreams were killing them, I can only imagine that they have seen some horrific scenarios. I hope not all their dreams are nightmares. But with three of them already dead and one narrowly escaping the same fate, I doubt they're experiencing all rainbows and sunshine.

I think about my own dreams . . . those that I remember. I do a lot of flying. So much that I know that feeling in my chest that lifts me up off the ground—lungs full of air, shoulders leaning just the slightest bit to change directions. It's as if I live another life in my dreams . . . one as real as this one. Real enough to give me sensory memories, and when I think hard enough about it, I feel my muscles flex, allowing movements my body has never made.

I dream about my dad too. I dream he didn't really die. That it was all a mistake. I walk into my parents' kitchen, and there he is, chopping vegetables for his famous Cajun stir-fry. I ask him why he let us believe he was dead. He always acts surprised, then pats me on the back. "What are you talking about? I've been here this whole time."

Those are the dreams I wake up from in tears. The ones that make me want to stay in bed for the rest of the day, half of me wanting the dream to return so I can see him again, and the other half wishing those dreams would stop so I wouldn't feel so ruined afterward.

Yes, my dreams are vivid enough to imagine what the test subjects could be experiencing. But a regular night of sleep only contains short periods of dream activity. These kids are living through dreams that are almost nonstop.

I look down at the charts I'm making. From what I can see so far, they started out with fifty minutes of heightened feedback and twenty of lowered. If my theory is right . . . and I am almost convinced that it is . . . they pass those longer periods in REM sleep and shorter in NREM. Fifty minutes of dreaming. Twenty minutes of rest.

But over the hours, the REM activity has become longer and the NREM shorter. I check the timing of the last few periods of heightened and lowered feedback. It's clear now that they are continually shifting by one minute each. More dreams, less rest.

No wonder their bodies are wearing out. Their heart rates are gradually getting weaker every hour. Their lungs are showing signs of exhaustion, their breathing becoming less regular. According to my calculations, their "rest" time is now down to twelve minutes. They're going to burn out. And if what has happened to BethAnn, Remi, and Brett is any reflection of what is happening inside the dreams, if nothing is done, they're all going to die.

I finish the charts. Why do the phases move by exactly sixty seconds each time? Perhaps because the Tower was regulated in minutes for the treatment. The sleepers' bodies were set, in a way, like a clock.

In any case, the regularity of the timing can't be questioned. 50/20, 51/19, 52/18, 53/17 . . . No one can dispute that data: not even the researchers. How they interpret it is another matter. Which is why I need to carry out phase two of my plan: finding the videos of the moments of death. The times when the sleepers woke up and spoke.

CHAPTER 15

CATA

A FUZZY WHITENESS GROWS FROM A TINY PIN-
point to spread across my entire field of vision as I become aware
of my surroundings. I'm lying on the ground . . . in the Void.

"What. Was. That?" I hear Sinclair's voice and turn to see the
others sprawled nearby. "I couldn't even dream up something
that freaky if I tried."

We all push ourselves up. Fergus weaves on his feet before
stretching out a hand to help me up. "You're okay," he says, checking me over.

"I don't even remember what happened." I rub my hand over
the back of my head. As usual, my clothes are in pristine condition, I have no cuts or scrapes, but I'm so tired I feel like I was
run over by a truck. Noticing me wobble, Fergus leads me to a
couch, wraps his arm around me, and lets me lay my head on his

125

shoulder. It feels so good that I close my eyes and just soak in the comfort of touching another person. Of letting go of all my defenses and trusting someone, if only for a moment.

Ant walks over to us, chin straps dangling—the chullo that was eaten by acid is back to its slightly worn state—and looks me up and down. Exhaling a sigh of relief, she makes her way, feet dragging, to the couch next to ours and flops down.

"What happened," answers Sinclair, perching on the edge of another couch, "is after you fell in the pool and landed on your head, we pulled you out with a rope and carried you through the Wall. But in between, there were rats and putrid water and a skinless guy doing a Freddy Krueger and coming back to life again and again. I mean seriously. What the fuck?"

He scowls at Fergus, clearly annoyed with the head-on-shoulder moment we're having. I couldn't care less.

"You're the one who's supposed to be a specialist in horror movies," he says to Fergus. "I would expect something like that from your dreams. But Cata? She could be screenwriting slasher films *and* doing all of the special effects." He looks me over with sour amusement. "If you have stuff like that living inside your head, you've gotta be truly and deeply messed up."

I think back to the dream and am horrified that those insanely violent scenes came from my mind. They came from me. Then my disbelief and shock turn on a pin and suddenly switch to anger. "I don't give a shit what you think, Sinclair. But it is comforting to know that with all my true and deep messed-up-ness, you have no choice but to tag along with me to revisit my traumatic past."

Sinclair blinks, but if he's surprised by my sudden show of spine, he masks it well. He looks at Ant and Fergus. "We need more weapons. If we didn't have those"—he points to the pile of backpacks and weapons lying in the middle of the space—"we would have been sliced and diced by the Flayed Man's fingernails or sucked into the concrete walls of that freaky basement place."

Ant rolls over, letting her arm fall limply over the side of the couch. "Too tired," she moans. "You make something. It's not like I have magical powers. If I can do something here, you can too."

Sinclair blinks again. Two people talking back to him is apparently too much. He lies flat down and folds his hands across his chest, but continues talking. "What we need is to train. Remember how we were talking about the Matrix? Neo trained when he was in that Voidlike space."

"That's different," Fergus responds, his voice flat. We're all exhausted. "In the Construct, the guys in the ship downloaded different programs to his brain that turned him into an expert in karate, sword fighting, whatever. We don't have downloads. We would have to learn how to do that stuff from scratch. And if we're losing a minute every time we're here, that's just not going to happen. We have a better chance of learning to fly in the nightmares than acquiring battle skills in the Void."

He says it sarcastically, but Ant perks up. "Wait, what did you say?"

Fergus yawns loudly, covering his mouth, and then says, "That's the whole thing about the Matrix. Neo learned that physical laws didn't apply to him because the 'real world'—as he had always known it—was a construct. I mean, they all knew it, but when he actually believed it, he started doing things like defying the laws of gravity, space and time, and all the rest. Have you never seen *The Matrix*?"

Ant shakes her head distractedly and gets out her notebook and pen. She flips open to a page that's full of her scrawling, and writes sideways along the margin. "So once he accepted reality, he was able to ignore the rules he previously thought applied and work outside of them?"

Fergus nods cautiously.

"So, in a way, our advantage is like Neo's. We know we're in a nightmare world. One that is a construct of our own minds."

Fergus looks confused, then a light goes on. "Yes," he says. He carefully unwraps his arm from around my neck and leans forward on his knees toward Ant. "Wait . . . I think you're on to something." He hesitates. "But the nightmares are real in a way. They're real enough to wound us."

Ant responds, "But the wounds aren't permanent. They hurt . . . yes . . . but they aren't real because they disappear as soon as we get inside the Void. The only thing that's permanent is if we die in the dream. And since that should also be a construct of our mind, I'm thinking that when we die in the Dreamfall it must trigger something outside of here—in the real world."

"Same with the Matrix," Fergus says. "I think they explain it as, if the mind dies it can't survive in either place." He sees me watching and looks sheepish. "I watch a lot of films."

"For good reason," I say, running my finger over his tattoo. He smiles.

"I'm not suggesting that we should follow the rules laid out by a science fiction film," Ant interrupts, "but I wonder if we might have more control than we think we do."

Fergus frowns. "You tried to create a gun in Remi's dream. That didn't work, and you're obviously the most focused of all of us."

Ant thinks for a moment, flipping among the pages of her notebook. And then a look of clarity dawns on her. "It wasn't my dream. If each of these dreams originates in one of our brains, maybe that person is able to control things in that world. The Void is neutral. But when we're in someone's dreams, we're at the mercy of their memories and imagination."

I think back to my dreams: the Flayed Man, the cathedral, and my house of horror. What if I could have manipulated things with my thoughts during any of those?

Sinclair sighs loudly. "Kudos to Ant for thinking outside the box. But there are so many things we're up against. So many things trying to kill us. At least Remi's no longer one of them."

Fergus flinches. "Remi seemed coldhearted and self-serving, but he did try to protect Brett in the end. And what if he had planned the whole thing to save us? I have to admit, I actually feel really bad that he didn't make it. I'm starting to wonder if I didn't misunderstand what the person in the lab told me."

"What was it exactly that the person in the lab *told* you?" Sinclair asks doubtfully.

"What, you don't believe me?" Fergus lifts an eyebrow.

"What if the lab itself was just another dream?"

Instead of looking offended, Fergus looks thoughtful. "There was a different quality to it," he admits. "It wasn't like any of the other dreams. But that doesn't mean it wasn't a dream. I hadn't actually even doubted it . . . until now."

Sinclair crosses his arms. "If there's a possibility that that was a dream . . . or even a near-death experience, it means we have reason to doubt any 'fact' you gathered in that place."

"It's because of that 'dream' that we remembered about the lab and the experiment," Fergus insists.

I shake my head. "No, the rest of us remembered it while you were unconscious. It's when we brought it up that you recalled being in the lab. Not that I'm doubting you. But maybe it planted something in your mind."

Fergus's brow knits in worry. "It's such a clear memory. Just like the memories of the nightmares."

"Exactly," Sinclair says. "It could be a nightmare itself."

Fergus starts to protest, but Sinclair cuts him off. "It doesn't matter. I mean, what other information did we get from that? That there was a problem with the experiment. That we were in comas. That the scientists were trying to find a way to get us out. All that tells us is that we need to stay alive while we wait for them to rescue us."

"Which is basically what we're doing. We haven't even begun to think of a way to break the Dreamfall cycle of nightmares and Voids," I say.

"Which brings us to the only relevant 'fact' that Fergus brought back from his dream," Sinclair affirms.

"What's that?" Fergus asks.

"That BethAnn died in the real world. Which doesn't really matter. Except if she survived, then we have a little more hope. Remi and Brett could be out there alive too, waiting for us. In fact, you know what that means?"

We all stare, unable to guess.

"It means if we all killed ourselves in the nightmare, we could come out alive on the other side." Sinclair leans toward us, hands spread out as if he's offering us the best deal we've ever heard.

"That is pretty extreme," I say.

"It's a risky move to make," Fergus agrees. "We'd have to be absolutely sure that my 'dream' was nothing but that . . . a dream. Otherwise we'd be . . . dead."

"But that's the only clue we've gotten to 'breaking the cycle,' as you put it," Sinclair rebuts. "I've been thinking about it, and it's the only way I can imagine to get out: by dying."

"I understand your logic," Ant says, and everyone turns to her, "but it's too big of a risk."

"How so?" Sinclair asks with an air of confidence.

"It's a matter of risk analysis," Ant says, just as confident. "Let's say Sinclair's theory is right: BethAnn woke up in the real world after dying here. And let's say we stay on the same course as we have been—trying to survive. We're getting more and more tired, and pretty soon we'll be stuck in the nightmares with no Void to take a break, let down our defenses, and plan. We'll die. No question. And if Sinclair's theory is right, at that point, we'll come back to life in the outside world.

"But if Sinclair's theory is wrong and we kill ourselves—or let ourselves be killed—in the nightmares, we'll just be dead on the other side.

"The only effective strategy we have is believing that Fergus's dream is true and fighting to live until we either stumble across a way out ourselves or are rescued by the doctors in the real world."

"I've got to say, I'm with Ant on that one," Fergus admits.

"Fair enough," Sinclair accepts. "But if any of you are risk takers, and I'm right, we could be out of here in a matter of minutes. No more pain, fear, struggle. We just die and wake up on the other side."

There is a moment of silence as we think about what it would mean for this to be over. I see it in the others' eyes. We want out. We're all so tired.

Ant sags. "I'm not willing to take that risk. It's the easy way out. And in my experience, the easy way is rarely the better way."

Sinclair directs his gaze at me. "However tempting that sounds at the moment, I have to say I'm with Ant," I say, feeling strangely out of sorts from the whole conversation.

Just then, the first boom of the door comes. We all groan.

"I know I should be afraid, but I'm almost too tired to drum up the energy," Fergus says, as he rises to his feet.

"Well, since Brett is gone, at least we know we won't be facing show-tune-singing unicorn corpses in nightgowns," Sinclair says. Which is a bit harsh, but he has a point.

Everyone starts putting on the backpacks and attaching the weapon belts. The boom comes again, and the wind begins to whip my hair around. We get into formation—in a circle facing outward with arms linked—but Ant hesitates and steps out of the group. She takes off her hat and gloves and tosses them aside, and then links arms with me and Fergus.

Seeing our astonishment, she says, "They were getting in my way. But I'm keeping the notebook and pen."

"Please do," I say, squeezing her arm in mine. "If anyone can figure out how to get us out of here, it's you."

CHAPTER 16

JAIME

"WE CAN'T WAIT ANY LONGER," ZHU SAYS. "I HAVE double-checked . . . triple-checked . . . with our colleagues, and they are all in agreement."

"And I have the go-ahead from all the legal guardians," Vesper replies.

"How are they doing?" Zhu asks.

"How do you think?" Vesper's expression is grim.

Zhu sets her shoulders and clenches her jaw. "This has to work."

She looks over at me. "Jaime, we are proceeding with five rounds of electroshock. This time, we are doubling the intensity and will not go to lowered continuous flow afterward, as we did in the trial."

I nod and jot down her words in my notebook. She looks

satisfied. "If you would like to watch us attach the electrodes, you're welcome to see how it's done."

I step down into the test area and make the rounds with them. They attach the patches to the subjects' temples with careful, methodical movements, double-checking each other's work.

I watch for a moment, but find my gaze drawn to the faces of these teenagers I feel I'm beginning to know. Not only have I read through their histories twice, but I've been studying their feedback for the last hour. Carefully sketching the chart showing this girl's heartbeats. Tracing the lines that follow the tension of that boy's muscles. They are no longer subjects to me. They are people who have lived through difficult circumstances. Kids who have been up against challenges that most teenagers will never have to face. They are people with pasts. And now that I know them more intimately— in some ways—than my own friends, I sincerely hope they will have a future.

"Back to our stations," Vesper says, and the three of us head for our desks. Like before, Zhu speaks into her microphone, laying out what they are doing along with the date and time. They will be recording every detail of this procedure, and they expect me to do the same. My notes are valuable because I'm not invested in the outcome like they are. Whether or not my testimony can be used in court . . . if things even get that far . . . I am a neutral observer. I am an outside voice that could corroborate the methods they used to the rest of the medical world.

"Administering general anesthetic," Zhu says as she types a key and the Tower begins to click.

Anesthetic. Of course. Even though they are comatose, they can still feel pain.

I remember seeing my father in the ICU. He had already died, but a respirator was keeping him breathing, so he looked like he was still alive. He had chosen to donate his organs, and the hospital had to keep his body going until the removal procedure took place. "We will give him anesthetic during the surgery . . . of course," the nurse told me.

"Why?" I asked. "He's dead."

"His brain is dead, but his body's being kept alive artificially. Because of that, many doctors believe anesthetics should be used."

It was an explanation for the bereaved. For a twelve-year-old. I looked it up years later, and understood why she hadn't explained further. It was troubling, to say the least. Not that I regret my father's death having helped some people. But knowing the body still reacts when the brain is dead is hard to take when the person in question is your own father.

These kids are a different case, though. They are comatose, and from interviews held with patients who recovered, pain can be registered—even in the deepest of comas.

My thoughts are interrupted by Vesper's announcement that he is starting the electroconvulsive current. This time I don't turn to watch. I saw it before—the flexing of fingers and toes each time the current flowed.

Instead, I watch on my monitor, where you can't even tell anything is happening. I listen to the static that signals each round, counting until it reaches five.

Zhu speaks into the mic, "Five rounds of electroshock complete." Vesper switches off the anesthesia and current. The doctors step down into the test area to check on the subjects, removing their electrodes one by one.

As she detaches the pads from Cata's temples, Zhu says for my benefit, "We will be monitoring their feedback continuously now, but might not see any change for a while."

I note it down. Finally, when the doctors have settled back in front of their monitors, I click to expand the screen I had minimized and discreetly plug my earbuds into the computer's audio feed. On my screen, BethAnn lies on her bed, plugged into the Tower, pretrial.

I pop the earbuds in, check the timing on her feedback chart, and drag the scroll bar to 11:25 a.m. I press play.

CHAPTER 17

ANT

BEFORE MY EYES EVEN HAVE A CHANCE TO OPEN, I hear a chainsaw.

I've never seen a chainsaw in real life. I don't remember ever having seen one on TV or in the movies. But there are some things you just know, and this sound is unmistakable. The sound bores a hole into my heart: first a tiny hole, then widening until a chasm of fear gapes inside me.

I reach up to pull my earflaps down, but they aren't there. I need my chullo. Why did I leave it back in the Void? I remember . . . It was getting in the way last time. But I long for it anyway.

I wonder for a second if I can make one materialize before remembering that in the dreams I have no power. Unless, possibly, it's my dream. And there's no way my dream involves a chainsaw. I give up and raise my head to look around.

We're in a log cabin. The room measures approximately ten by fifteen, so one hundred fifty square feet. Door in one end with a standard-sized window on either side. There are two sets of bunk beds—one on either side of the room—and a chest of drawers. A tall white candle sends out a weak glow from a bedside table. A door in the far wall is half-open, showing a dismal-looking bathroom beyond. It smells like heavy-duty mildew, copper pennies, and fear.

"You've got to be kidding me," says Sinclair from nearby. He rises to his feet and walks over to the bed, brushing his fingers over the blue-and-white pin-striped pillowcase. He stares straight at Fergus, who is being pulled to his feet by Cata. "Is this *Friday the Thirteenth*?"

Fergus rubs his forehead tiredly, looks around, and then nods. "Like I said, I watch a lot of horror films."

"Well, I've only watched a few, but I clearly remember Kevin Bacon being stabbed through the neck on this exact bed," Sinclair says, crouching down and looking cautiously underneath.

"What are you looking for?" Cata asks.

"Jason's mom . . . or a big-ass snake." He stands, satisfied. "At least we'll know what to look out for."

The sound of the chainsaw grows louder.

Sinclair raises an eyebrow. "I don't seem to remember a chainsaw in that film, though."

Fergus nods, biting his lip. "They all get mixed up in my dreams."

"So I guess that would be . . ."

"Leatherface. From *Texas Chainsaw*."

"Perfect. Just perfect. I didn't see that one coming. You?" Sinclair looks at me.

I can't tell if he's being sarcastic. "I'm not allowed to watch R-rated films unless they're foreign," I respond.

"Of course you're not," Sinclair says. This time I'm ninety percent sure that's sarcasm.

He turns to Fergus and says, "I guess we're depending on you, buddy. What comes next?"

"Weapons," Fergus says, unsheathing his sword. We draw our knives and Sinclair gets ready with the crossbow.

"Do you know what's going to happen?" Cata yells to be heard over the noise of the chainsaw. Heavy feet pound on the porch.

"No," Fergus yells back. "With these dreams, I never fight back. I'm always hiding or running."

"Well, that's about to change right . . ." begins Sinclair as the door explodes in a shower of splinters, ". . . now." His crossbow twangs.

A huge man wearing a weird leather mask sewn together with big black sutures crashes through the door and comes to a standstill as Sinclair's bolt plants itself firmly into the middle of his forehead. He roars in pain and fury, dropping the chainsaw as he grabs for the projectile sticking out of his head. The power tool thrashes around the floor like it's alive, and Sinclair has to scramble to get out of its way.

"Run!" yells Cata. She grabs my arm and drags me toward the bathroom.

"Not that way! Trust me!" yells Fergus, sticking out an arm to stop us. He pulls us toward the door, shoving the flailing masked man out of the way. The man stumbles to the side and slumps, motionless, over a chair.

Curiosity pulls me a step closer to the man, in spite of my fear. "Is he dead?" I ask.

"No one is ever truly dead in these films," Cata replies, and yanks me away.

Sinclair has already grabbed the doorknob, and pulls open what remains of the door. The four of us run outside into a dark, wooded landscape.

In front of us is a lake, the water black as ink. A full moon hangs low in the sky. I shiver from the cold and wrap my arms around myself.

A small rowboat is moored by the water's edge, and to our left is an archery range with four bull's-eye targets sitting in a row. Sinclair turns to Fergus. "You've got to be kidding me."

Something moves out in the middle of the lake, its epicenter spawning circles of waves. "What was that?" I ask, my heart in my throat.

"You don't even want to know," Sinclair replies.

"So this stuff is all straight out of various horror films?" I ask.

Fergus turns to me. "I've seen them all. Repeatedly. I have a lot of material to draw from."

"Why?" I ask. "You told George you don't even like them."

"Probably distracts from your less-than-perfect home life," murmurs Sinclair.

"Oh my God!" says Cata. She gives Sinclair a shove.

"What?" he says, shrugging. "His other dreams are about killing his dad. Or his dad killing him. I can't imagine it's all sunshine and roses at his place."

Fergus ignores him and pulls me into a protective side-hug as we set off into the woods ahead of the others. I don't flinch. Yay, me.

"It's desensitization," he says. We speed-walk side by side as he explains. "It's so I won't have a cataplectic attack. The fainting thing I did back in the Void. It's brought on by strong emotions. I've pretty much got fear under control. Laughing is still a problem, though. Even after watching all the comedies I could. I might not get freaked out by horrific things, but I have to remind myself not to laugh."

"Thus the DFF tattoo," Cata says from where she matches our pace on the other side of Fergus.

"What's the DFF stand for?" I ask.

"Don't Freaking Feel," says Fergus.

"Except it's not 'freaking.'"

"Correct," he responds with a sheepish smile. "I guess I thought if I cursed at myself, I'd take it more seriously."

Cata laughs.

"Then why can't you have a nightmare about a comedy? A little Bill Murray wouldn't kill us," says Sinclair.

"Unless it's *Zombieland*," Fergus responds under his breath.

I'm not getting any of the references here. It's like Fergus and Sinclair are speaking in code. It's not the first time I've felt left out. But I wish we weren't run-walking because I want to jot them down in my notebook so I can look them up later.

"Does that mean you're not scared?" I ask.

"Sure, I'm scared. But not terrified. That doesn't mean these things can't kill us, though."

"Like what?" I press. "What could kill us in these woods?"

"Allow me," Sinclair says, righting himself after tripping on a tree root. "As I remember from *Friday the Thirteenth*: throat slit with bowie knife, arrow through the heart, throat stabbed from back to front with a knife, face smashed by ax. There might have been a machete. But all I know of *The Texas Chainsaw Massacre*, since this is a Fergus movie mash-up, is the obvious chainsaw and something about huge meat hooks."

"There was a hammer and a freezer," adds Fergus.

"Helpful to know," murmurs Sinclair.

Just then, a cherry-colored balloon floats by. I see a red clown wig poke out from behind a tree.

"Um . . . Pennywise," Cata squeaks from beside me.

"Just ignore him," Fergus says. "He won't come after us. At least . . . he hasn't chased me yet."

Clearing the trees, we approach a winding one-lane road. We crouch below the embankment as an old station wagon sided with fake wood paneling drives past us and up a hill. As soon as it's safe, we scramble across the road. The landscape abruptly changes.

We're in a graveyard. I look behind us, and the road has disappeared, replaced by row upon row of old, crumbling graves.

"Where are we?" asks Cata, a tremor in her voice.

"It could be one of so many different places," Fergus says. "I can think of about twenty off the top of my head."

I'm standing next to a freshly dug grave with what looks like a bucket of blood and a tiara sitting on it instead of flowers. Cata glances at it and yells, "Ant, move!" just as a hand thrusts up from the pile of dirt. I leap aside, my heart beating so hard it feels like it's about to burst out of my chest. The hand disappears into the ground, the soil where it had broken through smooth and undisturbed.

"Ugh, Carrie!" Sinclair says. "Well, that's not too bad, unless her mother's lurking among the graves reciting Bible verses."

Then, from a nearby grave, another hand pushes out of the dirt, followed by an entire corpse that starts rising out of the ground.

"That one's not Carrie," yells Sinclair, fumbling with his crossbow. He points and shoots. The bolt goes wide, sinking into the freshly disturbed soil of a grave nearby, which has its own zombie emerging.

"We're not going to be able to fight all of them," Fergus says.

Cata shrieks and fumbles for her knife as other graves begin bulging and limbs start sticking through.

"Get your weapons out!" Sinclair urges.

"Daggers aren't going to do us any good," Fergus says.

"It's your dream, Fergus!" I say. "You can make us some weapons!" A moaning sound resonates from all around as an army of corpses starts rising out of the graves.

"I don't think I can here! Not in the middle of a zombie attack," he says. He takes my hand and pulls me away from the staggering corpses. "Just run!" he yells. We struggle back up the hill toward where the road used to be.

"How do we get out of here?" I ask. The road has disappeared, and all I can see is graves for what looks like miles around. Fergus doesn't answer. He just pulls me along as he darts through the cemetery, looking back from time to time to make sure Cata and Sinclair are keeping up.

The zombies are doing what I always thought they would: holding their hands either straight out in front of them or dangling by their sides as they stagger along really slowly. They're even wearing cheesy zombie clothes like an old wedding dress and a farmer outfit with overalls and straw hat. But as I watch the lumbering way they move and hear the groans emanating from their rotting throats, I find myself thoroughly terrified. Add that to the smell—a stench like when Dog dug up the neighbor's dead cat, who had been buried for three months, and dragged it into the kitchen through the doggy door.

I know what the smell is: the volatile organic compounds that come from bacteria breaking down animal tissue into gases and salts, like cadaverine and putrescine. But that knowledge doesn't console me like cold, hard, immutable facts usually do. Because in this case, facts don't matter. The smell, in my mind, equals evil.

A crow caws three times, and then others pick up the call, and a whole cloud of them lifts to the sky as more zombies pour out of the ground. One bird isn't so lucky: a putrescent hand grabs it before it can fly away. I hear it squawk, but I turn away so I won't see what the zombie does with it.

Do zombies eat other species' brains? I wonder. I wish I could write it down so I could look it up later. Not that I really believe in zombies. But it would be interesting to know what the lore says on the matter.

"No graves this way!" Sinclair says, waving us over to a section that is just an expanse of grass and mud—free of headstones.

He turns around, pointing his crossbow in the direction we came from, and waits for us to huddle behind him.

"I can't run any more," Cata pants, leaning forward, hands on knees, taking deep breaths.

"Man, you have to make more weapons. Or do something!" Sinclair says, swinging the crossbow from side to side, waiting for the zombie onslaught. But, besides the distant cawing of the crows, the night is totally quiet. With the imminent danger apparently left behind, we all begin to relax.

"I have to sit down," I say, and everyone throws themselves down on the grass, panting.

"Any idea of what comes next?" Cata asks Fergus.

Fergus shakes his head. "It could be . . ."

"Wait!" I say, my hands flying to my face. "Something's happening." A numbness is creeping through my body. My lips feel all puffy . . . like at the dentist . . . and then it spreads through the rest of my face.

"Whoa . . . major hit of narcotics going on here," says Sinclair, laying full-out on the ground.

"I feel like after my wisdom teeth surgery," says Cata, sinking back to lie next to him.

I can't sit up, and kind of slump to the side, where I'm practically eye to eye with a barely conscious Fergus. "What's happening?" I ask.

"Don't know," he mumbles. "This hasn't happened before."

A roar of zombies starts up from far away. "Oh no," I say, but the words kind of trip on their way out my lips and get lost in the buzzing sound in my head. And then it feels as if someone points a remote control at me and presses off.

CHAPTER 18

CATA

I PASSED OUT ON A HILL IN A CEMETERY. I WAKE up on the floor of a department store.

An elevator-music version of "The Girl from Ipanema" is playing over the speaker system. I hear Fergus groan nearby, and I force myself to sit up and look around.

We're in a ladies' sportswear section that looks straight out of the 1970s. The mannequins have shoulder-length, feathered-back hair that looks like my mom's school photos from junior high. They're wearing striped sweatbands around their foreheads and wrists that match their knee-length athletic socks.

Across the aisle from us is the men's section. The male mannequins are dressed in polyester suits with wide lapels and colorful shirts unbuttoned to frame gold medallion necklaces.

"Holy Bee Gees!" Sinclair says, squinting at them as if he

doesn't quite believe it. He shades his eyes from the bright white fluorescent lights, and attempts to push himself up to his feet. Reeling, he reaches out to one of the mannequins for leverage. It comes crashing down as he stumbles drunkenly to the side. Propping himself up with his hands on his knees, he asks, "Anyone else have a completely undeserved hangover?"

"What happened back there?" I ask Fergus, who sits with his head between his knees.

"I don't know," he says, raising his head to look at me. "I thought I was having another cataplexy attack. That's what it felt like, at least."

"Anesthetic," says Ant succinctly. "I had a tonsillectomy when I was four. It felt just like that when I went under."

"But why . . ." I begin, and then it comes to me. "Maybe something happened to us in the real world. Something in the lab." I look at Fergus for backup.

"Maybe they *are* trying to save us," he says. "They must have done something that necessitated our being anesthetized."

"Doesn't look like it worked," says Sinclair, holding his arms out and studying himself as if he expects a limb or digit to be missing.

"Where are we now?" I ask.

"Still in my dream," Fergus responds, looking around. "*Dawn of the Dead*, 1978, from what it looks like."

"The Dreamfall took us from one zombie movie to another?" asks Sinclair.

"At least this one's a little more comfortable," says Ant.

"Not for long," says Fergus. "Not with the racket Sinclair just made."

"Hey!" Sinclair says. "How was I supposed to know Disco Guy was such a lightweight?"

"Look," Fergus whispers, and points to the far end of the aisle. A zombie dressed in a security guard costume is staggering around, seemingly searching for whatever made the noise. Its skin is moss green, and blood the color of neon ketchup is smeared on its face and neck.

We scramble to hide behind racks of clothes, but Ant looks unsure. "That doesn't look scary," she whispers. "It looks stupid. I've done better zombie makeup than that for Halloween."

"George Romero, the director, wanted them to look cartoonish," Fergus says.

"They'll look scary enough when they're tearing your guts out with their teeth," Sinclair adds.

Fergus nods his agreement. "These ones move slowly. But they seem to pop up out of nowhere, and the danger is being cornered by too many at once."

"Wait. I think I've seen this movie," Sinclair whispers back. "Aren't we in a mall that has a gun shop smack in the middle?"

"We're in a *mall*?" Ant asks.

Fergus nods distractedly. "Yeah, but the gun shop is in the main section of the mall itself. That's where most of the zombies are gathered."

"What we should be thinking about is where the Wall is going to appear," Ant says, keeping an eye on the lost-looking zombie.

"Could it appear in the mall? Or do we need to go out into the parking lot?"

Fergus shrugs. "It came inside the cathedral, so it's possible. I think our strategy should be avoiding contact with the zombies for as long as possible until we hear the boom, and then make a run for it."

"I like that plan," Sinclair says. "But it doesn't look very feasible, seeing that Security Guard Zombie has called for backup."

Fergus rises slowly from behind the rack of clothes we're hiding behind and scopes out the room. He pops back down, frowning. "Two more. Even though they're slow, they'll eventually find us."

He thinks. "How much time do we have, Ant?"

"This dream was supposed to last fifty-eight minutes, and we used up about twenty before we passed out. But I don't know how long we were unconscious. It didn't feel that long, but who knows?"

"Okay." Fergus nods. "As much as I hate to say it, I think Sinclair's right about the weapons. Our knives aren't going to be enough. We can make a run for the gun shop, arm ourselves, and then fend them off while we wait for the Wall."

"Sinclair, can't you just shoot these three guys?" I ask.

"I only have one bolt left," he says. "I used all the rest on the zombies in the graveyard."

I glance over at the display of sports-playing mannequins next to us. "Okay, then you get the one that's closest to us. We'll get the other two."

"With what?" he asks.

"Just worry about yours." The moaning's getting closer. "Now!"

Sinclair pops up from his crouch and aims at the zombie guard. I jump up and wrench the golf club away from one of the sports-playing mannequins. "Ant!" I say and thrust it at her. It takes her a second to realize what I'm doing. Then she smiles and flips the club over, gripping it in both hands.

I grab the softball player's bat for myself, and Fergus takes what's left: a tennis racket. He stares between it and his sword, and then props it back against the mannequin's leg. "I think I'll stick with the sword," he says.

I hear the twang of Sinclair's crossbow. The zombie security guard crumples to the ground. The others aren't far off, and, alerted by the first zombie's death groan, they turn and spot us. "Just hit them hard in the head. That's enough to bring them down," says Fergus, and he runs toward one. I hurl myself toward the other, but it's already closing in on Ant.

She raises the golf club and watches the moaning, lumbering man uncertainly. In contrast to the green-skinned zombie, this one has an orange complexion with bloodless white eyes and lips. Glancing back at me, Ant yells, "I'm just going to pretend his head is a pumpkin." Then she swings the golf club with a wicked force.

It hits his temple, lodging deep inside. He totters and falls. Ant has to let go of her weapon and jump aside to avoid him crumpling on top of her. She watches to see if he's going to move again. When he doesn't, she edges up, grabs the putter, and wiggles it free from the cavity it carved in his head. Brains spill out on the department store's linoleum floor. She squishes her nose in disgust, and then wipes the gore off on Disco Guy's pant leg.

"That is seriously disgusting," she says to me, oblivious to the openmouthed awe with which I'm staring at her.

"Ant. That was awesome," I say. "George would be so impressed."

Ant gives me this little grin, and for the first time I can remember, she looks truly happy.

"I didn't take you to be the violent type," I catch myself saying before I even wonder how she'll take it. "I mean, not liking guns . . ." I let the thought meander.

"There's a difference between shooting people and bashing monsters," she replies.

I think of the exhilaration I felt while smashing evil statues in my cathedral dream and then my horror when Sinclair killed the guard in the jungle. "I get it," I agree.

"Over here!" Fergus yells. He stands at the top of a motionless escalator. "Gun shop's on the ground floor," he says as we follow him down the stationary metal stairs. We make a ton of noise, but there aren't any zombies waiting for us when we get to the bottom.

"Okay, this way." Fergus runs toward the double glass doors opening from the department store into the mall. He points to the sign above the door. "If we get split up, we meet back here: ground floor, Penney's. The gun shop is about halfway down the mall. Just go fast, and don't let yourself get cornered!"

We dart out into the mall, which has so much *stuff* that at first I don't notice its undead inhabitants. There are junglelike planted areas, fountains, art displays, and working escalators running between the ground and second floors.

But after a few seconds of taking it in, I spot the zombies. They're milling around like in a comedy routine, with zombies riding up and down the escalators and splashing around in the fountains, but mainly just shuffling and falling over things. With the green faces and neon blood, they don't look that scary, especially since they're not attacking anything.

But as a few of them get a glimpse of us, they are pulled in our direction like paper clips to magnets, and I start feeling a core of fear harden inside me. Fergus and Ant dispatch the first few before Sinclair and I even have time to catch up. But as we continue, they get closer, and our fight begins. Sinclair starts swinging his ammunitionless crossbow at them, while I do the same with my baseball bat.

Up close they don't look so funny. The way they bare their teeth and claw at me triggers a primal reaction that makes me want to strike. I cringe as my bat meets the first head. Maybe it's the woman's old-fashioned stewardess outfit and blue eyeshadow that make her still seem human to me. But I tell myself to ignore the details and, after feeling queasy on the next two, am able to block my emotions and bash heads without hesitating.

Ant is doing so well with the golf club, you can tell she's managed to turn off the part of her brain that usually gets freaked out. She set her own tone when she decided to think of their heads as pumpkins, and she's going at it with a gusto that makes that makes her seem like a completely different girl.

I overhear Fergus giving her instructions, and I realize that they're both treating it in the same way—as a spatial exercise. Ant loves to measure things, and he's having her look at the zombies like she would on a paper or screen, measuring the angles.

"Your two o'clock," he says.

"Sixty-three degrees," she corrects and whacks the guy in the forehead, spraying gore down the front of herself. As the monster crumbles, she's already looking for her next geometric equation.

Within five minutes, and with a trail of twenty slain zombies in our path, we get to the gun shop. After striking down a few stragglers in the immediate vicinity, Fergus opens the door and we all dash in. He turns the dead bolt, and we are momentarily safe. A horde of zombies that had been on their way to us begins to congregate outside the windows.

Maybe vintage zombies aren't as resourceful as modern-day ones, because none of them picks up a bench and throws it through a window. I mean . . . that's what I would do in their place. Instead, they ineffectively claw at the windows.

Fergus and Sinclair start pulling guns off the walls and lining them up on the counters. They find ammunition in the drawers and stack them next to the weapons.

Ant watches disapprovingly. "I'm fine with my golf club."

"You won't be fine with your golf club when we're trying to run for the Wall and there are a hundred zombies in front of us," Fergus explains. Noticing Ant's frown, he sets down his machine gun and says, "Listen, Ant. I'm not fond of guns either. But just pretend it's a game, like before. This time we're in a video game and these are virtual guns." His voice peters out as he watches her stony expression.

"All right. Keep your golf club, and you and I will go back-to-back. Does that work? I'll shoot in front of us, and you bash any that sneak up from behind."

Ant seems relieved by this plan. Fergus gives her a little smile and gets back to work.

"Okay, Cata. Come here," he says, and hands me a machine gun.

"Um, I wouldn't even begin to know how to use this," I say.

"Have you ever shot a gun?" he asks.

"Of course," I respond. "I'm from Georgia. My sister and I used to shoot cans in the backyard with our dad's shotgun."

"This is easier than a shotgun," he says. "And I'm going to set it up for you. See this string of bullets? It loads itself. All you have to do is pull the trigger and hold on tight, because it moves around a lot, like the kickback of a shotgun, but over and over."

"How do you know how to use a machine gun?" I ask.

"I don't," Fergus says. "But I've played enough video games to extrapolate."

When he grins, there's a playful mischief in his eyes that makes me smile back. And during this goofy exchange, something happens to my heart. Something that started back a while ago, but that I hadn't had time or energy to notice.

I glance over at Sinclair and find him staring at me with a

sardonic grin. He is more handsome than Fergus . . . in a glamorous movie-star way. But his smile has always made me feel uncomfortable, like I'm being judged.

Fergus has always been warm. Why hadn't I recognized it before? I wish it had been Fergus who had kissed me in that alleyway instead. I break Sinclair's gaze and watch Fergus efficiently loading the gun, and whatever's happening to my heart kind of solidifies and becomes a sure thing.

I look over to see that the windows are now full of zombies, clawing and moaning, and want to laugh at myself for having any other feelings right now besides fear and disgust. It's like we're in a B or even C movie, where, even though catastrophe is taking place, the characters have the time and composure to fall in love. This is neither the time *nor* the place.

Sinclair clears his throat, and the moment is gone. "Okay, everyone gear up." He has so many guns strapped to his body that he looks like a rich-boy version of Rambo. Fergus wraps a gun belt around my waist and steps back to let me buckle it. He drapes a strap over my right shoulder and another over my left, then attaches them at the back.

"Three guns?" I ask. "Why do I need three?"

"Because they're going to run out of bullets, and you won't have time to reload. So you shoot everything you've got in one gun, then you drop it and pick up another and start shooting again." There's that smile again. He knows what he's saying sounds ridiculous. I can't help smiling back.

Sinclair is attempting to fit Ant with a hunting vest . . .

unsuccessfully. "If you're not going to carry a gun, at least put this on."

"Why do I need a bulletproof vest for zombies?" she asks, shrugging it off.

"I doubt they'll be able to claw or bite their way through Kevlar," he responds. "It just gives you more of a chance to make it to the Wall."

This seems to make sense to her, because she shuffles it on, and then, noticing a pair of noise-reducing headphones, slips them over her ears. She grabs the golf club and practices a swing toward the grimacing faces in the window. "Smashing pumpkins," she says a little too loudly. "I think my mom has an album called that."

Sinclair has managed to put a few more guns on. I'm surprised he can still walk. "Isn't that heavy?" I ask.

"I'm looking it as both armor and weapon. I'd like to see those zombies bite their way through this!" He gestures to the complex web of ammo belts and machine guns draped across him.

Fergus's setup seems more realistic. He has three guns like me, but the one he carries in his hands looks a lot heavier than Sinclair's.

"Okay, let's do this thing," he says, and it's only from the slight strain in his voice that I can tell he's taking this seriously. He talked Ant into seeing it as a game, but he obviously doesn't believe his own hype.

I look in the direction of his gaze. The things outside the window are getting scarier the longer I look at them: their rotten, dripping teeth, the missing chunks of skin leaving exposed cavities, the fervor in their movements and hunger in their eyes—a clammy, cold feeling spreads across my skin. If we take much more time preparing, I'm going to be too afraid to move.

Fergus groups us together in front of the door. I avoid looking at the things now that there's just a pane of glass between us. "How do we do this?" I ask.

Sinclair lays three machine guns down on the counter next to us. "Okay, these can be our spares. We shoot these guns through the windows before going out. One each, except Ant. Empty them completely. That will clear out the zombies standing near the windows. Then pick up your primary gun and we rush out, locate the Wall, and run for it, clearing our way as we go."

Fergus and I nod, but Ant looks dubious. "You hide while we shoot out the windows," he advises her. "There's going to be a lot of flying glass." She nods and leaves us to crouch down behind the counter.

I set the more lightweight machine gun on the counter and pick up the heavy "spare" that Sinclair prepared for me. The three of us line up side by side and aim at the zombies, who don't seem to even see us. They keep scratching and moaning and baring their teeth. One of them pushes its hand too hard against the glass. It falls off, smearing black blood down the window. "I don't think I can stand much more of the gorefest," I say, feeling light-headed.

"Okay, go!" Sinclair says. I pull the trigger and try to hang on to the gun as I spray bullets back and forth toward the windows.

It's so loud, and there's so much glass and blood and brains flying everywhere that I want to throw up and cry and scream all at once. I settle for screaming, pouring all of my fear and disgust and anger into a high-pitched shriek that, if we were in the real world, could without a doubt land me a role in a slasher film.

Sinclair and Fergus are yelling too. It just seems to go together: shooting machine guns and screaming.

As the bullets run out, and there is a lull in the commotion, the first knock of the Wall comes booming through the space, shaking the ground we stand on. We look at one another, panicked.

Sinclair yells, "Let's go!" and we run out of the space left where the door used to be. Sinclair and Fergus shove decomposing bodies aside to make a path for us as we crunch over the broken glass.

I get to the middle of the mall and turn my head from side to side. "I don't see the Wall!" I yell.

The others look equally confused. Zombies that were out of range of our shooting begin to shuffle toward us, moaning. "It must be at one end of the mall," Fergus says. "Since the shops curve around, we can't see the whole thing. We have to split up. Ant and I will go down this way. Cata, you and Sinclair go down that way. As soon as you get a clear view of the end of your side, come back. We'll meet here in the middle."

Fergus and Ant peel off and head toward the left. "Come on!" Sinclair yells, and, shooting as we run, we go in the direction we came from—toward Penney's. We pass shop after shop, all empty.

The zombies that haven't noticed us yet are wandering around, doing weird things like sitting in a fountain and sifting through the coins that lay at the bottom. Or going through garbage cans and looking at each object like it's the holy grail. We shoot all the rest that come near us.

The elevator music has gotten louder, and the moaning chorus along with it is making the scene feel even more surreal. We turn a corner and spot our end of the mall. No Wall.

"It's got to be in the other direction," I yell.

"Let's go," says Sinclair, and we turn to run back toward the others. But he's so loaded up with weapons that he doesn't see a sunken garden area right in front of him. He trips over the edge and falls straight onto his face. There is a second of stunned silence before he starts cursing and trying to get up.

I grab his arm and attempt to pull him to his feet. The guns are heavy and he stumbles over the weird plant formations. He loses his balance and falls back onto his knees.

"Take some of those off!" I yell, and try to unbuckle the belts that are strapped across him. He's thrashing around, and I can't tell if he's trying to detach the weapons or get me off of him.

I feel something brush my back, and I turn to see a face next to mine. It looks as surprised as I do, and there is a moment of hesitation before it stretches its mouth wide open. Too fast for me to dodge, it throws its head back, lunges forward, and bites into my shoulder.

I scream as a burning pain radiates out from where the teeth are clamped into my flesh. I instinctually swing back and smash the zombie across the side of the head with my gun. It holds on, its mouth locked on me like those fighting dogs you see in videos that don't let go of their prey no matter how forcefully they're pulled away by their masters.

"Sinclair!" I scream as he staggers to his feet. He turns and sees me, and his eyes widen as he scrambles to grab a weapon. I take my gun in both hands and strike the zombie again with all my force. I feel the gun embed into its head. The jaw unlocks and the zombie falls back from me and hits the ground, the gun still planted in its skull.

I twist my head to inspect my shoulder. I'm bleeding so heavily that I can't tell if the thing has taken a chunk out.

Sinclair takes his gun and sprays bullets in a circle around us, downing every zombie in the vicinity. He grabs my arm, and we stumble forward, running toward where Fergus and Ant . . . and hopefully the Wall . . . should be awaiting us. But I've only gone a few steps before I'm literally blinded by pain. The world seems to erupt in yellow flames. "I can't . . ." I start to say, and then fall to my knees.

"You have to stay conscious!" Sinclair says, and tries to help me. I feel paralyzed. I don't have the strength to get back up, but I am locked there, determined not to fall over. He can't support my weight, and he sets me back down on the ground.

From behind us comes a pounding noise, and a double door with a "Personnel Only—Keep Locked" sign above it begins to buckle under the weight of some unseen force.

"Oh my God, there are more of them coming," I moan.

"Cata," Sinclair says, and his voice sounds so different that I glance up to catch his gaze. "If you don't want to run, you don't have to," he says, and there is a disarming warmth in his words. "Remember what I said about dying here? I really do believe it. This could be your time. You're close enough to death right now that it is actually a valid choice."

He leans in closer. "That thing got one of your arteries. You're bleeding out. If you stay here, you'll die. Which means you could come out on the other side. You could be with BethAnn and the others in the real world. They're alive. I just know it. I have this feeling."

I look at him, and for a second I am tempted. I'm in so much pain, and I feel so weak that I don't want to make another move. Sinking down to the ground and just lying there seems almost delicious right now. There would be comfort in giving up.

"Are you offering to shoot me?" I ask.

"I couldn't shoot you," he says. "But I could give you this." He hands me a pistol.

I look at it for a moment, and am so tired of running . . . of fighting to live. I raise it to my temple. Feel the barrel cold against my skin. Sinclair watches me expectantly.

As I start to squeeze the trigger, an image of my brother and sister flashes in my mind, and I stop. I remember that I'm not only making decisions for myself. I have to do my best to survive . . . for them. I've got to save them. I'm the only one who can get them away from our father.

I drop the gun and, leaning forward, start throwing up a green liquid. The pounding continues from behind the locked doors, and I hear the splintering of wood.

I barely register the second knock of the Wall, but the ground shakes, and a chandelier detaches from the ceiling and comes crashing to the ground.

The sound forces me into alertness. I look up to see Sinclair's face bobbing up and down, swimming in my blurry vision. "You go ahead," I slur. "Tell Fergus and Ant I'm here. But if you can't come back for me . . . don't risk your own safety."

We hear a shout. Two people are running toward us. I slump to the ground in relief as Ant wallops a zombie with her golf club and Fergus shoots at something near where we're crouching.

"You're hurt!" says Fergus as he huddles down next to me. Just then, the locked door splinters, and zombies begin pouring through.

"Do something," Ant urges Fergus. "It's your dream."

Fergus is puzzled for a second, then, understanding, he nods and looks toward the door. He concentrates, but nothing happens. The zombies are getting closer. And then, a few yards away from us, a red-and-white pin-striped cart with "Popcorn" written across the top in big puffy letters shudders and flies across the space. It slams into the door and cuts off the tide of undead. Sinclair and Fergus shoot the few who got through with blasts of their machine guns.

We all stare at each other. "It worked!" Fergus says.

"Oh man, that was *awesome*!" Sinclair yells, his eyes practically popping from their sockets.

Ant just stands there like she's working out the trajectory or velocity or whatever.

A lightning bolt of pain shoots through my shoulder, and I cry out. The three huddle around me. "One of them bit her!" Sinclair explains and, taking my arm, drags me to my feet.

Ant looks at me with scared eyes. "Can you walk?" she asks.

I wobble but take a step forward.

"Here, lean on me," Fergus says. Draping my good arm across his shoulder, he wraps his arm around my waist, and, supporting most of my weight, he propels me forward.

"The Wall's just past there," Ant yells, pointing to a bar called the Brown Derby.

We round the corner to see the Wall bisecting the entire two floors of the mall. It has cut the Craft Showcase and the Card Shoppe in half, and the stores beyond have disappeared. A crowd of several dozen zombies writhes in front of it, clawing at its invisible force field as enthusiastically as if it were hiding a mountain of brains. Unlike in the other dreams, the populace of this nightmare seems to see the Wall just fine.

"Oh. My. God," Sinclair says.

"Can you sweep them out of the way like you did with the popcorn cart?" Ant asks.

Fergus focuses on the wall of zombies, but nothing happens. "I think I used up my superpowers back there. Maybe it was better that I didn't have time to think about it."

"We have to shoot our way through," says Sinclair. He swings two guns that were strapped behind him around to his chest and wedges them under his arms, putting a finger on each trigger. "Dual wield." He chortles.

"You are enjoying this way too much," Fergus says, shaking his head.

"If we have to fight our way past a wall of zombies, we might as well have fun doing it!" Sinclair says.

Even Ant holds her golf club up like she's ready to smash some heads.

"We just have to push through them. It doesn't matter if we get bitten, since we'll be fine on the other side," Fergus says.

"Can you put a gun in my right hand?" I ask. He pulls my last remaining gun around so that it's supported on the strap, and I thread my finger through the trigger.

The third and final boom comes from all around us, shattering the chandeliers and glass storefronts and knocking half of the zombies off their feet.

"Go!" Ant yells, and the four of us barrel toward the line of undead. As they hear us coming, they turn and refocus their efforts from clawing at the invisible barrier to surging toward us.

I run with my left arm around Fergus's neck and my gun in my right hand. He's got one hand around my waist and shoots a steady stream of bullets with the other. Ant follows from behind, bashing any zombies we don't clear, and Sinclair is to our right, spraying back and forth with his two guns.

We're basically unstoppable. Or at least, I think so, until we're on the verge of pressing through the Wall and Fergus comes to a complete stop. The wind is whipping around us, and the zombies' clothes are flapping around as they stagger backward. But one stands stock-still in front of us, ice pick in hand and eyes rolled back in his head.

"Don't shoot him!" Fergus yells.

Beside us, Sinclair's momentum carries him through the Wall, whooping and shooting both of his guns as he disappears.

"Fergus! Get us through!" I say, loosening my grip on his neck, ready to pitch myself forward. But Ant comes up from behind, and swinging her club back, hits Ice Pick Zombie with full force. The top of his head splatters, pieces of it flying into our faces. I feel a small hand on my back, shoving me hard through the Wall. As we fall forward into the darkness, I hear Fergus say, "Dad."

CHAPTER 19

JAIME

THERE IT IS, AT 11:26 A.M. SUBJECT THREE—
BethAnn—moves her head slightly to the right, and a second
later begins to thrash from side to side, eyes squeezed shut, face a
rictus of pain.

I hear myself in the microphone mounted in the Tower just
under BethAnn's camera. "Dr. Vesper!" My voice comes from far
away. A loud beeping noise can be heard—the emergency signal
of the heart rate monitor.

In a slightly hysterical voice, Dr. Vesper calls, "What the hell?"

And there I am, appearing beside BethAnn, leaning over her,
but thankfully not blocking her face from the camera.

Her hands fly up to her chest, pressing on her heart. "She's
going into cardiac arrest!" Vesper's voice comes from nearby.

"What should I do?" My voice is frantic.

BethAnn's eyes pop open. I pause the video and note down the time.

11:28:10—Subject 3 conscious

I play with the image to see if I can enlarge it. Nope.

I tap open the computer's system file and look through the applications. Yes! There is a basic movie-editing application that came with the computer. I open it up. It's enough like iMovie that I'm able to figure it out, and within moments I have imported five minutes of the video and zoomed in on BethAnn's face.

I start the video back up, beginning at the point where she opens her eyes. My head is in the corner of the shot, and she is clearly focusing straight on me. Her mouth moves, and her eyes take on an expression of pure horror.

I scroll back and turn the sound up to the max. Her voice comes through my earbuds as a strained whisper, but the words are completely recognizable.

"Am I still . . . in Africa? Did Ant make it? The soldiers . . . guns . . . genocide . . ." She's making a huge effort to get each word out.

Vesper appears by my side and takes her by the shoulders. "BethAnn. Do you hear me?" But her eyes are now fixed on the ceiling, unseeing.

The heart rate monitor goes into flatline. Vesper checks her eyes and puts his ear to her chest. He begins CPR and says, "Call nine again, Jaime. Tell them we need a defibrillator down here now!"

I stop the video and, with the video-editing software, save and export this portion to the desktop. I run back through it again, writing down each word as she speaks.

Africa. Soldiers. Genocide. Those are all a part of Remi's past. Did BethAnn get shot in Remi's dream? And what did she mean about ants? I back up. "Did Ant make it?" Ant, not ants. Ant . . . and then it dawns on me. I shuffle through the test file to subject six. Antonia Gates. Could BethAnn mean her?

I open a window and search Facebook. There are a couple of Antonia Gateses, but they are much older than the thirteen-year-old. Same for Twitter. Maybe her parents don't let her have social media accounts. I Google "Antonia Gates," glance at her profile in the test file, and add "Princeton, New Jersey."

Several articles pop up, all concerning awards she's won. A mathematics prize. President's Award for Educational Excellence. Prizes at science fairs, regional and state. I click into one of them, which starts with:

New Jersey high school student wins $70,000 for science fair project on neurological factors in attention deficit disorder. Antonia (who prefers to go by "Ant") Gates impressed science fair judges and respected researchers in the field with her work exploring the connection between the areas of the brain that deal with language . . .

I stop there. She prefers to go by Ant. BethAnn wanted to know if Ant made it. Antonia was there in a dream fabricated by Remi's mind. A dream about the traumatic incidents in his past. About the African genocide that robbed him of his family.

I am numb all over. I can't feel my hands. I was right: they're conscious, and they're together.

The door to the lab opens. I pull my earbuds out and turn around. Mr. Osterman and a professional-looking man in his twenties, looking even more business formal than the director in tailored suit, tie, and silk pocket triangle, walk into the lab.

Mr. Osterman gives me a distracted thumbs-up and goes to confer with Zhu and Vesper. The other man walks up to me and places a bottle of San Pellegrino water and a bag of organic whole wheat crackers on my desk. I begin to stand, but he waves me back into my chair, squatting down, lowering himself to my level. "Hi, Jaime. I'm Jonathan, Mr. Osterman's assistant. How are you doing?"

"Uh, I'm fine," I say, caught off guard by the attention.

"This has got to have been a traumatic day for you, Jaime. I can't even imagine." He makes a face like he's trying to imagine, but it's just too traumatic, so he gives up and shakes his head, pressing his lips together in feigned empathy. "Did you have some lunch?"

"Yes, I went outside and ate just a little while ago."

"Good. Good," he says, scanning my desktop and focusing in on my charts and notebook. "I see you've been hard at work. My boss tells me you've agreed to record everything that's happening in your own words, and I just want to tell you how grateful we are for that."

I nod, rendered speechless by his fawning.

"I just wanted to say that you should feel free to call me, or even Mr. Osterman himself, if you prefer, with any questions or concerns you might have. We are one hundred percent at your disposal. I brought you a snack here," he says, gesturing to the water and crackers. "Let me know if you need anything else. I realize this will be a long day for you and want you to be completely comfortable." His face is so close to mine that I notice a red puffiness between his eyebrows. He plucks his unibrow, I realize.

"Thank you," I screw my face into an expression of intense seriousness. He seems to appreciate that and, standing, gives me a companionable clap on the shoulder. I have the uncontrollable urge to shudder from his touch—I've always had a low tolerance for insincerity—but restrain myself.

I wait until he and Osterman leave the lab before slipping my earbuds back in. I pull up the video of Fergus and, checking my time chart, drag the scroll bar to 2:50 p.m.

There it is: Fergus ripping out his IV tube with his left hand and his right hand flying to his chest. I see myself, a minute later, appearing at his side. He holds his fist over his heart, looking like he's trying to yank out an invisible object that's lodged in his chest before giving up and letting his hand drop to the side.

There I am, glancing back and forth between the defibrillator and the door—trying to decide whether to give him a shock or wait for Zhu, I remember. And then Fergus's eyes open and he looks around the room in panic. His eyes fix on me, and his lips move.

I select the area of video, import it into the movie-editing software, and zoom in, enhancing the sound. I press play. "Help me," Fergus wheezes.

"Fergus, can you hear me?" I ask.

Fergus nods. "Did BethAnn make it?" He can barely get the words out. It sounds like he's drowning.

"BethAnn . . . She died," I hear myself say.

Fergus squeezes his eyes shut and says, "It's the dreams. They're killing us."

I stop the video. Save and export. There's no way the researchers can dispute this evidence. But before I show them, I have one more to go. Vesper said it looked like Remi was trying to talk before he died. I open Remi's video window, scroll forward to 4:57 p.m., and press play.

CHAPTER 20

ANT

"IT WORKED! FERGUS, YOU MANIPULATED REAL-ity in your dream!"

We are back in the Void, assembled on the couches, which we've pulled together into a tight group of four. I try not to fixate on the other two, stranded by themselves outside the circle. They look wrong there. I want to turn them around so their backs are to us.

Fergus was looking at me weirdly when we arrived in the Void. Like it was him who I had bashed in the head right before coming through and not a creepy old-man zombie. He's looking more normal now, as he runs his fingers through his hair and shakes his head in amazement. "I can't believe it worked."

"Well, you must have believed it, or it *wouldn't* have worked," I say.

"That was seriously kick-ass," confirms Sinclair. "What did you have to do?"

"Well, like Ant said, I cleared my mind, even though I obviously couldn't give it my full concentration. But once I saw the popcorn cart start shaking, I actually began to believe I could move it. And as soon as I believed it, the thing just went flying across the space to hit the doors."

"That totally makes sense," says Cata, nodding thoughtfully. She takes Fergus's hand in hers and squeezes, and for some reason I want to hug them both. Not that I ever would. But it just seems like the right thing to do in reaction to the unidentifiable emotion I'm feeling right now. I block it out and try to focus on what we need.

"Okay, well, now that we're sure that it works, we should try to guess what's coming next and get ready for it," I say. "But we just used one of our minutes. Only ten to go."

"If the Dreamfall is alternating between our dreams, then who is left?" Cata asks.

I get out my notebook and read out loud.

"'Dream one—we all had our own dreams then saw each other at the end, so that doesn't really count.

"'Dream two—Cave with slime lake and monsters—Fergus

"'Dream three—Genocide in the African village—Remi

"'Dream four—Graveyard and coffin—Unknown

"'Dream five—Cathedral and crypt—Cata

"'Dream six—Circus—Ant

"'Dream seven—Alleyway with dead horses, subway, and asylum—Brett

"'Dream eight—Militant rebel camp in jungle—Remi

"'Dream nine—Skinless man and scary house—Cata

"'Dream ten—Horror movie mash-up—Fergus,'" I say slowly as I jot the last entry down. I add them up. "That's two for Fergus, two for Remi, two for Cata, one for Brett, one for me, none for BethAnn, none for Sinclair."

Fergus looks strangely at Sinclair. "You haven't had a dream yet?"

"I told you, I never remember my dreams," Sinclair responds defensively.

"So the graveyard dream could be yours," Cata suggests.

"It could also be BethAnn's or Brett's," Sinclair says.

Fergus shakes his head. "Too lucid for Brett. And it couldn't be BethAnn's. She was already dead."

"We haven't proven that," Sinclair says, holding up a finger. "There's just as much of a chance that she's alive as she is dead, as we discussed. And if she's alive, she could still be mentally linked to us."

"George didn't have any dreams because she was imaginary. Maybe that means *you're* imaginary too," Cata says jokingly.

Sinclair rolls his eyes.

"I didn't see you at the informational meeting," I say, flipping to his page in the notebook.

"What informational meeting?" he asks.

"The one we had a week before the experiment," I respond.

"I've remembered seeing some of you there. I saw Remi sitting with his aunt." I flip a page back. "I saw a man and woman sitting together alone, who I'm guessing were Brett's parents since he was probably too sick to come." I turn another page. "I think I saw you, Cata. Were you with a blond woman who didn't look anything like you?"

Cata looks surprised, and then nods. "That would be Barbara. My mom's best friend. She became my legal guardian after I . . . left home."

Fergus gets this strange look on his face, like he's trying to latch on to an idea that's just beyond his grasp. And then his eyebrows shoot up. "I remember you, Cata! I met you at the meeting. You were sitting one seat over from me."

And all of a sudden, it's like a switch flips and Cata gets all excited too. "Yes! You were on my right. You had these dark circles around your eyes and a big bruise on your chin. And you were trying to chat with me while a doctor gave a presentation on a stage below us. You were sitting with this beautiful Indian woman."

"That would be my mom," he says with a grin. "And you were joking about how we should hold each other's hands while they fried our brains."

Sinclair's face is turning red. And although I can't read his expression, he is obviously not enjoying Cata and Fergus's bonding moment. "Well, I don't remember any of you," he says.

"You don't remember your dreams. You don't remember the informational meeting. What kind of insomnia goes along with amnesia, Ant?" Fergus asks.

I click my pen five times (my hat and gloves were waiting for me when we got back, and I'm embarrassed to say that slipping them back on felt like reuniting with old friends). "Well, sleep deprivation can *lead* to amnesia . . ." I begin.

"That wasn't a real question," Fergus replies, smiling.

"Oh," I say, and read his smile as friendly, not sarcastic. I smile back.

"All of these warm fuzzies are making me nauseous," says Sinclair, scowling. "Can we get on to something more productive since we only have a few minutes left?"

"Four," I specify.

He ignores me. "The people who have had fewer than two dreams so far are Ant and Brett, and the people who have had no dreams are BethAnn and me. I don't remember my dreams, so I can't be of help. BethAnn and Brett are beyond asking. So, Ant, it's up to you to tell us what might be coming."

"Well, like I said before, I've got the robber who gives me a lethal shot in the nose, a nest of deadly snakes under my bed, and a scary house with ax-wielding ghosts. Dentists and/or terrorists pulling out my teeth. We did the clowns one already." I think for a moment. "There's the carnival dream."

"Carnival?" Cata asks.

"Yeah. I went to the state fair once, and it scared me so badly I've had nightmares about it ever since." I click my pen five times and pull my earflaps lower.

"What about it scared you?" Fergus asks. Though I half

expected him to think it was funny, his face is all seriousness.

"The rides," I say. "The guys who run the rides."

"Yeah, they always look like they're either drunk or just got out of prison," remarks Cata.

"Or both," confirms Sinclair.

I take a deep breath. "If you haven't noticed, one of my 'quirks,' as my mom calls it, is control. I don't like to be out of control."

"You don't say," murmurs Sinclair.

Cata shoots him an evil look. "Go on, Ant."

"And although the statistics for carnival ride fatalities are extremely low compared to everyday automobile accidents, the fact that someone I don't trust has my life in their hands is . . ." I can't finish my sentence because my throat has closed up so tightly. I pull my legs up to me, wrap my arms around them, and put my head down, basically rolling myself into a ball. *Hugging myself*, as my dad calls it. I squeeze tightly and the frantic beating of my heart begins to calm.

"You go. She likes you," I hear Cata whisper. A second later, I feel Fergus sit down next to me. He puts his arm around my shoulders. I don't flinch.

"You're really brave, Ant," he says, leaning in close to my ear. "You might even be the bravest of all of us." He picks up my notebook from beside me on the couch. "You're definitely the smartest. I think you're doing really, really well. And even though George isn't here to comfort you, the three of us are. We're all behind you. We believe in you."

It feels like warmth is spreading from his arm through my

shoulders, filling me up. Making me feel stronger . . . like George always did. I soak in the comfort for another moment and then look up into his eyes. "Thank you," I say.

He gives me a squeeze. "You're welcome," he whispers.

"It should be coming right . . . now," I say as the knock rings out from all around us, vibrating the air with its hollow wooden sound. The blue lights flicker on to one side of us, and the door appears between them.

I watch the others' faces as we gather up the backpacks and weapons. No one seems terrified. We all know what's coming. Maybe not exactly what, but we know it will be hard. That we will have to fight to survive. We've accepted our situation. And we're in this thing together.

CHAPTER 21

JAIME

IT'S BEEN AN HOUR SINCE THE DOCTORS APPLIED the five rounds of electroshock. Zhu hovers over Vesper's shoulder as they inspect the four remaining subjects' readouts. Although they're speaking in low voices, I hear enough to understand that they didn't achieve the result they had hoped for. After the electrodes were removed, the feedback settled rapidly back into what it had been before.

"The way they're wearing down, we're going to have to start targeted life support measures," Zhu says finally. Vesper reluctantly agrees, and five minutes later a couple of nurses are doing the rounds, anesthetizing the subjects before doing a small surgery on their necks as well as inserting tubes through their noses. These are hooked up to mechanical ventilators plugged into the Tower. I know enough about tracheal intubation to realize that the fact that they're inserting ventilation through the nose and not through the mouth means the doctors are thinking long-rather than short-term care. Just another sign of their desperation.

I know they'll want to update me soon, so I'm rushing to finish the video for Remi. I find the place in the recording where he and Brett begin cardiac arrest. I cut the section, paste it into the film-editing software, and zoom in. This time, Vesper takes up half of the picture, but I still have a clear view of Remi's face.

There it is . . . His lips move. I back up, enhance the sound, then press play. I can't quite tell what he says. Something about saving someone. I back up, jam the earbuds deeper into my ears, and make sure the sound is on maximum. Play.

This time I can hear. I write down as many words as I can, back up, and play it again, filling in the blanks. A chill creeps up my spine as I read back what I have written.

"Couldn't save Brett . . . at least he didn't die alone . . . hope my family saw that I tried."

Those were Remi's dying words. Oh my God. This was about the survivor's guilt mentioned in his file. Remi couldn't save his family. He felt guilty being the only one to live through the massacre. He couldn't let that happen again. So he died in one of their dreams trying to save Brett. I am shaken to my core. I feel like throwing up.

But this is it. This is the evidence I need to get the researchers to listen to me.

I put the earbuds down and gather my papers together as Zhu

and Vesper walk over to my desk. "Okay, Jaime. Please write this down however you wish. Seeing that the subjects' feedback has continued to decline since the last rounds of electroshock, Dr. Vesper and I decided to opt for basic life support. We have given them nasotracheal intubation for oxygen and put them on transvenous cardiac pacing, which is like a temporary pacemaker. They are already, of course, on artificial nutrition and hydration by intravenous feeding."

Zhu makes this speech with a tone of resignation. She waits for me to write it down. Instead, I summon my courage and look them in the eyes. "What's next?" I ask.

They seem surprised by my directness, but Vesper answers, "We are beginning discussions on our next step, conferring—as we have this whole time—with several of our esteemed colleagues."

I pull out my charts. "May I show you something I have been looking at?"

"Of course," says Zhu, leaning in to see. Vesper looks at me warily.

"Using the feedback charts that you gave me access to through the server, I consolidated all seven subjects' data onto one chart for each category of feedback," I point to the heart rate chart. "Each color stands for a different subject."

"Very good, Jaime," Zhu says. "That's exactly what we do at the end of a trial once all feedback has been recorded. Except, of course, it's the computer that does the work for us." She smiles encouragingly. "I'm sure your supervising professor will be very impressed by your work."

She runs her fingers over the up-and-down lines, which get weaker with each period of activity. "You've illustrated very nicely how the subjects' bodies are tiring over time."

She begins to turn away. "Uh, that's not why I made the charts," I say, rushing my words. "I made them to show you something."

She turns back to me. Vesper hasn't moved, but now he's crossing his arms, as if waiting for something unpleasant.

"When I looked closer at the lengths of time for the periods of accelerated and lowered feedback, I found a pattern." Zhu and Vesper are silent, waiting.

I pull out the time chart and place it on top of the feedback. "You see, starting after the first electroshocks, the period of heightened activity was fifty minutes. The next time it was fifty-one. And the next fifty-two, and so on. And, inversely, the periods where the feedback returns to normal have been getting shorter. They began at twenty minutes, and have been reducing by a minute each time."

Zhu picks up the time chart and looks between it and the feedback analysis. "Well, that *is* intriguing," she says. "It's definitely something we will look at . . . most probably due to some sort of glitch that occurred in the Tower during the earthquake. Perhaps a power surge that was integrated into the bodies' metabolism. How very interesting."

"And disturbing," Vesper adds. "It means that the subjects are quickly moving to a point where their vital signs will be continually elevated. We will need to consider that in planning where we go next."

"Yes," I say, relieved. "That's exactly what I was thinking."

"Well, Jaime, I am very impressed," Zhu says. "You were able to see something that Dr. Vesper and I hadn't noticed . . . or at least hadn't concentrated on because we were so concerned with the current status of the subjects. It is something we wouldn't have seen until afterward, so I am glad that we had a third set of eyes and ears here, free to concentrate on the details we couldn't."

"Yes, well, I think it is more important than that," I say, feeling my chest tighten in anxiety. The doctors look at me quizzically. Here goes nothing.

"You see, I think that the periods of heightened feedback correspond with REM sleep. I think that the subjects are dreaming for long periods of time punctuated with short periods of NREM sleep."

The doctors stare at me in shock. "Jaime," Zhu begins, "we've been over this before. The subjects can't be in REM sleep. Their brain waves are in delta. Comatose brains do not dream."

"But I have proof!" I turn to my monitor and click on the file on my desktop holding the video with BethAnn's last words. "BethAnn spoke to me before she died. So did Fergus!"

The file won't open. My hand is shaking so badly that I'm clicking and nothing's happening.

"What are you talking about?" Zhu's voice is suddenly cold.

"Not that again!" says Vesper.

185

"But if you'll just watch . . ." I say, clicking desperately on the file.

"Jaime, calm down. What are you trying to tell us?" asks Zhu in a strained voice.

It's now or never.

"I know this sounds crazy. But I believe that when the earthquake hit, the sudden loss and then surge of electrical charge threw the subjects into a shared state of consciousness. One in which they are living inside each other's dreams. If you heard what BethAnn said . . . and Fergus . . ."

"Jaime, do you even hear yourself?" Zhu says in a dangerously quiet voice.

"Fergus said that the nightmares are killing them. It's right there in the video." I click again—no luck.

"Jaime." Vesper's voice drips poison. "What you are saying is completely insane. It is beyond the bounds of science or reason."

"All I'm asking is that you watch what I recorded. And that we reset the brain-wave monitor. I think it either got damaged in the blackout, or that this state of consciousness they're experiencing is something that hasn't been recorded before. That the monitor can't pick up."

"That is QUITE ENOUGH!" yells Zhu.

"Get out," says Vesper, pointing at the door. "Don't you realize how much strain we've both been under? Spitting out your science fiction fantasies when we are in the midst of a life-or-death crisis just will *not* do. Out!"

"But Mr. Osterman said . . ." I begin, grasping for straws.

"I don't give a shit what Mr. Osterman says," Dr. Vesper growls. "This is *our* trial. And you are no longer a valuable contributor, as an observer or anything else. All it would take is for me to repeat what you just said, and any evidence you gave about the test would be rendered invalid."

"But you can't . . ." I gasp. "I have to help them!"

"*We* will help them," Zhu says, turning her back to me and walking to her computer. "And you will help us by gathering your things and leaving the building at once. Good-bye."

CHAPTER 22

CATA

WE STAND FACING OUTWARD, ARMS LINKED, IN the middle of a street in what looks like a picture-perfect middle-class suburb. Kids' bikes lay on their side in one yard, and a basketball net is attached above a two-car garage in the next. Perfectly proportioned trees, meticulously trimmed around power lines, cast shade upon lush green lawns. We have landed in the least dangerous-looking place possible.

But just as I begin to let my guard down, a horrible noise starts screeching from all around. It's like a hundred violin strings being played with bows strung with sandpaper, over and over again: *skreek . . . skreek . . . skreek*. It sounds straight off the soundtrack of a horror film. I drop my hold on Sinclair and shove my palms against my ears.

On my other side, Ant crouches into a squat, squeezing her

eyes shut and pressing her head between her hands.

"What is that?" Fergus yells.

Sinclair stands there, hands by his side, staring at us like we're all crazy.

"Don't you hear that?" I yell.

He nods. "Of course I do!" and claps his hands to his ears.

Keeping my ears covered, I move out of the street to the sidewalk. The noise decreases just a tiny bit. The others follow me, Fergus dropping a hand to put his arm around Ant and help her out of the street. Sinclair ignores us and walks toward the other side of the road.

"I think we should go this way," he says. I can barely hear him over the screeching.

"Why?" I yell.

"To get away from the noise," he says, casting an uncomfortable glance around the neighborhood.

I shrug and move toward him, but the noise gets exponentially louder with each step. I dash back to where Fergus and Ant huddle on the sidewalk. The noise gets softer. I shake my head at Sinclair. "Not that way," I yell.

The screeching is so loud and high-pitched that my eyes are watering. I hunch over and head toward the next street, but the noise gets louder. I start back toward Fergus and Ant, and it gets softer. On a hunch, I step up onto the grass of the yard and the noise lessens. Another step up the lawn, and it lessens more.

"This way!" I say, and though I hear Sinclair shouting something from behind me, I make my way toward the house at the top of the lawn. With each step the pain lessens, until I'm heading up a set of brick stairs to the front porch of the house. I drop my hands and wave the others toward me. "It's better here!" I yell.

As they make their way over, they straighten from their defensive crouches. "What the hell?" Fergus asks, looking confounded.

"I wonder if it's some sort of alarm," I ask. "Like a hurricane warning or something."

"It wouldn't get softer by us just moving across the yard," Fergus responds.

"It's the dream," Ant says, looking like she's trying not to cry. She blinks back tears, frowning at the yard like she can see the noise. "It's directing us."

"Are you okay?" I ask her.

She's still covering her ears even though the noise is no longer at an earsplitting level. "I'm oversensitive to auditory stimulation, especially high-pitched repetitive sounds."

"Why didn't you bring the hat? It helps, doesn't it?" I ask.

She nods. "And it squeezed my head. That makes me feel safe. Like the gloves. They squeeze my hands." She sighs and her gaze drops. "I know that sounds weird."

"Weird is good," I say. "All my friends are weird. Normal people are boring."

She smiles and answers my previous question. "I took them off as we went through the door. They got in the way in the other dreams."

"Does the noise still hurt?"

She nods. I take a step toward the door, and the sound gets

lighter. "I think you're right," I say. "We're meant to go inside."

"What?" Sinclair asks incredulously. "We don't know what's in there. The other nightmares haven't been exactly kind to us. Why should this one be any different?" He has this are-you-stupid-or-what? expression on his face that makes me want to smack him.

"This is the first time it's felt like we were being led in any particular direction," I say. "Plus, I'm not going back out there. It's torture."

Fergus is already trying the door. He taps the doorknob in case it's booby-trapped like in my dream. When nothing happens, he touches it again lightly and then twists, leaning back in case something horrific is about to leap out. Instead, the door swings open to show a well-decorated living room.

"They leave their bikes in the yard and their front doors unlocked. This must be a safe neighborhood," I say.

Ant just stares at Fergus, hands still over her ears. The noise continues at the same rhythm, *skreek skreek skreek*, but as we step over the threshold, it gets softer.

"Unless this is a trap, we seem to be going the right way," says Fergus. He waves us forward.

"It's got to be a trap," says Sinclair.

"Yeah, well, we'll keep our eyes open," replies Fergus, not even looking at him. He's been ignoring Sinclair ever since he made fun of Ant in the Void, and I can't say that I blame him.

Ant drops her hands from her ears, but still looks uncomfortable. She peers back over her shoulder at the front door, shuffles away from the living room into an open-plan kitchen, and breathes a sigh of relief. "Better."

Fergus passes her, walking through the kitchen to a hallway beyond. "This way," he says, and we follow. Sinclair groans in protest, but no one pays attention.

Fergus places his fingers on a doorknob on one side of the hallway, and I touch another. "Louder," we say simultaneously, and continue down the hallway. I grab the doorknob on the right, and the noise cuts out completely. "Here," I say, and twist the door handle.

The room is as much a stereotype for teenage girl as the neighborhood is for middle-class suburbia. One wall is monopolized by a bulletin board with dried flowers, movie tickets, summer camp photos, and piano recital programs skewered haphazardly across its surface with colorful thumbtacks. Substitute the people in the photos for me and my friends, and the one in my old bedroom was practically identical.

There are a couple of band posters, some vintage-print curtains with pink poodles, and a full-sized white wooden bed with matching bedside table, dresser, desk, and chair. A huge fluffy blue oval rug takes up the rest of the floor space, and I can imagine the room's inhabitant lying sprawled across its soft faux fur while she talked on the phone or read.

"The screeching sound is gone," Ant remarks.

"This must be where the dream wants us," Fergus responds. "But why?"

"Well, since we don't have to run for our lives for once, we should take our time and look around," I suggest. "Besides, the sound might come back if we leave."

"I think this is all a bad idea," says Sinclair. He flinches when I look at him, and walks across the room to look out the window. "How do we know that the dream isn't doing something malevolent? Like drawing us into the most dangerous place by reducing the beeping?"

"All I know," says Fergus, looking away from where he's inspecting the bulletin board, "is that if you prefer to go back out into that noise, you're either stupid or deaf."

He carefully pulls a thumbtack out of one of the pictures and brings it over. "Judging from the fact that this girl is in all of the photos, I'm guessing the room must be hers."

He points to a dark-haired girl with thick bangs standing between two other girls. She's pretty in a wholesome kind of way. Not too much makeup. Freckles.

"Does anyone recognize her?" Fergus asks. We all shake our heads, but I'm not completely sure.

I take the photo from him and turn it over. *Last week of freshman year. BFFs! We're going to miss you, FayFay! New schools suck!* That doesn't mean anything to me.

"I feel like I might have seen her before," I admit. "But I'm positive this isn't my dream. Maybe she just has an easily mistakable face."

"Nice," Sinclair says.

"You know what I mean," I retort. "Like the ultimate girl next door."

"There's something strange about her," Ant says. "Her lips are smiling, but her eyes aren't."

"That's a weird way of putting it," Fergus says.

"Facial expression recognition cards," Ant replies.

"Facial what?" Sinclair asks, confounded.

"Nothing," Ant says.

"No, wait, I've heard of those. They're used to teach autistic people to read body language," Sinclair says.

Ant ignores him.

Sinclair has leaned in to take a better look at the photo. He snatches it from Fergus's fingers. "Look," he says, pointing to the girl on the right. "That looks like BethAnn."

We all lean in. "A little bit," I concede.

"Didn't she say she had a sister who died?" Sinclair asks Fergus.

Fergus nods.

"Well, maybe this is the sister's room and we're in BethAnn's dream."

"That would mean BethAnn's still alive. And that Fergus's experience in the lab was just a dream," Ant says, a glimmer of hope in her voice.

"If that's the case, then the graveyard dream with the coffin could be hers too," I say.

"We still haven't established why none of the dreams are yours," Fergus says to Sinclair.

"Maybe I *am* a figment of one of your imaginations," Sinclair says, a wry smile curving his lips. "Or BethAnn's. Or Remi's. Or even Brett's. Or I could be a complete fabrication of the Dream-fall."

Ant shifts her gaze to Sinclair and frowns. "Even allowing for George, that doesn't follow any of the rules we've seen so far." She goes for her notebook and then stops herself. "We must have been brought here to find something. So let's look."

We spread out and begin combing through the girl's things. I take the bulletin board and study the photos. Another has the same "FayFay" nickname written on the back, and a third has a list of girls' names. "I think her name's Faith," I say.

"Faith . . ." Ant says, and looks like she's trying to remember something.

"It goes with the initials," Fergus says, pointing to large letters—*FPL*—that have been covered in floral paper and hung above the door.

"What was BethAnn's last name?" asks Sinclair.

"She never said," Fergus responds.

Ant moves to the side of the bed and picks up a plasticine pouch sitting by a glass of water. "There's a tiny bit of powder left in this. I wonder what it was?" she asks, raising it to her nose to sniff it. She picks up the glass and swirls it around. "Must be medicine. Looks like she poured it into this glass. There's white sediment that settled to the bottom."

A buzzing noise comes from the corner of the room and, as I turn, the computer lights up. Everyone scrambles toward the desk. On the screen, an instant messaging window is open showing a long conversation between two users called FaithAndLove016 and Nick-At-Night. I pull the chair back, sit down, and begin skimming through it.

"What's it say?" asks Fergus.

Ant has crowded in beside me and moves her lips as she reads. "Oh my God," she whispers.

"What?" asks Sinclair testily.

"Faith . . . I'm assuming that's her . . . is talking to someone else about wanting it to 'all be over.' And the other person is telling her that she'd be better off getting it over with," I summarize.

"He's telling her to kill herself," Ant concludes. "Listen to how it ends."

FaithAndLove016: You'll give my parents the note, right?

Nick-At-Night: Promise. What time did you choose?

FaithAndLove016: Midnight. My clock is set.

Nick-At-Night: That's in fifteen minutes.

Faith: I know. I'm ready. But I'm scared.

Nick: I'll stay here with you. You can keep writing me 'til the end.

Faith: Thanks. Don't worry, though. I'll click out of the window after we're done, like you suggested. I wouldn't want you to get in trouble for helping me. You're the only person I've been able to talk to about it. You've been my only real friend at my new school.

Nick: 👍♥

Nick: Do you have it?

Faith: Yep. Can't thank you enough for getting it for me.

Nick: You're supposed to take the entire thing in a glass of water.

Faith: I know. The last thing I want is to wake up being resuscitated in an ER. Thanks for worrying about me.

Nick: Be brave.

Faith: Five minutes.

Nick: Are you scared?

Faith: Yes.

Nick: You can tell me how you're feeling, if that helps.

Ant stops reading and meets my eyes. I haven't seen her this devastated since George disappeared. She studies the plastic pouch still clutched in her fingers, then flicks it away from her, rubbing her fingers frantically on her leg as if she touched something radioactive.

"This Nick guy was egging her on," I say, turning to Fergus and Sinclair. I feel the blood draining from my face as the realization sets in. "He gave her poison and encouraged her to take it." I'm so horrified, my face and fingers are numb.

"That is the sickest thing I've ever heard," remarks Sinclair, covering his mouth with his hand, his forehead furrowed in horror.

Fergus puts his hand on his stomach. "I feel physically ill."

A bell starts ringing, and we all jump. It's not the screeching violins. This sounds more like an alarm clock. Fergus goes to the bed and, crouching, grabs something lodged between the bedside table and the mattress. He holds it up, tapping the button on the top to stop the ringing. "My Little Pony," he says, looking amused. The glitter of the horse's rainbow-colored tail sparkles in the overhead light. The hands both point to twelve: midnight.

My head spins. "No!" I gasp.

"What?" asks Fergus.

"What's wrong?" asks Ant at the same time.

"It's from the other dream," Sinclair says, visibly shocked.

"One of the corpses in the coffin . . . She was holding it in her hand. Wait . . . that's where I've seen her!" I say. But I'm unable to think any further, because the bed has started trembling. It's like we're in an earthquake, but the only thing shaking is the bed.

"The walls!" Ant cries, pointing.

Water has begun to course down the walls on all sides, running in streams across the floor and puddling around the bed. Fergus slips and falls. The clock crunches under him, and he yelps. He holds up his bloodied hand to his mouth and then looks up in surprise. "It's salt water," he says.

A loud creaking noise comes from the floor, which cracks down the middle and starts caving in toward the center of the room. The bed gives one last shudder and, with a crash, falls through the hole that has opened in the floor. Underneath is dark, churning water, fed by the water streaming from the walls. I grab on to the desk for leverage, but it's no good. The entire floor is caving in and taking us with it. Water splashes across my face as I feel myself slipping, grabbing on to the soggy rug, and falling into the watery pit.

I'm sucked into a waterfall, tossed around by the crazed currents, and then carefully deposited, feet on the ground, on a city street at night. Fergus, Sinclair, and Ant stand around me. It's raining hard, but we're all already soaked, and it feels like a warm summer night, so it doesn't make much of a difference.

"Where are we?" Ant asks.

"Look," Fergus says, pointing to a row of lit-up skyscrapers in the distance. "I think we're in New York, but I can't tell where. Sinclair, you're from New York, right?"

"It looks like we're way uptown." Sinclair looks toward where Fergus points then scans the street. "I'd say either Harlem or the Bronx."

"Doesn't look good, wherever it is," I say, looking at the decrepit buildings around us. Some look abandoned, and others—with lights in the windows—don't look habitable. The walls are covered in graffiti, but not the kind that qualifies as street art. More like tagging of property. The traffic light at the nearest crossroads is broken. A rat climbs out of a trash can with something that looks like a finger in its mouth and makes a dash for the nearest gutter. I shudder and wrap my arms around myself.

All of a sudden, the screeching violin pulses start up again, full blast. Our hands fly to our ears. Unable to communicate, we nod to each other and spread out, walking in four different directions. "This way!" Ant yells, crouching over so far she's almost bent double. We follow her, jogging to get away from the sound.

We turn right at a corner and run down another street, still holding our ears. I wonder what we must look like to anyone watching, but there's no one on the street besides us. Finally, we turn right onto an alleyway and the violin sound fades and finally becomes silent.

We are standing below a web of fire escapes, drying clothes draped over the sides of the ladders and on clotheslines strung from building to building. The walls are so full of graffiti that they remind me of the Jackson Pollock splatter-paint canvases we studied in art class.

On the ground where we're standing, it looks like someone spilled a gallon of dark red paint. The rain has slowed to a drizzle, and the red stain glimmers in the light cast from the windows above.

Something moves on the periphery of my vision, and I turn to see figures coming toward us from the nearest avenue. "Um, guys?" I say.

"Oh, great," murmurs Fergus, and turns to move in the other direction. But there are people coming from the far end of the alley as well.

"Looks like someone noticed us running through the rain like maniacs," Sinclair says.

Ant looks like a wet mouse and is tapping the side of her leg repeatedly.

"Should we draw our weapons, or would that be a bad idea?" I ask.

"Well, if we had guns like someone suggested earlier," says Sinclair, throwing a poisonous look at Ant, "that might make a difference. We draw our blades, and these guys will shoot us before they can get close enough for us to scratch. And I can only take out one at a time with the crossbow."

"Aren't you out of bolts?" I ask.

"Nope. Automatic refill in the Void," he responds.

"So we don't draw our weapons," Ant summarizes.

"No weapons," I repeat, as if convincing myself this is the best plan.

As their faces pass under sheaths of light shining from the apartments above, I can see that they are all boys—some would qualify as men—of all different shapes, sizes, and skin colors. But there's something they all share: a tattoo on their upper arms. As they draw near, I can make out what it is: a stylized wolf face with numbers on either side.

They stop about five feet away from us, hands in pockets except for those holding cigarettes. One steps forward. "You're obviously not from around here. What business you got in our 'hood?"

His eyes flick to me, and I see him note that I'm the same color as he is. It doesn't look like that's earning me any points, though.

"To be honest, we're in the middle of a nightmare, and you're just figments of our imaginations. Or at least one of our imaginations," Fergus says in a steady voice.

The guys all look at one another, some with confusion, others verging on rage. The hands previously in pockets begin to draw out objects.

"Fergus!" I whisper, suddenly cold with fear.

"What? It's true!" Fergus says, turning to me. "What are we supposed to do, play some stupid game? If this is BethAnn's dream, she can't manipulate reality like I was able to in the last one because she's not here. We're basically fucked."

"Excuse me," comes a voice I haven't heard before. And then I realize I have. It's Ant. But she sounds confident. She sounds like George. "We didn't mean to come here. It was kind of an accident. But we're happy to leave if you let us."

"Haven't you heard the saying?" the leader says. "There are no accidents. At least not in my book. Now tell us why you're here . . . in the very spot"—he gestures at the red stain on the ground— "where we had to teach another intruder a lesson."

He looks at a tall lanky boy on his left. "Hey, Tommy, do you think they might be here because they're doing their own investigation into that tragic accident?"

The tall boy folds his arms across his chest and shakes his head in mock regret. "Yeah, Dutch, that was really sad how the guy just kind of fell on his own knife. I'll bet they're friends of his."

We stand there, speechless.

"Fine," Dutch says. "Fish here has a really good way of getting people to talk. Why don't you show them, Fish?"

A guy steps out from behind them. His fingers are threaded through a set of brass knuckles, and he pounds them into his fist as if to demonstrate what they're used for. He strides straight up and sticks his face into Sinclair's. Sinclair flinches but stands his ground.

"*Do* something," Ant says to no one in particular.

"Yeah, *do* something," says Fish to Sinclair, and draws his fist back.

But before he can carry through, Fish spins and punches Dutch in the face. The gang leader falls back, cupping his nose in both hands. "What the fuck, Fish?" he gurgles.

Fish drops his fist and gapes at Dutch in shock. "I don't know what happened!" He stares down at his hand like it doesn't belong to him.

"Get him!" Dutch says to the tall guy beside him, who raises the knife and steps toward Fish with a look like he wants to cut him in half. But instead he turns and drives the knife into his leader's stomach. Dutch doubles over and falls to his knees.

"Tommy!" says Fish in horror. "Why'd you do that?"

But before Tommy can answer, the other gang members start piling on top of them—some helping their leader and the others attacking the two traitors. Only two guys stay with us, one with his eye on Sinclair, like he wants to ask him a question.

"The bloodstain!" Ant says. I look down and see that the red mark beneath us has begun to rise and thicken, as if the pavement itself is bleeding. It's halfway up my Converse, lapping up over the toes.

"I can't move!" Fergus murmurs from behind my right shoulder. I turn to see his worried expression. He's trying to walk, but he's stuck in the blood. He's able to pull his foot up about an inch before it snaps back down, splashing into the red slush as if he's stepped in liquid cement.

"I'm stuck," Ant says. I can't tell if the blood is rising or she is sinking, but the red stuff is lapping around her ankles. She holds her fingers to her wrist. "We're only forty minutes in. Nineteen to go," she says, looking panicky.

Sinclair is mesmerized by the fight taking place a couple of yards away. His eyes are glued on the gang members, even though the blood is halfway up to his knees. Our guards are staring at us with something like fear in their eyes, but neither of them moves until we begin to sink through the puddle of blood.

I'm struggling, blood up to my chest, when one steps forward and hands something to Sinclair. "I think you should have this," the boy says, and presses a huge hunting knife into Sinclair's outstretched hand, slicing through his palm. Sinclair screams with pain.

The blood puddle makes a horrible slurping noise, and I feel myself being pulled forcefully downward. I take a deep breath and hold it as I am sucked into the ground.

CHAPTER 23

ANT

WE'RE IN A HALLWAY FULL OF DOORS. THE DOORS and ceilings are painted a shade of gray so bland that it shouldn't really count as a color. I hold my arms out. The hallway is four feet wide, and I count twenty doors on either side. A standard door measures, on average, thirty inches across, and the spaces between the doors are a little less than the height of Fergus, who is six four (when I asked how tall he was, he didn't even look at me weird). So that is twenty times one hundred two, which is two thousand forty inches. Meaning the hallway is one hundred seventy feet long. Ticking that box in my head makes me feel safe enough to turn my attention to other details.

Each door has a number on it. We are standing in front of 327.

Judging from the fact that several of the doors are padlocked, and the entire place is made of uninviting gray concrete, I am guessing we are in a storage facility. It smells like cleaning products, with just the slightest whiff of mildew. The place is spotless, unlike my family's storage space under our house, which Mom says she'd rather just avoid than clean.

Sinclair is moaning, his hand dripping with blood from where the gang guy sliced him with the knife. It's dripping in a puddle on the painted floor, and for some reason I can't stop looking at it. I like the patterns made when things drip, but realize it is probably strange to watch someone bleed, so I try hard to avert my eyes.

Sinclair catches me looking. "Why couldn't you put basic first aid supplies in one of the backpacks?" he asks.

"I thought about that a couple of times, but then I forgot when we were in the Void," I explain.

Frowning, he pulls his yellow button-down shirt up over his head, then tosses it to the ground. Using his foot to anchor it, he rips an arm off and winds it around the bleeding palm, squeezing his eyes shut against the pain.

Cata takes a few steps away from the rest of us, and the horrible screeching noise starts back up. I press my hands to my ears. Everyone's covering their ears and looking around, like some kind of obvious clue is going to pop up and show us which way to go.

"I guess it wants us to figure out which door to look behind," Fergus yells.

"It looks like there's another hallway around the corner from this one," Cata says. "There have got to be hundreds of doors down here!"

Fergus heads in the opposite direction from Cata and holds up a hand. He goes a few more steps, then says, "It's getting quieter this way!"

"Couldn't the Dreamfall be a little less evil and just play really annoying elevator music instead of exploding our eardrums like this?" Cata says.

"If it wanted to be nice, it could have set us up with a widescreen TV and comfortable chairs in the Void," Sinclair says, then looks at me. "Hey—that's an idea!"

"Seeing that we have ten minutes in the next Void, and a minute less in each subsequent Void, I don't think light entertainment should be our priority," I hear myself say. Wow. I'm channeling George again. And, based on Sinclair's scowl, I'm doing pretty well at it. It feels weird, but knowing that she came from my brain anyway, I guess I can embrace it instead of feeling like I'm possessed.

The farther we move down the hallway, the softer the screeching gets, until we're standing outside door 303 and the noise stops. There's no padlock on this door. Cata turns the knob. "It's not locked!"

Cautiously poking her head in and looking around, she flicks a switch to the right of the door. An overhead light goes on to show . . . nothing. With the exception of a few dust bunnies in the corners, the cement room is completely bare.

"Um, what are we supposed to do here?" says Fergus, stepping in past Cata and looking around. I follow him in.

Sinclair hesitates, "Isn't it considered stupid to go into a place . . ." And then he shrugs and steps into the room.

"Well, the sound has stopped," Cata says. "The dream must want us here. But why?"

"How much time do we have?" Fergus asks.

"Fourteen," I reply.

"Well, then we'd better hurry and find whatever we're supposed to find, because I can't imagine the Wall showing up in a storage space."

There's a faint smell of something I can't quite place in here. It resembles the zombie smell from the mall, but not quite. Instead of sinister, it smells sad. I sniff again. It reminds me of the time a squirrel got in the house and died behind the washing machine. At first it smelled like this, and no one could figure out what it was. Then it started smelling like the Porta-Potties at the state fair, and Mom and I went on an "odiferous treasure hunt," as she called it, and found the decomposing culprit.

This was before we got Dog, of course. He would have found it straightaway.

So maybe it smells like new death. But that sounds weird, so I don't say anything to the others.

"Wait! There's something over here," says Cata, looking behind the door.

"Well, it looks like someone's been partying in the basement," says Sinclair, plucking an empty bottle of vodka from the ground.

"These aren't cigarette butts," Fergus says, retrieving an ashtray from next to it. "What kind of person would have a vodka-fueled pot party in a storage space?"

"A minor whose parents were at home. Not speaking from experience or anything." Cata holds up her hands in innocence. She scans the room. "Is there anything else?"

I pick up a nail from the other side of the door. It has a trace of gray paint on the sharp end.

"Well, we've got a nail, an empty bottle, and some joint butts. What does the Dreamfall want us to do with that?" As the words leave Fergus's lips, the door slams shut.

I try the handle. "It's locked!" I say. Actually, I don't say it. It's more of a squeak. My throat has closed up tight in terror. I try again, jiggling the handle.

Cata comes over and kicks the door, then puts her weight into it while turning the handle, but it doesn't budge.

"I was going to say something about it maybe being stupid to walk into a small, lockable space before we came in, but I thought it was stating the obvious," says Sinclair.

"Well, it was either come in here or put up with the screeching, so small, lockable space won," Fergus says testily.

"Okay, let's figure this out," I say, trying to quiet my panic enough to hear myself think. "How can this be a part of Beth-Ann's dream? The first place we were—the bedroom—could have been a horrible thing that happened to a friend of hers . . . or even her sister. The second place . . . maybe she had had a frightening experience with a gang, or was followed down a scary street . . . or maybe she's just afraid of them in general."

"It doesn't have to be something from our direct experience," says Fergus. "Like the dream in the cave. I've definitely never been anywhere like that before in real life."

"But this place?" asks Cata. "What would an empty storage space have to do with BethAnn? I can't imagine her coming down here for a drink and a smoke."

"Maybe she lived in this building?" suggests Sinclair.

"If that was BethAnn's sister's room we were in, then Beth-Ann *didn't* live in this building," I say.

"It doesn't really matter, as long as we figure out how to get out of here before the Wall comes," says Fergus.

"Wait! There's something here." Cata crouches and inspects the back of the door. "Someone scratched a message in the paint. I'll bet they used that nail you found, Ant."

I hold up the nail. It's flecked with the same dark gray paint that coats the door.

"Why would someone scratch a message into the back of the door?" asks Sinclair.

"Because the walls are made of cement," I say.

"That's not what I meant." Sinclair rolls his eyes.

"Okay, let's try to read this," Cata says. "'Griffin Anderson. Born 2000. Unless someone comes soon . . . died 2014. I've knocked until my knuckles are bleeding. I've screamed until my voice is gone. I'm starving. Weak. I keep hallucinating, thinking I hear footsteps. I keep thinking he'll come back. Never, ever trust your friends. They might just turn out to be your worst enemies. Bye, Mom and Dad. I love you. Griff.'"

Cata turns. The blood has left her face. "Oh my God. Someone died down here." She backs away from the door like it's got a contagious disease.

Griffin Anderson. Why does that name sound familiar? There's something . . . a memory . . . just on the edge of my consciousness, but I'm not making the connection.

"How much time?" Fergus asks me.

I give up on the name and switch to my internal clock. "Six minutes."

Fergus lays a comforting hand on Cata's shoulder. She reaches up to hold it. "We can figure this out in the Void," he says softly. Comfortingly. He likes her. "But right now, we need to get out. Let's see how strong the doorknob is."

Cata backs up and Fergus starts attacking the doorknob with his sword, but it only dents the metal.

"How about the air vent?" I point to the far end of the ceiling. "If you lift me up, maybe I can crawl through."

Sinclair leans against the wall with his arms crossed, lost in thought.

"Come help me!" I insist.

"I'm thinking!" he replies with a scowl.

Fergus gives him a disgusted look, and walking to the back wall, makes a cradle out of his hands. I put a foot in, and he lifts me up. "Step onto my shoulders for balance," he suggests.

I maneuver myself up to a standing position, then Fergus grips my ankles while I run my fingers over the screws holding the metal grill in place. "I wish I had thought of making a screwdriver in the Void." I pull my knife from its sheath and use it to wedge the vent cover open.

I've only succeeded in popping one screw out when the first boom comes. It sounds hollow and farther away than usual, but it still shakes the ground where we are. The knife drops from my fingers as I flail and then push my hands against the ceiling to stabilize myself.

"Okay?" Fergus asks, tightening his grip on my ankles.

"Fine," I respond and, taking the knife from Sinclair, renew my efforts at the screws.

On the other side of the room, Cata is attacking the doorknob, wiggling it and forcing it up and down, trying to unstick the lock. "This is not going to work, you guys." There's a note of hysteria in her voice.

I keep working. The other screw comes out and the plate falls with a clang to the floor. I reach up into the hole, and feel around to measure the size of the metal air shaft. "It's definitely too small for me!" I yell.

The second boom comes, stronger than the first. I can't keep my balance this time, and topple forward off Fergus. Luckily, Sinclair is in the way and breaks my fall, half catching me, half dropping me to the ground.

We stare at each other, breathless and panicky. "What happens if we miss the Wall?" Cata asks.

"We go to the next dream," Fergus says. "But when I did that, I woke up with a clown sitting on my chest, peeling my face off. No time to prepare or even look around."

"We'd better not come out on top of that Leatherface guy," I say. "Because I don't think I can handle running from a chainsaw again."

Then, out of nowhere, Sinclair lets out this enormous sigh. He reaches into his back pocket and pulls out a set of keys.

"The keys from the coffin!" Cata gasps as Sinclair strides over to the door and, choosing one, fits it in and opens the door with one smooth move.

Fergus, Cata, and I stare at each other in shock.

"If you want to make it to the Wall, you'd better move," he mumbles without looking back, and sets off running down the hallway, turning right when he gets to the end. He knows exactly where he's going.

I dash out behind him, with Fergus and Cata following me. Turning the corner, I see Sinclair jam the up button of an elevator, change his mind, and throw open a door next to it. I trail him as he sprints up a flight of stairs and opens another door. We burst out into a luxurious, red-carpeted lobby, lined in mirrors. A doorman in a uniform stands behind a desk.

"The Wall's just outside!" Sinclair bolts in the direction of a revolving glass door.

"No running in the lobby, Mr. Hartford!" the doorman shouts.

"What's going on?" I yell as Sinclair dodges an elderly lady in a fur coat.

"Really! Thomas, stop these hooligans this minute!" the woman screeches at the doorman.

Sinclair runs into the revolving door and, as soon as he gets to the other side, disappears into the blackness of the Wall. I step into the turning glass and push on it for all I'm worth. The machinery grinds to a stop, and I'm stuck between the lobby and the black Wall outside. Fergus and Cata are squeezed into the compartment behind me.

"Don't push it," the doorman yells, "it has to move by itself!"

"We're going to miss the Wall!" I yell, my voice hoarse with terror. I knock on the glass five times. It doesn't help me or the door. Then there is a scraping of gears, and the door lurches forward. Before it gets completely around, I slip through the crack and into the darkness of the Void.

CHAPTER 24

JAIME

I GATHER MY THINGS. MY JACKET. MY BOOK BAG. My notebook. I fold up the charts and shove them into my bag, waiting for someone to say something, but they don't. I leave everything else as it was.

The doctors are so angry that they don't even watch me go. I cast one last look at the four subjects, sending them a kind of half prayer, half wish of positive vibes, and then walk out the door.

I stop at the front desk and ask the receptionist for my phone. "Sign out," she orders as she reaches into the drawer and places it on the counter in front of me.

I step through the glass doors into the cold March evening. The parking lot is almost empty. I have the same sense of stepping out of a spaceship onto another planet, and walk zombielike toward my car.

What now? I can't just go back home. I can't leave things like this. Those kids are going to die, and I'm the only person on earth who knows what's really going on. Even though I have no delusions of being the expert who's going to save their lives, I still have a responsibility. I can't explain what happened. But if I could only get them to watch the videos, Zhu and Vesper could approach the situation in the way it should be treated: with the knowledge that the kids have some kind of psychic link and are stuck together in a collective subconscious, while continually going up against deadly situations.

If Zhu and Vesper can't wake them up, at least they could try to stop them from dreaming. Put them into real medical comas, where their brain waves are not active, until they recover.

I go to the parking lot and sit in my car for what seems like forever, not knowing what to do. I keep going over and over what happened. What could I have said differently to make the doctors listen?

After ten minutes of indecision, I turn the ignition and start driving. I have no idea where I'm going. I don't know Larkmont that well, even though it's only forty-five minutes from school.

It's almost seven thirty p.m. I'm not really hungry, but I do need to sit down and think. I keep an eye out for a restaurant or café. And at the next intersection, I see exactly what I need. Denny's. Nothing like twenty-four/seven breakfast to get the brain cells hopping.

I park near the front door and slide my laptop out of its regular hiding place under the passenger seat. I take a corner booth, ask for the Wi-Fi code, and order a Grand Slam breakfast. It doesn't matter how bad the coffee is; I'm in such shock that my taste buds don't work.

What can I do?

Or maybe I should be asking what I *would* do if I *could*.

My plan A had been that if we restarted the brain-wave monitor it might prove my hypothesis. Zhu nixed that. Plan B was showing the doctors the videos. It would have provided enough evidence that the subjects were dreaming, so that the doctors would take the necessary steps. That was one big fail.

So forget about proving my hypothesis to anyone. The only plan I have left is direct intervention. But that seems so crazy, I can't even imagine how it would work.

Something has been bugging me about the videos. It's the knowledge that three of them actually came out of the dreams. They emerged back into a conscious state. And it happened when they were flatlining.

In two of the cases, Remi and BethAnn, they sounded like they were on the verge of dying in the dream . . . almost dead. BethAnn said she'd been shot, and Remi actually claimed to be dying.

Fergus was different. He was making that movement like he was pulling something from his chest. He said he'd been injured, but not that he was dying. It seemed like he could have woken up, but that he chose not to. He said he had to go back.

What if the trick is getting them close enough to death to allow them to wake up, but not close enough to kill them? Then they would need to be resuscitated.

I face-palm. That's the stupidest plan I've ever heard. And even if it were feasible, how could I do it? Zhu and Vesper think I'm crazy. They aren't going to listen to anything else I say. I would have to sneak in and do it on my own. But how? The researchers have already said they're not leaving the room again.

What is clear is that if the teenagers aren't woken soon, they will die. The doctors will try to stabilize them, but after the failed attempt at electroshock, they have no further plan.

My breakfast comes. I gobble down the bacon and start picking at the eggs while I run the whole thing through my mind. The images of the three subjects waking. The words they had spoken. What their messages had been: *They killed me. I'm dying.* And *I can't leave them.*

It seems that the subjects have to make a conscious decision to come back—something Fergus wasn't ready to do—and have to be stable enough to make the jump. The more I think about it, the more I believe it might work.

I open my laptop and connect to the Wi-Fi. I write my hacker friend Hal a note.

Guess who? Back for another favor. I swear I'll make this up to you. My last and final request: are you able to send a text message to two cell phones from a number that isn't your own?

CHAPTER 25

CATA

"THAT WAS YOUR DREAM!" I YELL BEFORE MY EYES are even open. I swing my head around to locate Sinclair, and then I charge. He is struggling to his feet, and I push him so hard that he falls over backward. "What the hell, Sinclair? Why were you pretending that was BethAnn's dream when you knew it was yours the whole time?"

"Because the cemetery dream was his too." Fergus joins me to loom over Sinclair. "Isn't that right? You knew exactly what that key was for. You barely looked at it before you fit it in the lock."

Sinclair crab-walks away from us before scrambling to his feet. He crosses his arms as if daring us to come closer.

Joining us, Ant opens her notebook and studies a page. "Cemetery dream," she says. "You guys were buried with three dead kids. I didn't have time to write down the names, but I remember them now. The gravestone said Faith Lemaire, Etemad Khayyam, and Griffin Anderson; sixteen, sixteen, and fourteen years old."

George had a photographic memory, I think. *So, of course, Ant does too.*

Sinclair continues staring at us haughtily, not even trying to defend himself. Fergus looks at me. "Cata, you said the My Little Pony clock was in the coffin. And the keys. What was the third kid holding?"

"A knife," I say. I think for a moment. "The clock goes with the part of the dream in the girl's bedroom. The keys go with the part in the storage area. There were lots of knives in the street gang part of the dream . . ."

Ant looks at Sinclair. "When we were sinking in the blood, that guy said to you, 'I think you should have this,' and cut your hand with that knife. Why did he think you should have it? They talked about a 'tragic accident' where a guy 'fell on his knife.' Did they recognize you from that?"

Sinclair watches us like a trapped animal: like he feels he is threatened and is searching for a way to escape. He throws his hands up. "Okay. You got me. Those were my dreams. So put me in handcuffs. I have dreams of vengeance. Doesn't everyone dream of hurting the people they hate?"

"That's why you didn't seem terribly surprised about lying in that coffin with maggoty corpses," I say, remembering how calm Sinclair seemed under the circumstances. I let myself return to that horrible place in my memory. "You knew the coffin was underground, so you must have been there before. You knew that the ticking in the coffin was a clock, even before we found it. And I had my doubts when you freaked out over the hunting knife. I wondered then if the dream might be yours."

"Well, aren't you the perfect little Sherlock Holmes?" Sinclair replies. His face is getting uglier by the moment. Like an ocean of hate and spite that he has been holding in is now seeping through his pores.

"What was the poem on the gravestone?" Ant says, ignoring us. She reaches back into her memory and pulls it out:

"'The traitor spread honey atop pretty lies.

Only the love of his victims he asked.

For deceiving the lamb is the wolf's cherished prize.

And only in death is the true beast unmasked.'"

"You tricked those kids," Fergus says. "You befriended them and tricked them."

"You all seem to be forgetting one thing. These are freaking DREAMS. They come from our subconscious, but they do not represent real life. Cata, was there really a skinless man living in your house?"

I start to answer no, and then, because of the way he phrased it, I pause. Skinless man *living* in my house. What is skin? A barrier. My dad had no barriers with me. *The Flayed Man is my father*, I realize. I feel like someone has punched me in the stomach and turn away from the group.

"O . . . kay," Sinclair replies. "And how about you two?" I hear him continue. "Blue Gollum Dad in the slime cave and Stephen King–style clowns running a circus of death? How much real life was there in those dreams?"

No one answers. "There was something different about your dreams," Ant says.

"Why did you lie about the cemetery?" Fergus presses. "When all the rest of us were owning up to our deep, dark dreams, you denied it."

"I don't like to let people inside my personal space," Sinclair replies.

"We were almost killed in your personal space," Fergus replies. "It would have been helpful to know more about it."

Sinclair shrugs.

I have managed to shove the revelation about the Flayed Man's identity back into the box in the corner of my mind that comes in handy in situations like this: ones that threaten my sanity.

I turn to Ant. "You remembered seeing everyone at the informational meeting before the experiment. Do you remember Sinclair? Because I don't."

"Hey," Sinclair says. "I'm standing right here."

"Yes, but you haven't participated in solving things in the past. Why would you suddenly be helpful?"

Ant flips back to a page in her notebook and thinks. Her eyes widen, and she stares at Sinclair. "I remember seeing everyone except Fergus, but he and Cata saw each other. I saw BethAnn, I saw Remi with his aunt, and I saw those two parents without a kid. Brett's parents is what I'm guessing. But now I remember the last group. Sitting in the middle right of the room." She squeezes her eyes shut to summon the image.

"There were a man and woman sitting together. They were tanned. Well dressed. Rich-people hair. And they were sitting with this boy who doesn't look a thing like you. He had dirty-blond hair and freckles. And didn't look like a movie star."

Sinclair looks visibly uncomfortable.

"Hey, I remember him!" I confirm. "And . . . oh my God . . . I saw him again! In the dream in my house. There was this second . . . split second . . . where you didn't look like yourself, Sinclair. You looked like him! But when I blinked, you looked like this again."

"Like that actor in the zombie love movie. That Nicholas guy," Fergus adds. "The similarity is striking."

Sinclair sighs and rolls his eyes.

Ant looks at him. "We appear in the Dreamfall as we think of ourselves. You see yourself as a handsome movie star. And you've been able to maintain that image for hours, under extremely stressful circumstances. Cata only noticed you slip once. It would take a truly delusional mind to pull that kind of stunt. Someone suffering delusions of grandeur."

"A psychopath," Fergus finishes for her.

I gasp. "Oh my God, you're the psychopath! And you tried to make us think it was Remi!"

"Well, I'm not the one who came up with that theory," Sinclair rebuts. "And who knows? He might have been a psychopath!"

"You slaughtered that guard without even flinching. Just like you did the tiger. You're the one Fergus was warned about," I insist.

"In his *dream* about the lab?" Sinclair asks critically. "I'm not sure how seriously we need to take that warning."

"Even if the warning wasn't real . . . if it was just a creation of Fergus's mind," Ant says, "then it seems his subconscious was perceptive about your true nature."

"What makes you so sure about that?"

"I can't read any of your expressions," Ant says.

Sinclair's face is blank for all of a second, and then he responds, focusing directly on Ant. "Listen. You're the one who said you don't like to be put in a box. So don't put me in one. Even if I have traits that fall under the category you call *psychopath*, they also fall under the diagnoses of *sociopath* and *narcissist*. I think the acceptable term, in any case, is 'antisocial personality disorder.' And, like you've said before, it's not always a bad thing."

"Manipulating people, playing people against each other, lying . . . Those aren't bad things?" I say accusingly.

"It turned out to be a good thing when I manipulated that gang in the alleyway," he says with a grin.

We stand there in shocked silence. "That's why they attacked each other. It was your dream, so you were manipulating them!"

"And in the process, saved our lives," Sinclair comments smugly.

"But . . . wait a minute," I say. "You tried to turn me against George, saying she was ordering us around too much. You tried to pal up with each of us when you wanted something from us. You palled up to those kids too, didn't you? That's the 'traitor spreading honey,' wanting-the-love-of-his-victims part of the poem, right?" I say.

"Everyone does things to make people like them. And even if I have thoughts of revenge or manipulation, that doesn't mean that I follow through on them."

"And you know all this because you studied it?" Ant says, giving him the stink-eye.

"Bam," says Fergus.

"I'm telling you, my dreams are just as fictional as yours have been. It doesn't matter if you believe me. Even if I were a dangerous, violent, murderous psychopath, which I assure you I'm not . . . it wouldn't be in my interest to hurt any of you. We all need one another to get out of here."

And as he says it, I see the fluorescent blue out of the corner of my eye and hear the first knock sound out.

"What the . . ." Fergus says, looking wide-eyed at Ant.

"That was ten minutes," she says, shrugging. "That's all we've got. Next Void will be nine."

We stare at Sinclair. Everyone's thinking the same thing . . . even him. "Don't look at me like I'm going to murder you all as soon as we get into the next dream," he says. "Which, by the way, should be yours, Ant, from the way things look."

He holds out his arm for me to link mine through. I hesitate, wrinkle my nose, then wrap my arm through his. Fergus steps in to take his other arm so that Ant doesn't have to.

"You don't have to keep trying to look like a movie star now that we know who you are," he says to Sinclair as the second knock comes.

"Who's trying?" Sinclair says. "Like Ant said, this is how we perceive ourselves. What's wrong with having really high self-esteem?"

Fergus shakes his head. "Delusional," he mumbles.

Ant squeezes my arm hard in hers. "It's going to be okay," I reassure her without thinking.

"How do you know?" she replies. "How can you imagine that anything's ever going to be okay again?"

CHAPTER 26

JAIME

I'M JOTTING DOWN TIMES AND LOCATIONS. THIS
is going to be tight . . . if it's even doable. I need to get back to the
clinic and down into the lab before the subjects hit the next window of NREM sleep. From my calculations, they are currently in
REM, will come out of it in forty minutes, and then have only
nine minutes of stability before they are plunged into the next
dream.

It will take me fifteen minutes to drive back to the clinic. I
have to leave now. I raise my hand for the check and toss back
the rest of my coffee. I haven't heard back from Hal, and I don't
have a phone number for him. I'll just have to trust that he gets
my message, is willing (and able) to do what I asked, and can get
it done in time.

I study the pages on resuscitation I found on the internet one last time: *What happens when a respirator is turned off for a period of minutes? How long can a patient flatline before being resuscitated? Manual shutdown of pacemaker and the effects upon the human body.*

I can do this. I know I can. And if I can't, there will still be a window of time for the paramedics to resuscitate them. They don't have to die. They just have to get close.

My hands are clammy, and I feel shaky all over as I leave a ten on the table and pack my laptop into its bag. I can't think about the danger or I'll lose my courage. Walking into the parking lot, the frigid air sweeps under my collar and up the back of my neck. I shiver, but not from the cold.

I climb back into my car and head back to the Pasithea clinic, switching on the radio as a distraction. When I hear the song playing on the classic rock station, I'm not sure if I want to laugh or cry.

Dreams of war, dreams of liars
Dreams of dragon's fire
And of things that will bite
Exit light
Enter night
Take my hand
We're off to never-never land.

Metallica seems to have read my mind and is singing about the sleepers through my beater car's speakers. But, unless Hal comes through, the four kids might never escape from their never-never land.

I pull into the clinic's parking lot and check my phone. Eight twenty-five. I've got eighteen minutes before the subjects transfer into NREM sleep.

Eighteen minutes to go through the door, get past the receptionist, and sneak downstairs into the lab. And still no word from Hal. I rest my head on the steering wheel. It'll never work. What am I . . . completely insane? Do I have a Messiah complex or something? Who am I to think I can do anything . . . should do anything . . . for these dying kids?

And then the alert sound dings on my phone. It's a text from Hal: *The eagle has landed.*

I jump out of my car and race toward the clinic entrance.

CHAPTER 27

ANT

WE ARE SITTING IN A BOAT. WELL, NOT REALLY A boat, but one of those fake boats that run on tracks through any carnival attraction that includes an indoor river exploration. Pirate rides, tunnels of love, some haunted house rides . . . wherever, they want to force you to look at what's on display by strapping you into a small space encircled by murky water.

It's a four-person boat, and Fergus is beside me, thank the gods. I grab his hand without any hesitation at all, and he takes mine in both of his. Cata and Sinclair are in the seat behind us. She has scooted all the way over away from him and is shoved up against the door on her side. He's acting like he doesn't notice, but his face is a gray cloud of fury.

It's dark for a moment, with just the smell of chlorine and murk and the lapping of water against the boat, and then all the lights

230

go on and we're in a low-budget version of "It's a Small World."

No question we're in my nightmare. When I went to Disney with my parents at age three, I had such a major freak-out that they had to stop the whole ride and send someone to come out in those plastic fishermen's wader overalls to carry me to "land" and take me out through a door hidden behind a miniature Eiffel Tower.

"'It's a Small World'! I used to love this as a kid!" says Cata.

I can't even talk I'm so horrified. "Why are you scared, Ant?" Fergus asks me softly. "It's the least frightening ride of any amusement park. It's the one they take babies on."

"Everything about this ride is unnatural," I say. "The water is exactly five feet deep and is dyed a shade of green so dark that you can't see the bottom. The boats don't even float; they're on tracks. Someone in Florida recently got two of his fingers chopped off when he got his hand stuck underneath."

"Well, we won't put our hands under the boat," Sinclair says, sarcasm dripping from his voice. He no longer has anything to hide.

"Look at their faces," I say, ignoring him. "Three hundred audio-animatronic dolls, each with exactly the same face. They've just been painted different colors and wear different wigs. Which, though it avoids regional facial differences (and thus racial stereotyping), it means that three hundred versions of the exact same face are staring at us."

Everyone is silent for a moment, I guess checking out the identical features on the creepy dolls. A shepherdess with blond, curly locks and a blue fluffy pinafore, waves her staff to welcome us as her sheep gleefully jump on a rotary wheel that makes them go around and around in a never-ending fluffy loop.

On our other side, Dutch children ice-skate in figure eights next to a windmill with tulips in its windows, which have apparently been biogenetically engineered to bloom during ice-skating season.

Everything's fake. I hate fake. I am terrified of fake, and my hat with its comforting earflaps and my soft, tight gloves are not enough to insulate me from that fakeness. To protect me. I hold on to Fergus for all I've got.

"I don't understand what's scary," Sinclair says. "They're all cute and smiling and dressed in stupid national clothes that I'm sure no one actually wears, but what's wrong with that?"

"They're smiling," I say.

He looks confused.

"It's the kind of smile baristas use in coffee shops. It's the kind of smile that *you* make sometimes where it doesn't match your eyes, and so it isn't on my flash cards. It's not real."

"Hey!" Sinclair says. "Don't take your trust issues out on me. And if you can't even tell what someone is feeling without memorizing flash cards . . ."

Fergus turns fully around, and Sinclair's tirade peters out. "Listen," he says. "Whether you're the psychopath I may or may not have been warned about, until you can prove for a fact that all the violent shit happening in your nightmares is just your own weird notion of vengeance, I'm watching you. So don't even try to mess with the rest of us.

"We all have our challenges. But we need one another to get out of here. Since you're so good at pretending to be something you're not, why don't you fake being a nice normal human being . . . just for the rest of the dream."

Cata looks like she's about to burst out laughing. Sinclair gets this look of pure hatred in his eyes that only lasts about five seconds, and then it's like he's processed what Fergus said and pretty much accepted it. I squeeze Fergus's hand hard to show him how amazing I thought he was and turn my attention back to the dolls.

"You're right, they *are* all smiling at us," Cata says after a minute. "Their eyes are all trained right on us."

Another boat rounds the corner and bumps fake boat bumpers with ours. I want to throw up when I see what's in it: more gleeful animatronic dolls. The ones in the front row are wearing Mary Poppins–style clothes, with the boy doll taking its top hat off and on and the girl doll swirling its parasol above its head. Behind them are French cancan dolls who kick their legs in the air and whoop.

They are all staring straight at us. And as we watch, their smiles morph from plastic grins to horrible, leering grimaces, their lips stretching back to show brown, rotting teeth. The music slows down just a beat, transforming from a song that's meant to sound joyful into a creepy-sounding dirge.

"Fuck me sideways!" yelps Sinclair.

"Okay. Now I'm scared too," Cata says.

"What's going to happen, Ant?" Fergus asks.

"Honestly, I don't know," I say. "I have nightmares about this, but nothing happens. I know we shouldn't try to get out of the boat, but almost anything could be next."

"Um, yeah, getting out might not be the best idea anyway," Sinclair says, staring down into the water. "What did you say, it's five feet deep? Well, those five feet are chockablock full of extras for *Chucky Twelve: It's a Small, Small Massacre.*"

I look down. Floating dolls clog the water. They face in different directions but move the way they were made to: Hawaiian dolls doing the hula dance, their grimacing faces marked with red dye as if they had been slashed with machetes. Scottish dolls with bagpipes, large knife marks painted across their plastic skin. And then some categories of dolls I've never seen in real amusement parks. They look like a line that the creators decided to reject—one featuring professions. Doctors holding scalpels, tiny white masks stretched across their faces. Butcher dolls in blood-stained aprons, holding cleavers high above their heads, smiling grotesquely as they bring them up and down.

With unmoving lips, the dolls sing about a world filled with love and sunshine and laughter, while the background music is piped from invisible speakers in a ceiling that seems to stretch as far as the universe.

Out of nowhere, Cata lets out a bloodcurdling scream and holds up her hand. Half of her index finger is missing, and blood is spurting out of the end. She stares at it in horror, then leans over, curling up in a ball around it and rocking back and forth.

A small hand clutches the edge of the boat next to her, and a head appears as a doll hoists itself up. It's the butcher doll, and it's carrying a bloody cleaver.

Sinclair leans back and kicks the thing in the face, sending it into the murky water with a splash.

I grab my backpack and pull out the small bag of medical supplies I produced as we were leaving the Void last time. "Bandage!" The horrific music has gotten louder and slower, the words warped and dragging out. I have to yell for her to hear me.

She won't uncurl. "Fergus, help," I say, and he leans back and grabs her gently by the shoulders. She holds the finger out, not even looking at us, and I bind it as tightly as I can with a white sterile strip, taping it to hold it on.

Sinclair whips the crossbow off his back and aims behind the slowly moving boat. He pulls the trigger, and the cord twangs.

"Why are you even shooting a doll?" Fergus yells. "It's not like it's alive . . ." But he stops talking as a dark cloud of blood floats to the surface of the dyed green water from the pierced belly of the floating butcher.

"Oh, shit," Cata moans softly, as she looks up and sees what's happening. The underwater dolls have begun to rise to the surface and are bobbing and floating around like fish in a net.

"Look!" Sinclair says, and points at the dolls on land. They're all leaving their castles and cottages and mountaintops and heading down toward us, still singing, faces stretched with the grotesque smiles. Sinclair raises his crossbow and shoots the Alpine doll in lederhosen who descends from his summit while yodeling. It tumbles over and over, plumed hat flying into the middle of the Italian piazza nearby, blood spurting from its chest as it comes hurtling toward us, splashing next to our boat in the water.

"Don't shoot them," I yell at Sinclair. "It's going to make it worse!"

"They chopped Cata's finger off. They started it." He aims at a bullfighter in bolero hat and tight red pants.

A tiny hand attaches itself to the side of the boat, and the doctor raises its surgeon's mask and leers horribly as it swings its scalpel toward me.

Fergus grabs me and pulls me back, out of its way. "This is your dream, Ant. Do something," he urges, and then yells as a pirate doll fires its pistol from close range, grazing his temple. Blood courses down his forehead as he sits there, stunned.

I close my eyes. "Stop!" I say. The boat jumps its tracks and slams to a halt against the riverbank to my left. I focus on the mob of dolls racing toward us, weapons brandished, and I make a sweeping motion with my arm. They fly backward, knocked into the water as if by a strong wind.

"Hurry!" I say, pulling Fergus by the arm. As I drag him from the boat onto land, he seems to come to his senses. And even though blood is pouring from his head, he turns to Cata and helps lift her from her seat.

"Oh my God, Fergus," she says when she sees him. She looks

like she's going to throw up, but leaps out of the boat, holding her wounded hand in front of her chest. Sinclair follows her, and we run away from the dolls into the blackness. Just ahead, an exit sign glows red, and I run straight through it, without thinking about what might be on the other side.

Everything goes black. It feels like I'm falling.

And then a voice speaks. "I'll bet this is your favorite ride, little missy." I feel myself being shoved into a seat with a cold steel bar situated ineffectually between me and the front of a roller coaster car. A black woven seat belt with metal clasps lies on either side of me, but the fabric is shredded and the lock is broken.

I look up, and a man with a long scar across his cheek, breath like the wino who begs for money outside the A&P, and two blue-black teardrop tattoos at the corner of one eye leers at me. I fixate on the tattoo, and think, *Don't they get a teardrop each time they kill someone in jail?*

"You don't really need that seat belt," he says. "We're just legally required to provide them. But hey—you aren't really living if you're playing by the rules!" He walks over and presses a button on the control box, and hard rock blasts out of the speakers. It's a song called "Crazy Train." I've only ever heard it at fairs, and they always play it on the scariest rides.

The ex-convict presses another button, and the train lurches forward.

I hear a voice yelling and look back to see Fergus seated in the car behind me, blood matted to his forehead. Behind him, Cata fumbles with her seat belt. Sinclair is behind her, struggling to get out of his car, but the carnie guy keeps pushing him back in.

"What happens in this part of the dream?" Fergus yells.

The music screeches, "I'm going off the rails on a crazy train . . ."

I point to the speakers. "What he says." And the train lurches forward.

CHAPTER 28

JAIME

ADRENALINE IS PUMPING THROUGH MY VEINS SO hard that I have to fight to keep my voice steady. I avoid the receptionist's eyes as I pick up the pen and write my name on the sign-in sheet.

"You're checking back in?" she asks.

I nod. "Took my dinner break and I'm back." I try to say it flippantly, but my heart pounds out of my chest as I write down the time.

The receptionist is silent. Does she know I'm not supposed to be here? She picks up the phone, dials a number, and puts the receiver to her ear. I can hear the tone ring on the other end, over and over. I finally have the guts to lift my eyes to hers.

She isn't even looking at me, only holding out her open hand. "Yes, it's the Pasithea clinic. Could we have three pepperoni-and-mushroom pizzas delivered to the back entrance, please? Put it on our tab." She looks up at me. "Phone!" she whispers, still reaching her hand toward me.

"Oh. Right," I say, and fish my phone out of my pocket and place it in her hand. She stows it in the drawer, and now I am left without a timepiece or any mode of communication, but I am in.

I walk to the end of the hallway and lurk in a space between a beverage machine and the wall until I see the door to the basement lab open. Zhu and Vesper barge out and scurry down the corridor leading to Mr. Osterman's office. "I can't imagine what is important enough that he would insist we come see him instead of him coming to us," Zhu says, worriedly.

"It's got to have something to do with the parents," Vesper responds. "Anything else could wait. Unless he's gotten some useful feedback from one of his colleagues, that is. Maybe he has some valuable information for us."

"He could have told us that over the phone."

They round a corner. I squeeze out from behind the drinks machine and dash through the door they just came through and down the stairs. Within seconds, I'm back in the laboratory.

Everything seems like a freakish dream: the darkened room, diodes blinking ominously in red and green from the octopuslike tower, which has been amputated of some of its arms. Only four beds are occupied: Catalina, Antonia, Sinclair, and Fergus. And their feedback is steady, slow. They are still in REM, as I calculated. My window of time is tight. I have to act now.

I rush straight down to the floor, dropping my bag by the door and ripping my coat off as I go. When I played back the video of the sleepers, I noticed which angle the cameras caught. So I stand well out of sight as I press the buttons on the Tower that operate each subject's video camera.

I've given my plan twenty-five minutes. Ten minutes for Zhu and Vesper to walk through the building and across the courtyard to Osterman's office. And then a few minutes for them to figure out he's not there. Or, if he *is* there, some moments of confusion as they discover that the text he sent them asking them to come directly to his office wasn't actually from him. Then ten minutes to walk back. I've used five of my minutes getting down here. Twenty left. I'm going to need every second.

I'm shutting down the Tower. Not just the pacemakers and respirators . . . the whole Tower. There's no time to try this out on each subject individually, and I can't count on the doctors to replicate my process with the others if I only resuscitate one. I've thought this through. It's all or nothing.

I go over my timing. Once the heart stops beating, brain cells begin to die after approximately four to six minutes without blood flow. After ten minutes, brain cells are effectively dead. My window is frighteningly short.

I check Fergus's charts. The first time he woke up, he was in cardiac arrest for five minutes and stayed flatlined for three.

Even if I unplug all four subjects at the same time, everyone's body responds differently. They could suffer cardiac arrest all at once, or one at a time. The important thing is getting them to that point of awakening . . . the point of imminent death. And then resuscitating them before any damage occurs to their brains.

That is why I can't count on doing it all myself. I'm going to need help. It will pretty much ensure I'll be caught, but I'll just have to try to talk my way out of things.

I check the clock. They've been in REM for more than a half hour. I don't know if there's an overall on/off control switch for the Tower, but I did see an electrical cord running underneath a plastic cover stretching all the way to the wall. I walk over, crouch down, and place my hand on the heavy-duty plug attached to the wall socket. And pull.

The Tower makes an eerie sighlike noise as it shuts down. The sound is one I've heard before: after the second quake. The flashing lights don't all extinguish at once. They sort of fade until the whole thing is dark.

The room is silent. There is no feedback. The monitors are dead. From now on, we're on manual. Old-school. Flying with no wings.

With a chill, I realize that's the same thing as plummeting.

CHAPTER 29

CATA

I HATE OZZY OSBOURNE. ESPECIALLY "CRAZY Train." Just stating that for the record . . . not that I have much time to think about it as I am hurled forward, my chest jamming painfully against the metal bar barely holding me in the roller coaster car. After jerking forward a few inches and then grinding to a stop twice, the train sits at the entrance to a tunnel.

Working carefully with my severed finger, which is shooting a laser of pain through my hand and all the way up my arm, I detach the seat belt from the empty seat next to me and use it to tie the two of mine together. I still don't feel safe, but it's better than nothing.

Sinclair is arguing with the carnie behind me, and I turn just in time to see the guy's jackboot meet the side of Sinclair's head . . . with knockout force. Sinclair slumps over like a rag doll:

out for the count. "What the hell are you doing?" I scream at the man, struggling to get out of my homemade seat belt.

"No climbing in and out of the cars. It's against regulations," the carnie says with a sneer. "Besides. I didn't like his face." He calls to someone in the shadows, "Take 'em away, Carl," and the train lurches forward with a jolt.

"Sinclair's unconscious!" I yell to Ant and Fergus. "He can't hold on!"

In an instant Fergus is up, out of his seat, crawling over the back of his train car. He perches for a second on the beam connecting the cars, and then throws himself over the front of mine. He scrambles past me, lurching toward Sinclair as the train enters the tunnel.

We are plunged into complete blackness, and it's not until we pass under a series of tubes of fluorescent blue that there's enough light for me to see that Fergus has climbed into Sinclair's car, wedged himself in next to him, and propped him upright, holding his head against the corner of the train car so it won't get jerked around.

I don't trust Sinclair any farther than I could throw him, but I still don't want him to get mangled in this carnival ride from hell.

I turn my attention forward to two cars in front of me, where all that is visible of Ant is her hat, the earflaps waving wildly in the wind. She looks so tiny and alone. The train jerks to the left, and we go through another series of fluorescent tubes. We seem to be picking up speed. And then something happens.

Everything stops in exactly the same way it did in the very first

244

dream, when I was frozen in midjump while running away from the Flayed Man. That time I was caught in a bubble, and could see outside of it into everyone else's individual dreams.

It's the same now, but the bubble surrounds the four of us. We're suspended in time, trapped in our roller coaster cars, as images race by us at breakneck speed.

As the images slow down, I recognize them as scenes from my life interspersed with ones of Fergus, Ant, and Sinclair. Finally, they stop flicking by. We're presented with a fuzzy, out-of-focus image of my little sister screaming.

The picture grows superclear: Julia's face is beet red and soaked in tears. She falls to the ground, and there I stand: me, my face scrunched up in fury. Me, with my I-won't-cry-no-matter-how-badly-you-hurt-me expression. My jaws are clenched so hard my teeth hurt just remembering it.

There's my dad with his razor strap held in one hand, its copper metal socket shining in the light. He lifts it up and back. "I'm not going to stop until I see you cry. I'm going to break your spirit, Cata," he growls, saliva flying from his lips as he brings the leather down toward my bare skin.

At the point of impact, the image is shattered into a million pieces, and inside our bubble we are drenched with a liquid that douses all of us. My mouth had been open in a horrified gape, and now it's full of the coppery penny taste of blood. I sputter and choke and let go of the metal bar to pull up my T-shirt and wipe the blood out of my eyes and nose and from around my mouth.

My father disappears and the images begin to shuffle again,

stopping at one of Ant . . . hatless . . . gloveless . . . in what looks like a puffy little-girl party dress. She sits in an old-fashioned school room, no teacher visible, but a large group of students standing around her, jeering.

"It doesn't matter if you ace all the tests. You're still retarded."

"Girls can't do science. You probably memorized the answers."

"You must have cheated."

"Why can't you talk like normal people?"

"Because she's autistic. That's the same as being retarded."

Ant in the picture is doing something with her hands, and I see that she's trying to tap her fingers against the table, but the awful kids are holding her arms down and she can't move them.

"What's the tapping for? Are you sending Morse code to your alien friends?" sneers one boy, hatred practically steaming from his pores.

"Why don't you give her a hug?" jeers a girl with perfectly wavy long hair. "Antonia loves hugs."

A boy leans forward and pinions Ant in his arms, squeezing her against him. There is a close-up of her face. She is so past scared that her pupils are pinpoints, and her eyes start rolling back into her head.

"I know what she needs!" the hateful girl says. "What Antonia needs is a good wet kiss." In an extreme close-up, a single tear leaks from the side of Ant's eye, and then the picture goes static and disappears.

Oh my God. Was that real? Did something like that actually happen to her? I'm pretty sure she would never wear a party dress to school, but that whole scenario might be a composite of her worst fears. Looking girlie. Being restrained. Being touched or groped without being able to fight back.

Oh, Ant. I want to crawl two cars forward so I can be with her. Not hug her, of course, but just be there with her, letting her know someone is on her side.

But I'm immobilized in my seat, my body weighing a thousand pounds, the scenes shuffling by again. It stops on an image of Fergus. He's face-to-face with a huge man—not just tall but portly—with pasty white skin and red hair.

The beautiful woman I saw with Fergus at the introductory meeting is standing in the background, pleading, "Chip, leave him alone. He can't help it."

"He can help it," the man yells as Fergus cowers beside a huge mahogany desk. "We can all help everything. Wellness is in the mind."

He grabs Fergus by the T-shirt. "Your illness is a figment of your imagination."

"Dad, I have about a thousand medical evaluations that prove you wrong," Fergus is saying.

"Western doctors don't know anything. You have to will yourself free. Take control of your mind. Heal yourself. But you don't want to, do you?"

"It doesn't work like that!" Fergus pleads, holding a hand up to protect himself. But he's too late. His dad has reared back and punched his son on the jaw. "You're pathetic!" the man yells as Fergus falls in slow motion to the ground. His mother rushes to his aid, but his father holds her back with one hand.

"People pay a fortune to hear me speak, and my own son won't even listen to my free advice. He's a failure, and he always will be."

The picture closes in on Fergus's face. His nose is bleeding. His eyes close slowly in defeat.

The images shuffle once more. I look backward to try to see Fergus, but his face is in the shadows. Sinclair's eyes are back open, though, and from the concentrated look on his face, I know that the girl now staring at us from outside the bubble is meant for him.

I recognize her immediately. She was in the coffin, the girl whose bedroom we were in. Faith. She holds her My Little Pony clock in one hand and shakes it like it's a hand grenade.

"Why'd you do it, Sinclair? Why did you lie to me? You told me things would be better if I were gone, but guess what, they would have gotten better if I had stayed. There are all sorts of things you learn in the afterlife. One of them is how to know the truth. You probably don't even know what that word means.

"Did you know what you were going to do the first week you befriended me as the new student in your rich-kid school? Had you already laid your plan to spread lies about me, get people to hate me, get me to hate myself? Thanks a *lot* for finding the poison for me and for 'being there for me until the end.' I doubt someone like you actually has feelings of remorse. So all I have to say is . . ."

And as she says this, her face goes from looking like a teenage girl's to moldering into a rotted corpse face: "I wish you a very short life, and hope that as you die you have one moment of clarity to see yourself for the monster you are. Don't worry. I'll be waiting for you. I hope to see you extremely soon."

The corpse girl stands there, holding her clock, as a handsome boy with light brown skin and curly black hair walks up to stand next to her. A knife is stuck in his chest, his shirt completely drenched in blood. "Great idea to leave our parents' party to taxi it up to the Bronx at midnight for a little 'pickup.' You said you knew some guys with excellent shit. Some 'solid' guys that you were tight with. I'll bet you had an inkling they didn't like Arabs. And it seemed so handy you had this knife on you." He gestures to his chest.

"With the way they let you go, once I was down on the ground, one might even say it was a setup. What was the deal? Did they give you something for bringing them a 'rich fucking Ay-rab' as they called me, kicking me as I bled out? Or did you do it for free . . . just for fun? Maybe because you and your parents didn't like our upstaging you at your precious social club. Bet you kept the knife too. You seem to like souvenirs."

A second boy walks up and joins them. He is gaunt, and his eyes look like they hold all the suffering in the world. "You said you had the keys to an empty storage space. You said you had booze and weed. I didn't even want that. I was just happy you wanted to hang out with me. You tricked me. You never came back." He holds up the set of keys that I recognize so well by now. "What did I ever do to you? Nothing. I never did anything."

The girl has almost completely disintegrated now, and the Arab kid's face has begun to cave in and become sepulchral. The third boy lowers himself to the ground, rolls himself into a ball with his arms held around his legs, and becomes very still. He has taken the position of his death.

They disappear, and in fast succession come two scenes I recognize immediately.

The first is in a bombed-out house in Remi's village. Sinclair sits next to BethAnn on the floor. "I won't tell the others you killed your sister," he says as she weeps.

"I didn't really kill her. I just left her alone for a few minutes," BethAnn manages to squeak out.

"It's the same thing isn't it? You're responsible for your own sister's death. If you think about it like that, you don't really deserve to be alive," Sinclair says. And then, as two soldiers pull up in a jeep, he abandons her, sprinting away to safety.

Then we are at the top of the watchtower in the jungle. Sinclair has just shot the guard and is scrambling up to stand next to a frightened Remi. "Guess you're feeling pretty bad right now about abandoning your family"—Sinclair says—"seeing you've gotten us all into this dream where we'll die the same way they did. Nothing like being responsible for other people's deaths."

"My family's death was not my fault," Remi says. His eyes are as big as saucers and filled with tears.

"I highly doubt that," Sinclair says. "You're the only one who lived. And here and now you know you'd save yourself and let the rest of us die if it came down to it."

"No!" Remi says, shaking his head. "No!"

"Then prove it," Sinclair says, narrowing his eyes, before he turns around to wave us over.

The images disappear, and the bubble bursts. The roller coaster begins moving again, picking up where it had been, and going so fast that the three knocks come almost in succession, the first shaking the whole roller coaster, the second splitting our cars apart, and the third jettisoning us into the air, flying like bullets, spinning in God knows what direction, over and over and side to side.

As the wind whips us around, a voice comes through the chaos, confident and firm. It's Ant's voice, but it's Ant times ten. "Take us through the Wall!" she commands. And we are swallowed by the darkness.

CHAPTER 30

JAIME

I SPEED-WALK TO THE CLOSEST SUBJECT—CATA—
and grab the stethoscope from the table next to her. Placing it on
her chest, I hear her heart accelerate from slow and even to fast
and irregular as the pacemaker loses control. But it's not speed-
ing up rapidly, like Fergus's did last time. Fergus's heartbeat is
accelerating too, but not at a rate that will wake him up. Same for
Sinclair, accelerating slowly. Ditto Ant.

Okay, Jaime, don't panic.

It's probably better that they take a few minutes to move into
cardiac arrest instead of launching into death mode all at once.
It just increases the possibility that the doctors will return before
I've succeeded in resuscitating them.

My face and fingertips are numb with alarm. This has got to

work. I look at the sleepers and don't even care about myself anymore. I could go to jail for the rest of my life. But at least I will *have* a life. If I fail, *they'll* all be dead.

CHAPTER 31

ANT

WE'RE IN THE VOID, BUT IT'S LIKE AN ALTERNATE version of it. The couches are gone. The light is not bright like before. It's more like the hazy air of twilight. But I can't focus on our surroundings. All I can think about is the boy sprawled on the floor in front of me, his fake movie-star face perfectly tanned, yellow button-down shirt unbuttoned one from the top and tucked into his designer jeans. He doesn't look like a killer. *But he doesn't even look like the real him*, I remind myself. *Everything about him is a mask.*

"You're a murderer." The words are out of my mouth before he even has time to look up.

He raises his head and fixes his gaze on me, then smiles. "Ant, Ant, Ant, how many times do I have to tell you: These are dreams. This is not reality."

Cata pushes herself up to a sitting position. "My part of the nightmare was reality."

"Your dad beat you with a razor strap?" Sinclair asks incredulously.

Cata takes a deep breath, then crosses her arms over her chest. "Yes. And worse."

"No wonder you left home," I say, but she's so focused on Sinclair that she doesn't hear me.

"And I suppose you really got in punching matches with your dad?" Sinclair says to Fergus. We're all rising to our feet, and from the way we face him in a semicircle, it looks like we're going to have what old gang movies call a "rumble."

"It wasn't a match. I never hit him back," Fergus says.

"Mine's true too, more or less," I say, "although my bullying wasn't as bad as what you guys got. At least my family loves me." Then, seeing Sinclair gawp in unabashed glee, I grasp for words. "That's not what I mean. I'm sure your families love . . ." I stop. Can there be love where there is violence? I can't think about it now. I settle for, "I'm sorry."

"So if all three of our 'episodes' from the roller coaster are true, why wouldn't yours be?" Cata asks.

Sinclair is silent. "I didn't actually kill any of those people," he says finally. "Not with my own hands." His look bridges pride and vindication. Finally, expressions that I recognize.

"You are a sick, sick person," Cata murmurs, shaking her head in disgust.

Sinclair just smiles, like this is all a big joke.

My anger is making me weak. I stagger backward and grab my chest. "Something's wrong," I say, just as the others make similarly alarming gestures.

Cata slumps down to sit, pressing her hand to her heart. Fergus bends over, putting his hands on his knees. And Sinclair's hand is on his throat as he starts fading back and forth between his real dirty-blond, freckled self and his movie-star persona.

"What's happening?" Cata says.

"The way we froze in the last dream"—Fergus pauses between words as if he's running out of air—"it's like what happened when we got thrown into this place after our first dreams."

"Something's happening in the outside world," I say. "They're doing something to try to get us out of here."

"I hope it doesn't kill us first," says Cata, leaning her head forward weakly.

"How long until the next nightmare?" Fergus asks.

"Now," I say as the first knock comes. The fluorescent outline of the doorway takes shape. . . hovering in the air nearby. Fergus helps Cata to her feet, and he waves me over.

"What, you're not inviting me to join the party?" Sinclair asks as the second knock comes and the wind begins to whip around us. I pick up the backpacks and hand them out, leaving Sinclair's on the ground for him to get himself. My dagger is still strapped to my waist, unused during the last dream. The three of us link arms, leaning on one another to stay upright.

"The Dreamfall will send us to the next dream together, whether or not we hold arms," Fergus says to Sinclair. "I can't do anything about that. But I can refuse to help you anymore."

Cata's and my silence speaks for us. And then Cata turns away and starts gasping for air. "Can't breathe," she says.

There's a pressure on my lungs, and I feel like I have been holding my breath underwater for a bit too long. "Not enough oxygen," I say. "I feel like I'm going to faint."

"Come on!" urges Fergus. His face is turning red.

The third knock comes, and I weave my arms between Fergus and Cata's. Sinclair scoops up his backpack and slings it across his shoulders. Setting his jaw, he stares at us with a hatred that must have been fermenting under that pretty face this whole time. And with a boom like an explosion, we are swept off our feet through the door.

CHAPTER 32

CATA

SOMETHING'S WRONG. WE GOT SUCKED INTO THE door, and then dumped right back into the Void. Sinclair sits a few yards away, his back to us. He gets up and comes over, acting like nothing's happened.

We drop arms and turn around in circles, checking to see if anything is out of place. "Is this the Void?" I ask.

"It looks like it," Sinclair says, reaching down and touching the ground. "Feels like it too." He sees me staring. "What? Like Fergus says, the Dreamfall's forcing us to be together. Might as well make the best of it."

I back up a careful distance from him, then turn to Fergus and Ant. "Something feels different," I say. I press against my chest. "I don't feel like I'm dying anymore."

"How much time went by?" Fergus asks.

258

"Only thirty seconds," Ant says. She takes her notebook out of her pocket and flips through it. "This is nightmare number thirteen. The amusement park lasted sixty minutes. This one's supposed to be sixty-one. And as for whose dream we're in this time, it could be any one of ours. All of us"—she pauses—"who are still here, that is, have each had two."

"Well, the last one started with Ant's. But then when that bubble thing happened, our dreams all ran in succession in the same space," I say.

"I don't think we can count on anything being the same after that," adds Fergus. "Especially if they're messing around with us in the outside world."

"Um . . . I think this *is* actually a nightmare," Sinclair says, as the colors of the Void begin to shift to a dark shade of green that reminds me of the men's smoking rooms in British historical TV series. Walls begin to rise from the ground, and a large solid desk sprouts up in the middle of the newly formed room. Shelves are everywhere, holding either leather-bound books or gilded trophy cups fronted with little statues of golfers or of men in suits shaking hands.

The huge redheaded man I saw during the roller coaster nightmare appears next to the desk, leaning on it with one hand as if for support. Behind him stands Fergus's mom. She holds her hands tightly in front of her, looking like a scared referee: she has to keep the game going, but doesn't want to make anyone upset.

"I refuse to have this discussion with you again," the man roars at Fergus, who disappears from between us and is suddenly standing directly in front of his father. Ant, Sinclair, and I step back to get out of the way, but the man notices us and points.

"Who are these . . . people?" he asks.

Fergus looks around, clearly surprised that his dad can see us. "They're friends."

"Friends?" his dad roars. "*They're* your friends?" He looks at us like the motley group we are. "You've never brought friends home before."

"I wonder why," Sinclair murmurs, plunging his hands into his pockets and pretending to study a nearby golf trophy.

"Don't worry, we were just leaving." Fergus turns on his heels to head toward a sliding glass door. Outside is a sunny patio leading to a swimming pool.

"Stop right there, young man. We have not finished our discussion."

Fergus turns. "You just said you refused to discuss whatever it was we were discussing, so I assumed that automatically meant 'end of discussion.'" He rubs his tattoo, and I can tell he's trying to stay calm.

Ignoring Fergus's attempt at logic, his father barrels ahead. "I refuse to let you live in the school dorms. I refuse to let you get an apartment, even if it is with another 'adult' who will take responsibility for your health, as required by your precious Dr. Patterson. That requirement is one of the only things I actually agree with him about. Because it forces you to stay here, under my authority, where you need to be until you accept the fact that your illness is all in your mind."

"Now, Chip, really," says the woman, "you can't force our son into seeing things from your point of view. Because that's what this is all about. *Your* point of view. Fergus does not need to accept it."

"Like hell he doesn't!" the man yells, pounding his fist on the table. "I am supporting this family. I am paying for his school. And for his ridiculous medical bills. My point of view is the only one that counts." He twists around to glare at Fergus's mother. "And quit your bitching, Amrita. This isn't about you. Don't you have some pottery to make? I didn't have that studio built for you in the garden just to have you creeping around undermining my authority."

"Oh my God," Ant says, and then presses her hand to her mouth like she can't believe she actually said it out loud.

"Is there something you want to say, little boy?" the man asks, directing his fury toward her.

Ant just kind of gapes at him, and then says, dead serious, "It's just that I didn't know that there were actually people out there who were as misogynistic and . . . offensive as you! I mean . . . I didn't think they actually existed outside of bad reality TV."

Sinclair gets this look on his face like he's about to explode with laughter. Fergus's dad turns beet red and heads for Ant with hands outstretched like he wants to throttle her. With a quick motion, she draws her knife from its sheath and holds it protectively in front of her. The man stops in his tracks, face frozen in surprise.

"What the hell is going on here?" he asks in a strangled voice.

Fergus looks at Ant, who seems ready to take on his huge father with her tiny frame and simple knife, and something seems to click. "What's going on is that I am leaving," he says.

His father lets out a guffaw. "Now *that's* a good one! What are you going to do? You don't have money to live on. You can't drive. They wouldn't even hire you at McDonald's because you could have one of your 'attacks' and set the place on fire. You're completely dependent on me. You have nowhere to go."

Fergus hesitates, and then his shoulders slump.

"Yes, he does."

The words are out of my mouth before I've even thought them through. Fergus turns and looks at me like I've grown a second head. "Cata, what are you talking about? My dad's right. I'm stuck."

I shake my head. "No. You're never stuck. Barbara"—I'm coming up with a plan even as I talk—"my mom's best friend, she took me in. Agreed to be my legal guardian. But you don't even need a guardian; you're eighteen. She has a huge house and dogs and horses. I know Barbara, and she would be thrilled to have you come stay and help her with the place—for as long as you need until you found a job and a school."

Fergus just stands there staring at me. "But . . . you don't even know me."

"For God's sake, Fergus, I've been inside your head. How much closer do you have to be to actually know someone?"

"Really? Barb . . . your friend . . . she would . . ." He can't seem

262

to get the words out, he's in such shock that a stranger would do something kind for him.

"Really," I say, laying a hand on his arm.

"But Mom," Fergus says, turning to the woman cowering behind her husband. "How can I leave you alone here with *him*?"

His father looks like he's just been slapped, and then turns in astonishment to look at his wife.

"You go," she says, a strength in her voice that wasn't there before. "I've put up with a lot to make sure you got what you needed. If I know you're safe, I can take care of myself."

"Now, wait just a bleeding minute here!" Fergus's dad yells. He grabs his son's shoulders and draws back one arm as his wife scrambles to pull him off.

Fergus just watches his father impassively.

"Go ahead. Hit me," he says. "You're bigger than me and you're stronger than me, and you can knock me off my feet with a punch. We both know that. But I've got witnesses this time. And for some reason, I think you care a little too much about your public image to ruin it by assaulting your son in front of his friends."

His dad looks at me, then at Ant and Sinclair. He lowers his arm and shakes it out like it was all an empty threat.

"Well, I obviously can't stop you from going, son." He chokes on this last word, like it irritates him to claim such a close rela-tionship to Fergus.

"You got that right," Fergus says and, taking me by the hand, starts toward the door. He slides it open, and a fresh breeze comes in from outside, along with the tinkling sound of water falling over rocks coming from the pool.

As his foot crosses the threshold, he turns and gives his mom one last look. "Love you, Mom. Take care of yourself." And then it's like a huge eraser sweeps the entire landscape clean and we're back in the Void.

"Well that was . . ." But before Sinclair can think of a sarcastic enough description for what just happened, huge beige stuccoed walls begin growing from out of the ground far on either side of us, in the form of an amphitheater. Rows and rows of chairs appear, arced around a circular stage and climbing probably fifty rows high. We are standing between the front row of seats and a finely crafted wooden stage lifted a good five feet off the ground. A row of steps runs up to the stage on either side.

"Oh, crap," says Ant.

"Where are we?" I ask.

"It's an award. Some kind of award ceremony," she says, pulling her chullo down over her ears. She wedges herself into one of the chairs and begins using the armrest to do some heavy-duty tapping.

As I watch, the chairs begin filling with people who just appear, already seated, legs crossed, chatting to one another in an atmosphere of expectation. A podium rises from the stage, and a line of chairs begin popping up one by one to form a row behind it.

Fergus and I plop down in the chairs on either side of Ant before they can be filled, and Sinclair takes the seat directly in front of us.

"What's wrong, Ant?" Fergus says, tentatively taking her hand. She lets him lace his fingers between hers.

"I win prizes," she says. "I like competitions. I like projects. But I don't like winning, because then I have to stand up in front of people, and sometimes I even have to say something."

"What'd you win here?" Sinclair asks, looking out at the enormous hall and the crowds of people jammed into the space. "The Nobel Peace Prize?"

Ant kind of hiccups. She grabs her heart, gives a pained look, and then breathes out. "No. It's part of a big science competition. I won seventy thousand dollars. They wanted me to talk."

"You won seventy thousand dollars!" I yelp. "Doing what?"

"Research about neurological factors in attention deficit disorder," replies Ant, like winning a major science award is the most natural thing in the world.

"Why am I not surprised?" says Fergus.

Ant turns to him with a hurt look. She thought he was making fun of her but, seeing the proud look in his eyes, she smiles instead.

Fergus gestures toward the podium. "This probably *will* be the Nobel Prize one day . . . in medicine or chemistry or something that will save the world."

"Not if she's in a coma," points out Sinclair.

"Don't even," I say, furrowing my brow. He holds his hands up in innocence. How can he act all jokey now that we know about him? He honestly doesn't seem to care.

Ant ignores Sinclair. "I didn't even get to go up to accept this prize," she tells Fergus. "My mom had to get it for me."

"Well, it's normal to be nervous about getting up in front of a big crowd when you're thirteen," I say.

"No," Ant explains, "I said I would go up, but I had to have seven things, and my mom said they wouldn't let me."

"What was the extra thing?" Sinclair asks. "Besides glove, glove, chullo, pen, notebook, and George?"

"No one could see George," Ant says, "so she wouldn't have been a problem."

"What was the last thing?" I press.

"Dog."

"You wanted to take your dog with you onstage?" I ask incredulously.

"Yes, but Mom said people would think I was visually impaired. And that they wouldn't understand about the hat and the gloves. So I wouldn't do it, and she did it instead."

"Oh, Ant," I say, stopping myself from taking her other hand because I know how uncomfortable it would make her.

Sinclair rolls his eyes.

Fergus speaks up. "Ant, I just stood up to my dad. He's my greatest fear. One that has always popped up in my nightmares in one form or another. And when I did, we all moved on. It's your turn now. I have a feeling we'll be stuck here until you do something."

Sinclair looks straight at Ant. "Dude, if your test is walking up eight steps onto a stage, taking an envelope from some guy in a tuxedo, saying a few words into a microphone, and then leaving, then I say . . . fucking DO IT! What are you, crazy? Can't you just suck up the tics and freakiness for five fucking minutes to save your . . . and possibly all of our . . . lives, depending on how this thing works? I mean, get a move on! We're wasting precious time sitting around saying, 'Poor Ant. That must be really hard to have a brain the size of a watermelon and get all that money and praise thrown at you. We really feel for you.' Well, fuck that shit! Buck up and go!"

Ant stops tapping and stares straight at Sinclair through his entire tirade. She doesn't even look upset. It looks more like she's listening . . . really listening . . . and thinking it through.

"You," Fergus hisses. "You do not deserve to talk."

Sinclair scowls.

"I hate to add anything to that elegant, heartwarming speech," I say, "but I think you're getting something wrong. Thinking back through the dreams, Ant has been up against some scary stuff. A lot of it's been about control. And about fear. In the beginning, Ant was the brains and George was the brawn. She was her shield. But what's become increasingly clear, now that George is gone, is that Ant is becoming more and more like her."

I turn to address Ant directly. "It's not that you aren't brave. Or that you can't communicate 'normally,' as you put it. It's that you don't know how to connect to that part of yourself that *is* George. The kick-ass part that doesn't hesitate from saying what she thinks and doesn't shy away from *thinking*."

Fergus picks up my stream of thought. "Cata's totally right. In that last dream, all of those kids were making fun of you. Bullying you. You were hiding from them . . . not reacting. That was obviously something from your past. Because the you that I've gotten to know over the last however many dreams would not take that shit. You have too much George in you. And with her gone, you're learning to connect those two halves of yourself."

Ant looks between the two of us. It's like a flame has ignited in her soul and is shining through her eyes. "She is inside of me, isn't she?" she whispers.

"She *is* you," I say.

Ant stands, hesitates just a second, then, without looking back, begins walking toward the stage.

In a flash, everything around us disappears: chairs, people, amphitheater . . . and we're back in the Pseudo Void.

We barely have two seconds there and then we're standing in my front hallway. The one that was in flames in my last dream, the Flayed Man fighting his way through my front door. But now the house is quiet. Three figures stand before me: my father in the middle and my sister and brother on either side, holding his hands.

"Cata!" Julia says. She looks like she wants to throw her arms around me, but, remembering our father, she stares down at the floor.

"Who are these people?" he says, staring at the others with suspicion.

"Friends," Fergus says.

"I've never met you before," Dad replies.

"Oh yes, you have," Sinclair reposts. "But you were wearing a monk's outfit and had blood coming out of your eyes."

My father gawks at him, incredulous. "Is this part of your rebellious, drug-abusing crowd, Catalina? The ones who led you astray?"

"No one led me astray, Dad," I say. "I did the straying all by myself. Well, with the help of law enforcement and child protective services."

"Has she been telling you people her lies?" my father asks, looking between Fergus, Ant, and Sinclair. "Catalina is a compulsive liar. She has false memories. I had a certified therapist confirm that the things she said I did . . . they weren't true."

I feel myself fading. My head is buzzing and my vision starts swimming. I want to be anywhere—*anywhere*—except here. I realize I'm dissociating. I look at my sister's face and think, *Sorry*.

And then I remember Fergus pushing my monk dad over the balcony in the cathedral. I realize to what extent the Flayed Man has terrorized me for the past few years, night after night. And I decide I'm not going to avoid it anymore. I'm strong enough now to face him head-on.

I straighten and take a step toward my father. "Dad, it wasn't a therapist. It was a church counselor. And you manipulated them into diagnosing me without even meeting me. How would they know I'm a liar . . . or have false memories, or whatever . . . if they'd never even talked to me? People trust you. You manipulate them. It's the only way you've been able to keep Julia and Fred."

"What do you plan to do about it?" Dad tightens his hold on my siblings' hands, who wince from the pressure.

"I don't know what I can do. But I will do everything I can. I'm not afraid of you anymore because I'm finally safe. And *finally*, I don't feel guilty about telling people what you did. About turning you in. Even if no one believes me besides the judge, I know I was right."

Dad yanks Julia and Fred behind him, as if to shelter them from me.

I take a step toward him, and he flinches. "I've been running away from the monsters in my dreams since I was a little girl. But the only monster I've ever known in my life was you."

I look my siblings in the eye. "I'm coming back for you," I say. Fergus throws the door open, and we walk out.

Before I even have time to react to my unprecedented display of courage, we're back in Pseudo Void. Fergus reaches out and wraps his arms around me. "You were amazing," he says.

I don't have time to bask in his affection, because seconds later we're standing in a funeral parlor. Five empty caskets are laid out, end to end, with enormous bouquets of flowers on either side.

Three of them have chairs set in front, and in each sits a child wearing funereal clothes. The air smells sickly sweet—the perfume of a hundred white lilies.

"Not them again!" cries Sinclair.

"Well, what else would it be?" Ant says. "You killed them! Do you have any worse skeletons in your closet that you have to confront? Because now's the time to dig them out. Pun completely intended."

Fergus and I look at each other, and he mouths, *George.* I smile and feel like a proud mom on the first day of school.

"I didn't really kill them!" he shouts, as the three of them lift their gazes to stare at him.

"I didn't kill you!" he yells, but keeps his distance. "It was your own stupidity . . . your own blind faith . . . your need for acceptance that killed you. I was just there to help you along your self-destructive paths."

"That's a lie," says the girl.

"We were your conquests," says the youngest boy. "You just wanted to see how much power you had. What you could make us do."

"The wolf and the sheep," the third boy says.

"I don't know what you want from me!" Sinclair yells, shaking his fists toward the corpses. "My sincere condolences? True heartfelt regret? A get-down-on-my-knees apology? Well, I'm not fucking doing it because I don't fucking care!"

He raises a hand, and suddenly the three children are bound

to their chairs by several strands of rope. "This is my dream, and I'm the one who says what happens."

He turns around and points at Fergus, Ant, and me, and suddenly I can't move. I look down to see that I'm sitting bound by rope to a chair identical to those of the dead children. I try to move my legs. They're bound too.

"How many minutes?" Sinclair asks Ant.

"Two," she says. She and Fergus are tied up like me. And to judge from her expression, I'm guessing that if her eyes could shoot flames, Sinclair would be burned to a crisp.

"You all have become deadweight," Sinclair says. He walks over to me and runs his hand over my hair. I shudder violently and try to bite his wrist. "I thought you might be worth keeping around," he says to me. "But you're just like everyone else. A loser. And in this game, only winners survive."

"I would have to disagree with that," comes a voice. I look up and see two figures standing in front of the two empty coffins. They are hidden in shadow. They take a step toward us, and Sinclair recoils when he sees their faces. It's BethAnn and Remi.

"How can you be here?" Sinclair asks, a note of fear in his voice. "When you die in the Dreamfall, you die in real life."

"We still exist in your consciousness," says Remi, "and that's what counts in this place."

They take another step toward Sinclair. Something glints in their hands. They're holding the knives that Ant made for us, back several Voids ago.

Sinclair looks alarmed and takes a step backward. "You can't hurt me. You're ghosts, like them." He points toward the three corpse children.

BethAnn and Remi brandish their knives and then, changing course, head our way. Just then, the first knock comes, shaking the room, and sending the gigantic urns full of flowers spilling off their columns.

"Are you all right?" BethAnn asks me as she bends down and starts sawing at my ropes.

"BethAnn," I say. "We saw what Sinclair said to you. Your sister's death wasn't your fault. You didn't deserve to die."

She frees the bonds on my legs and looks up. "I know that now." She gives me a sad smile.

"Does this mean that you're going to be alive in the real world?" I ask hopefully.

She shakes her head and moves behind me, slicing through the ropes in one quick gesture. "No. But I remain in your memories. It's the only reason I'm here."

I look up to see the three corpse children surrounding Sinclair. They're blocking him from running away. The second knock rings out, and the force is so strong, I am knocked to the ground. I push myself up to see Ant handing the corpse girl her ropes. Remi finishes sawing through Fergus's ropes. Fergus turns to him. "I'm sorry I doubted you."

"Forgiven," Remi says. His eyes are full of tears. "Everything I did, saying we should leave you . . . I always meant well."

"I know." Fergus draws him in for a hug. "Forgiven."

As the black wall appears, bisecting the funeral chapel to my left, the wind blows all of us back a step. Sinclair flails and lands in a chair BethAnn shoves right behind him. "Hey!" he yells.

The corpse girl hands a length of rope to Remi and another to BethAnn. They begin binding Sinclair to the chair as he struggles to get free. The corpse boys step forward and help to hold him down.

"What do you think you're doing?" Sinclair screams. He is now a hundred percent his real self: dirty-blond hair, freckles, and an expression so sour that it distorts his features into a mask of hatred.

"We're keeping you here. With us," says the corpse girl. Sinclair begins to flail and knocks his chair over, continuing to struggle as he lies on his side on the ground.

"You can't do this!" he screams, thrashing his body to no avail.

"Go," BethAnn says to us, raising a hand in farewell. She looks exactly the same: huge eyes, blousy cover-everything shirt, and pink Converse. I don't want to leave her here.

But Fergus takes me by the hand and, pulling me and Ant beside him, runs toward the Wall. This time, as we are enveloped in the darkness, the pain in my chest returns with full force, twice as strong as it was in the last Void. I gasp for breath and clutch my heart. Fergus's eyes are wide as he struggles for air. Ant is pressing her hand against her chest, a terrified expression on her face.

The wind swings me around so that I'm looking back out at the scene we're leaving, and I get one last glimpse of the funeral home. The five children are grouped around Sinclair, staring down at him. A look of pure terror is on his face. And just before the darkness swallows us, the corpse girl turns her head. The slightest of smiles blooms on her lips.

CHAPTER 33

JAIME

I HOVER, MY EYES FLICKING BETWEEN THE CLOCK and the sleepers as I run from one to the next, checking their heart rates with the stethoscope. They are accelerating at a dangerous pace. What scares me most is that Antonia has begun to gasp for air, and Cata is making wheezing sounds. I can't turn the Tower back on yet. If they don't get to the point of cardiac arrest, the pacemakers could kick in and save them before they have a chance to wake up. Cata wheezes loudly, and this time it sounds like words. *Can't breathe.*

I scramble over to the plug and ram it into the socket. The Tower begins to whir, but the lights stay muted as the power slowly builds up, feeding the machine section by section. I hear the air flow through the respirators, and all four sleepers gasp in oxygen. Their wheezing turns to regular breathing in mere seconds.

This is it. I'm calling it.

I rush to the phone and dial nine. "Send a team of emergency medical responders immediately to the basement laboratory in building one."

I run back to the sleepers, arriving just as Antonia's eyes fly open. "My heart. It hurts. Going so fast." Her hands clutch at her hospital gown like she wants to rip it off.

"Did we make it?" Fergus's lips barely move, his face a rictus of pain.

Cata yells, "Help! Someone help!"

I race over to Sinclair. His jaw is clenched, and his eyes are open, staring at the ceiling. That's good enough for me.

The door flies open, and a team of three paramedics pours through. They look around for the doctors and see me. Luckily, they're the same ones as before, so I don't have to explain who I am.

"I was out of the building," I say, "and when I came back, the power was out. It just came back on a few seconds ago."

"Where are the doctors?" they ask, rushing over to the subjects.

"I don't know."

"The monitors aren't working," one says, tapping a screen.

"Oh my God, I think they're awake!" says another. Each takes a patient as they scramble to put on their stethoscopes.

"You know resuscitation?" one asks me.

I nod.

"Take subject two," she says.

I stand next to Fergus and place my stethoscope on his chest. His heart is beating wildly. He's in cardiac arrest. He grabs my arm. "You guys figured it out. It worked," he wheezes.

"That part worked," I say back. "Now you have to survive."

"The pacemakers must have been turned off with the power," Ant's paramedic says. "Mine's beginning to flatline. Starting resuscitation by defibrillation."

"Same here," says Cata's EMT.

"Mine's already flatlined," says the man monitoring Sinclair.

Fergus's eyes lose their focus. As I listen, his heart stops beating. I pick up the paddles and step back.

Everyone's counting out their own beats as each of us tries to resuscitate our subject. I apply the first charge. Fergus doesn't react. I lean in close enough for him to hear. "Come on, Fergus. You've already resurrected once today. Let's make two times a charm." I apply the paddles again and press the charge button.

There is an explosion at the door as Drs. Zhu and Vesper burst into the lab. Their beet-red faces drain white with shock as they register the scene in front of them. "What in the name of God is going on in here?" yells Vesper. Zhu just stands there in shock.

I look down at Fergus, whose head has rolled to the side. The Tower makes a clicking noise as all the monitors restart at once, and there's Fergus's heartbeat . . . going strong. His second round of defibrillation worked.

Zhu walks up to me, gives me a look of pure hatred, and shoves me aside as she checks Fergus's vitals. Fergus turns his head slowly upward, opens his eyes, and blinks. "Hey, Doc! Looks like we're back."

Zhu lets out this half shriek, half gasp and turns to the paramedics. One by one, they step back and reveal successfully resuscitated subjects.

Cata blinks and raises her hands to her lips. "Thirsty," she says.

Antonia peers at them through half-closed lids. It looks like she's been to hell and back. "Could someone get my parents?"

Sinclair turns his head as the doctors approach. "Hey, it's our favorite sleep specialists," he says, his voice a rasp. "I just want to say . . . great job curing our insomnia." His eyelids begin to sag as his words slow. "Tell the others . . . it isn't over." His eyes roll back as the beeping of his heart rate monitor slows into a steady rhythm.

"Muscle tension relaxed, brain waves in delta," reports the paramedic standing by his side. "He's slipped back into the coma."

Zhu tears herself away from the subjects and marches over to me. "Explain. What are you doing sneaking back here? What have you done?" Vesper joins her and hunches over me menacingly.

"I haven't done anything," I say. "And I'm not sneaking. I left and went to dinner. And when I finished, I realized I'd forgotten my bag and came back to get it. I signed in with the receptionist. You can check!"

They wait, listening, so I continue. "When I came in, it was dark in here and the Tower was off. So I called the paramedics, like you had me do before. And when they got here, they asked me to help with the resuscitation."

Zhu narrows her eyes. "You have something to do with this. I can tell."

I lift my hands and try for the most innocent expression I can muster.

"They're alive," Vesper reminds Zhu.

Zhu's shoulders slump, and she lets out a sigh so deep, it's like she's been holding her breath for the last nine hours. "They're alive, but are they healthy? Let's start checking vitals and getting them warmth and nourishment. Someone notify the parents immediately."

They walk a few steps away before Vesper turns around. "Don't you even think about leaving now," he says. A muscle twitches beside his eye. I can tell he knows something, but even he doesn't know what it is. "Do you have your notebook?"

"It's in my bag." I gesture toward where I dropped it beside the door.

He turns away from me. "You have a lot to catch up on, Jaime. Better start writing."

EPILOGUE

JAIME

IT'S BEEN SIX MONTHS SINCE THE EXPERIMENT occurred, and you won't be surprised to hear that it will be the last of its kind. Zhu and Vesper quietly ended their research and are moving on to delve into the intricacies of fatal familial insomnia. They have already located the gene sequence and are taking the first steps toward finding a vaccine that will eradicate the disease completely.

And for the record, they never did ask me what really happened. My suggestion during the test about shared dreams had been too far out there for them to accept, so they preferred not to push me on what I thought had occurred. Ignorance is bliss, I suppose. Or at least, it keeps you from doubting your very sanity.

The clinic settled out of court for the deaths of BethAnn and Remi. Brett's family didn't sue. This had been their last-ditch effort, and no one had really thought it would work. Besides, with Zhu and Vesper turning their attention to curing the disease that took their son, Brett's parents were comforted that his experience had served as a trigger for action in the medical world.

The sleepers were up-front about everything. They answered all questions honestly, but no one believed that what they had experienced were anything more than hallucinations: delusions created by minds that were fighting to survive.

Osterman used my notes in court, although I refused to testify in person, knowing that I would have to lie. I passed premed with flying colors and, with the help of my adviser, secured a grant that will see me through medical school. I'm still set on specializing in public health. I had a friend make an architectural drawing of the future Detroit Free Clinic. It hangs on the wall above my desk.

Antonia, or Ant, as she makes me call her on the occasional times we have seen each other, made the courageous decision to skip high school, and this month she started university. The paper she wrote for her applications, laying out her spectrum theory of neurologically based behavioral differences, had universities fighting over her. She's on a full-ride scholarship and has about a million internship offers. She ditched the chullo and gloves as soon as the experiment was over, and is merely thought of as "eccentric" by her new friends in her dorm.

Cata went to court and won a conviction against her father for child abuse. Her brother and sister were taken in by Barbara, who I have met on a couple of occasions. She is the kind of person who thrives on caring for people, which is a good thing, because with

Fergus already having moved in, she had a full house.

It took Fergus under two weeks to settle things at home. He took the bus and arrived in Tennessee with his whole life in a suitcase. Barbara set him up with a local artist—one you've probably heard of—who is mentoring Fergus and showing him how to grow and develop his own style.

Cata enrolled in a college close to Barbara's house, and is majoring in journalism. Her goal is to become a writer and live in upstate New York in a cabin in the woods where the snow falls deep during the winter and she can write in the light of a crackling fire. Funnily enough, that plan would work perfectly for Fergus as well, since he wants to be near—but not too near—the New York art world.

He sent me one of his paintings, which has pride of place on my miniscule apartment wall. It takes me back to that day when the impossible became possible and I took a risk that could have cost me everything. Instead, that choice has set me on the road to the life I always dreamed of, and saved the lives of what I hope will be three enduring friends.

Sinclair passed away soon after the experiment. Convinced by the doctors that he would never wake from his coma, his parents had him unplugged from life support. On an anonymous tip, all three of the deaths he had been linked to were immediately brought to court, and he was convicted in absentia, bringing peace to the families of the deceased.

A couple of weeks ago, on one of those whims you never think you'll follow through on, I visited his grave. It was well situated under an oak tree on one of the cemetery's rolling hills. On the front of the gravestone was the typical information: name, birth date, death date, and words about beloved son. But for some reason I decided to walk around the back. There, inexplicably carved into the marble with an expert hand, were a clock, a knife, and a key.

ACKNOWLEDGMENTS

A huge *remerciement* to my editors at HarperTeen: Tara Weikum and Christopher Hernandez. For THREE WHOLE SERIES you have been the gentle hands that nudged me in the right direction. You asked the questions I needed to think things through and bring the best I had to the stories. Huge gratitude to both of you.

Thank you to the lovely Stacy Glick for finding *Dreamfall* and *Neverwake* a home with HarperTeen.

Thank you to Jenna Stempel for creating yet another incredible cover. The way you wove *Dreamfall* and *Neverwake* together into one beautiful nightmare is truly a work of wonder. And to Janet Robbins Rosenberg and Alexandra Rakaczki for performing their own magic on my crimes against punctuation. You are copyeditors extraordinaire.

I owe a huge debt of gratitude to my sensitivity reader, Jenna Gephart, who read both books from an Aspie teen's point of view and gave me her thoughts. She and her lovely mother, author Tina Gephart, invited me into their world and opened my eyes to the host of amazing people involved in the autism spectrum community. Thank you, Jenna, for loving Ant and for reassuring me that I got her right.

Thank you to James Hetfield, Lars Ulrich, and Kirk Hammett for letting me reprint lyrics to "Enter Sandman" in *Neverwake*. Metallica's song was constantly going through my mind as I wrote the nightmare sections of the book. It fits the story perfectly.

Neverwake had three wonderful beta readers: Lori Ann Stephens, Kayla Canfield, and Claudia Depkin all weathered through one or more drafts for me. Fergus, Cata, Ant, Jaime, the rest of the gang, and I are all extremely grateful for your comments and cheerleading. Laura Lam, thank you for confirming that my Small World scene was creeptastic enough. It's good to know someone else is terrified by those smiling dolls.

Thanks to my parents for renting the most terrifying rundown antebellum mansion in Alabama—the old dean's house of Samford University—during my junior and senior years of high school. Complete with an ancient bathroom connected to my bedroom, dilapidated concrete shower rooms underneath the house, and an Olympic-sized swimming pool filled with green sludge and rats. I planned this book as a teenager while lying in my bed listening to the house creak and imagining the Flayed

Man and the bloody slime dripping through the ceiling. How could anyone possibly live there and not write about it?

Thank you to my friends for your encouragement and cheer-leading during the planning and writing of *Neverwake*, including Kim Lennert, Diana Canfield, Alex Goddard, Mags Harnett, Cassi Bryn-Michalik, Christi Daugherty, Jack Jewers, Gretchen Scoleri, and Celeste Rhoads. Having your love and support means the world to me.

Thanks to Dr. Lewis Foss for advice on how to manage the lifesaving techniques Jaime needed at the end of the book. Giving fictional medical advice when you're used to dealing with real-life situations is quite a stretch, and I appreciate the support!

Thank you to Cata for telling my teenage story the way it would have gone if I had chosen a different path. To all of those who lived through abusive childhoods, I wish you healing. To all of those still living with abuse . . . don't be afraid to tell someone about it, even if you don't think they'll believe you. Report it. Protect yourself. Let Cata inspire you to take that step so that you don't have to handle it by yourself like I did.

Thank you to Humphrey for inspiring Remi. May you rest in peace.

Thank you to the visionaries behind the horror films that Fergus and I binge-watched to prepare for this book, including *Friday the 13th, Carrie, It, Children of the Corn, Halloween, A Nightmare on Elm Street, Night of the Living Dead, Dawn of the Dead, The Texas Chainsaw Massacre, Zombieland, Let the Right*

One In, Rosemary's Baby, The Shining, Amityville Horror, The Exorcist, and so many others. Also, thank you to *Flatliners* and *The Matrix* for being major influences for *Dreamfall*'s world-building.

Thank you to my children for egging me on to make things scarier, especially the brainstorm on how to make the amusement park creepy AH.

And above all, thank you to my readers for their enthusiasm over *Dreamfall*. Especially to those who said they don't read horror, but read *Dreamfall* because I wrote it, and ended up falling in love with the characters. What an amazing compliment! And for all of my readers: thank you for allowing me to entertain you with the stories in my mind and the characters of my imagination.

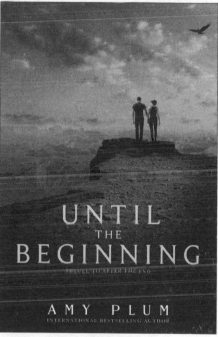

Can't get enough of the DIE FOR ME series?

Don't miss these digital original novellas
set in the world of the Die for Me series!

Available as ebooks only.

COULD YOU SURVIVE
THE DREAMFALL?

"**Remarkable, riveting, disorienting, and dark.**"
—Madeleine Roux, *New York Times*
bestselling author of the Asylum series

JOIN THE

Epic Reads

COMMUNITY

THE ULTIMATE YA DESTINATION

◀ **DISCOVER** ▶
your next favorite read

◀ **MEET** ▶
new authors to love

◀ **WIN** ▶
free books

◀ **SHARE** ▶
infographics, playlists, quizzes, and more

◀ **WATCH** ▶
the latest videos